Jill Sorenson

Wild

For my family

CHAPTER ONE

HELENA FJORD LOVED being an elephant keeper.

She'd worked at San Diego's Wildlife Park for ten years now, and she never got tired of studying the African elephants. Their size and strength awed her. She could watch them for hours, interpreting every tail twitch and ear flap. Communication among the herd was an endless source of fascination to her. But she always admired the animals from afar because keepers were required to maintain a safe distance.

These "gentle giants" could be extremely territorial. They were intelligent creatures, prone to mood swings and fits of temper. Elephants in captivity had been known to throw logs at electric fences and climb over the backs of their comrades to escape. They attacked zoo employees and trampled circus workers on a regular basis. Tending elephants used to be one of the most dangerous jobs in America.

Now that protected-contact methods had replaced free contact, accidents were less frequent. There was no elephant show in San Diego, no tricks performed for the crowd. Helena didn't wield a bull hook for intimidation purposes. She didn't even touch the animals without a sturdy gate between them.

This morning she followed her typical routine. The maintenance crew had already cleared away several hundred pounds of dung, a normal amount. She inspected the yard, ensuring that the animals had fresh water and other amenities.

After a thorough check, she headed back toward the barn, where the elephants were eating breakfast. A large hydraulic gate separated the barn from the yard. Her coworker, Kim, was in the keeper area of the barn. It had a roof, open sides and access to the feeding troughs. The animals were on the other side, behind thick iron bars.

Instead of joining her coworker, Helena stayed in the sunshine, enjoying its warmth on the top of her head. The park wouldn't open for another hour, and they were ahead of schedule. It was rare to get a quiet moment like this.

Helena scanned the ten-acre yard with pride. This was the largest elephant enclosure in the country. It boasted huge wading pools, wide-open spaces and dusty hills. Faux rock walls created an eye-pleasing border, and sturdy tree-shaped structures offered enrichment. The elephants had to solve puzzles to reach the snack rewards inside. They required mental tasks to stay sharp, as well as long walks and regular pedicures.

Over the past ten years, Helena had handled wild animals of all sizes and temperaments. She'd been bitten, scratched and urinated on more times than she could count. And she wouldn't trade a second of it. Because she'd also bottle-fed a baby chimp. She'd watched Bengal tigers mate, resuscitated a newborn giraffe and assisted with elephant labor. Every day at the zoo promised a new adventure. This was exactly what she wanted to do with her life.

Soon the park would be bustling with visitors. The weather was perfect—cool and bright. Many of the local schools were on spring break, which meant more families. More children.

Helena had always been more comfortable around animals than people, but lately she'd found herself staring at young parents with envy. She'd watched the pretty mothers pushing strollers and the cute dads with toddlers on their shoulders.

San Diego was full of rich, attractive people. They procreated just as beautifully as they did everything else.

Her musings were interrupted by an approaching golf cart. It rocketed up the path and sped through the entrance to Heart of Africa, the section of the park where she worked. The vehicle zigzagged around the play structures in the nearby kid zone before hitting a slick section of paw-print-covered concrete. There, the driver slammed on the brakes and cranked the wheel to the right, executing a flashy 180-degree turn. The maneuver had no purpose, other than showing off.

Helena recognized Josh Garrison's signature style. The chief security guard was an idiot. A handsome, charming idiot. Somehow his reckless behavior and juvenile stunts hadn't resulted in any injuries. He'd even managed to get promoted.

His lack of professionalism irritated her. She shoveled elephant crap by the truckload, sweating her ass off, while he cruised around the park, popping wheelies and cracking jokes. He came in to work straight from the beach, his hair wet from surfing and sand on his neck like he didn't give a damn. His pranks were legendary with the guys in the herpetology department. This winter, he'd sported a goofy mustache. Maybe it was supposed to be ironic, but all of the female employees had twittered about how cute he looked.

Helena wasn't sure why she had such a negative reaction to him. Her father had been the same type, brash and devil-may-care. He'd lived fast and died young. There was nothing dreamy or romantic about burning alive.

Josh was doing a basic grounds check, which didn't require spin-outs in the kid zone or stopping to say hello. He glanced across the elephant exhibit and touched his temple in mock salute. Kim smiled and waved. Helena didn't.

Her antagonism toward him wasn't a secret. He seemed to find it amusing. He'd even asked her out once, perhaps to spite her. She'd avoided him ever since. He didn't need any more attention from women.

Josh exited his golf cart and removed the lid of a nearby recycling bin to peer inside. Maintenance emptied the containers every night, so there was nothing to see. He leaned too far forward and fell in, doing a handstand with his legs akimbo.

Kim laughed at his antics, delighted.

Helena returned her gaze to the elephants, annoyed. She never knew what he was going to do next. He made her feel like she was on a rollercoaster, anticipating a steep drop or wild curve.

His behavior had never cross the line into harassment, so she couldn't complain. For a man with a relaxed work ethic, he was good at his job. Park visitors loved him. He responded to emergencies, escorted rowdy tourists to the exit and recovered lost children with ease.

After he left, zipping away in his golf cart, Kim glanced at Helena. "What are you doing this weekend?"

Helena pictured her empty social calendar. "Nothing, why?"

"I'm having a housewarming party Saturday night. You should stop by with Mitch."

Kim had just gotten married in Las Vegas—to a man she'd only been dating six weeks. Helena couldn't imagine making such an impulsive decision. She'd been with someone for six years and she still had no idea where they were going.

"Mitch is in Denver," Helena said.

"Oh, right. When's he coming back?"

"I don't know," she said.

Maybe never.

Mitch had accepted a new job at an engineering company in January. He'd been unemployed for most of the previous year, so she couldn't blame him for making the decision to move away. They needed to have a serious talk about their relationship, however. She'd been putting it off too long.

"Just come by yourself, or bring a friend," Kim said. "It'll be fun."

Helena's idea of fun was watching movies or reading on the couch. Kim was sweet to ask, and Helena had no other plans, but she hesitated to say yes.

Kim didn't seem bothered by Helena's nonresponse. "The cows are restless today," Kim said, changing the subject.

Helena took a closer look inside the barn. Kim stood on the opposite end of the stalls, behind a protective yellow line. The elephants could extend their powerful trunks through the bars like an arm, and were capable of delivering a powerful blow, so the keepers had to stay alert.

Helena noted that all of the animals had backed away from the feeding troughs, leaving half of the hay uneaten. The females hovered near Mbali, the baby of the group. Elephants often made low-frequency sounds that human beings couldn't hear. Helena could feel the vibrations in her chest, like the phantom twang of a bass guitar string. The animals also used body language to communicate.

While she watched, the matriarch curled her trunk into an *S* shape and stuck out her ears—a clear sign of distress.

Helena was about to slip through the gate and join Kim on the other side when a strange rumble came out of nowhere. It wasn't an animal vocalization, rolling thunder, or a new jungle rhythm on the loudspeakers. The noise reminded her of a huge semi-truck rattling down the freeway. But they couldn't hear that kind of traffic from inside the park. The low thrum grew into a dull roar, closing in fast. Several elephants trumpeted shrilly, adding to the chaos. Helena retreated a few steps on instinct.

Before she could brace herself, the ground bucked beneath her feet. She flew up in the air and came down hard on her stomach, slapped with a mouthful of dirt.

Oh, God. Earthquake.

Helena scrabbled for purchase and found none. She felt as if she'd been thrown from a speeding vehicle—or worse, tossed from an airplane. The loss of control over her body and surroundings was terrifying. She bounced across the flat, dry surface, tasting grit and grasping at pebbles. Her knees and elbows slammed against the ground. This was a major quake, no ordinary tremor.

She'd been living in California for most of her life and she'd never experienced anything like this. Dust filled her eyes and nose, choking her. A refrigerator-sized boulder near the wading pond broke loose and tumbled into the water with a terrific crash.

As she struggled to orient herself, Helena recognized a larger problem than the beating she was taking. The elephants were in a state of panic. Trumpeting in high-pitched blasts, they bumped into and climbed over each other. All of the animals managed to stay upright, but the real danger was underfoot. They were going to trample the calf.

Helena rolled onto her back and reached for her utility belt. She had a remote control for the hydraulic gate. If she opened it and released the elephants from the barn into the main enclosure, they might trample *her*.

Mbali made a sound she'd never heard before, a sharp cry of pain. Tears sprung into Helena's eyes. She'd witnessed the baby elephant's birth about a year ago. There was no other animal in the park she was more attached to.

Before she could rethink her decision, she pressed the button on the remote and held it down for five seconds, clenching her jaw from the effort.

Then the elephants were free.

Roaring, they fled the barn. Their massive feet pounded across the space, frighteningly close to Helena's prone form. She was tall for a woman, long and lean and not the least bit delicate. But she felt tiny in that moment, cowering on the unsteady ground as beasts that weighed ten thousand pounds stormed past.

Helena curled up on her side and tucked her arms around her head. She had no illusions about the animals she loved, no fantasies of being swept onto their backs and carried to safety. It was more likely that they would crush her without missing a step, or attack her in confusion.

None of the above happened. The elephants ran into the yard, leaving a cloud of dust in their wake. She stayed in the fetal position, shivering like a fresh-hatched lorikeet, until the tremors ceased.

A voice on her radio broke the silence. "Code three, lion enclosure."

She lifted her head in dismay. It was Greg Patel, her boss, and the head lionkeeper. A code three meant a compromised structure. Code one was an animal escape, the highest alert. Code two signified employee down.

Helena scrambled to her feet, wiping a mixture of blood and dirt from her mouth. She didn't feel any broken bones. Her elbows were scraped, her teeth aching. Kim was lying on the cement floor in the keeper area of the barn. Her eyes were closed, blonde hair streaked with red. Mbali was on the other side of the feeding troughs, motionless.

With a trembling hand, Helena grabbed her radio. "Code two," she said into the receiver. "Elephant enclosure."

She had no idea which problem to tackle first. Kim was hurt. So was Mbali. Greg needed help with the lion enclosure, which was only a few hundred yards away. The keeper area of the elephant barn was open and unprotected.

If the African lions got out—God help them all.

While Helena waited for instructions, the radio blew up with other emergencies. There were damages throughout the park. Many animals had escaped their enclosures. The lead herpetologist called in a code three for the entire reptile house.

It was mayhem.

She took a deep breath and tried to concentrate on safety procedures. Although she was trained to use a tranquilizer gun and a rifle, the weapons were locked in the director's office at the front of the park. Unarmed, she wasn't prepared to approach the lion exhibit. If she couldn't provide direct assistance, she was supposed to take shelter, along with any other employees and visitors in the area. Helena couldn't leave her fallen coworker behind, however. She wouldn't abandon Mbali, either.

Squaring her shoulders, Helena walked toward the elephant barn. The bars were wide enough for her to slip through. As she crouched on the concrete floor next to Kim, more trumpeting and distress calls echoed across the yard. The ground rumbled beneath her feet.

Aftershock.

Helena threw her arms around Kim, cradling her head to protect her from further injury. This jolt felt just as powerful as the first. The jarring motions seemed to threaten the barn's foundation, even though it was built to withstand ten tons of elephant rage.

She could only imagine what was happening in other parts of the city. In small homes and apartment complexes. The historic buildings downtown.

Freeways. Bridges. Hospitals. *Jesus.*

Helena pictured the happy families who visited the zoo every day. The mothers with strollers and the handsome dads. Dead. She smothered a sob at the thought. She was glad her mother had moved to Oregon. Helena didn't have any close relatives in San Diego, but her best friend lived here. Helena hoped Gwen was okay.

When the shaking stopped, she blinked the dust and tears from her eyes. Kim was like a rag doll in her arms. Mbali hadn't moved. Helena was struck by a memory of riding in a small-engine plane as a child. Her father had been in the pilot's seat, her mother at her side. She'd been frozen with fear, almost catatonic.

It had been the most terrifying moment of her life. Until now.

She squeezed her eyes shut, praying for her friends and coworkers. For every animal inside the park, including Mbali. For complete strangers.

After a moment, the radio began to buzz with keepers checking in. Josh Garrison was managing the communication between employees. His requests for more information from Greg had gone unanswered. Josh sounded as relaxed as ever, exchanging emergency information in the same tone he used to shoot the breeze. Even a devastating earthquake couldn't harsh his mellow.

"Helena, come in," he said.

Sniffling, she reached for her radio. "I'm here."

"What's your status, elephant lady?"

He liked to call her silly nicknames. Mount Saint Helena was another one. She felt a twinge of pique, which was more bearable than sorrow. "Kim is unconscious," she said, keeping her voice steady. "Her head is bleeding."

"Is she breathing?"

Helena watched the rise and fall of Kim's chest. "Yes."

"Scalp wounds bleed a lot."

That was true. Helena couldn't tell if Kim had any other injuries.

"Are you putting pressure on it?" Josh asked.

"No."

"Good girl. If you can find a clean towel, hold it over the wound, very gently. I'm on my way to get you."

Tears pricked her eyes again—this time, from relief.

"Have you heard from Greg, by chance?" he asked.

"No," she choked out.

"Don't go looking for him. Just stay put."

She agreed not to and signed off, lowering the radio. Her mouth felt bruised, her knees ached and there were tiny pebbles embedded in the flesh of her palms. These minor injuries throbbed like a distant heartbeat. It was almost as if her body belonged to someone else. She felt numb and disconnected, even lethargic.

Forcing herself to focus, she reached into a nearby drawer for a clean washcloth. Kim had a nasty cut on her forehead, along with a lump the size of a golf ball. Helena pressed the cloth to Kim's temple and glanced around warily for a better place to take shelter. Kim was a small woman. Helena could stash her in the cabinets if she had to.

There were two African lions in the zoo, a mated pair. They were both mature adults, healthy and strong. The male weighed about four hundred pounds, but the female was twice as aggressive. Zuma had been born in a game park in Namibia. She was perfectly capable of stalking and killing prey.

Helena was about to drag Kim across the floor when she opened her eyes. Her pupils looked strange, one larger than the other.

"What happened?" she asked.

"An earthquake."

Kim moistened her lips and frowned. "My head hurts."

"You bumped it."

"I should get up."

Helena kept a firm hand on her shoulder. "Let's wait for Josh. He's coming right now, and he'll take you somewhere safe."

"How bad is it?"

"You'll be fine."

"I mean…the park."

"It's bad," Helena said, surveying the space between the elephant barn and the path to the lion enclosure. She saw no movement, heard no vocalizations. She didn't tell Kim that any animals had escaped.

Mbali's mother came back to the barn for her injured calf. In the chaos, the herd had run away without her. Now Stani touched her trunk to Mbali's slack ears and mouth, as if trying to rouse her baby. Though temperamental, elephants were caring, compassionate creatures. The love between mother and child was obvious.

Helena studied the pair through the iron bars that separated them, touched by the scene. Mbali appeared unconscious, rather than dead. Helena wanted to examine the calf, but she doubted that the protective mother would allow Helena to enter their space.

After several more nudges from her mama, the little elephant awakened. She ambled upright, swaying. Stani curled her trunk around the calf protectively. As soon as Mbali gained her bearings, she scampered off, seeking the comfort of the herd. Stani followed close behind, touching the calf's twitching tail with her trunk.

Helena's chest swelled with emotion as she watched them cross the yard. Mbali was her favorite elephant and Helena couldn't stand the thought of losing her.

"I have to call Steven," Kim said suddenly, grasping Helena's hand.

"Where is he?"

"At our apartment."

Zoo employees communicated by radio only. They were required to leave their cell phones in lockers. Even if the lines were clear, they couldn't call anyone until they returned to the staff buildings.

"You're so lucky Mitch is in Denver," Kim said.

Helena realized, with some chagrin, that she hadn't spared a single thought for him. She'd worried about her friends and coworkers. The animals, of course. Her boss. She'd shed tears over total strangers, and been thankful her mother was in Oregon.

Mitch? Nothing.

In her defense, she'd been distracted, and Mitch was probably fine. Even so, she felt particular no urge to call him now. The distance hadn't made her heart grow fonder.

She'd wondered, more than once, if there was something missing inside her. An empty space or short circuit that prevented her from connecting with others. She'd always been reserved with her affections—toward humans, at least. Animals were easier. Safer, in a way. Their needs weren't as difficult to interpret.

"I'll try the front office," Helena said, picking up her radio. Maybe one of their coworkers could get in touch with Kim's husband. It was security's job to communicate with local police and request emergency services. Helena figured Josh had his hands full, along with every other first responder in the city. Kim might not be able to get medical treatment for hours. Before Helena pressed the button to speak, she heard Greg's voice.

Her spirits lifted. He was alive!

"Code two," Greg said, panting. "Lion enclosure."

Oh, no. He was injured, perhaps badly.

"I've been trying to block the exit—"

A low growl erupted in the background. It was the sound a lion made before charging. Sometimes they rushed forward as a warning and stopped short.

This was not one of those times.

"Zuma, no!"

Greg's stern shout was cut off abruptly. There was a heavy *thump*, followed by a strange gurgling noise. It sounded as if he'd been knocked down, but he hadn't dropped his radio or let go of the talk button. Helena listened with horror as the lion chuffed air through its nose and continued to make throaty vocalizations.

Then a sinister silence fell.

CHAPTER TWO

HELENA EXCHANGED A horrified glance with Kim.

They both knew how lions killed prey. The first strike was quick and brutal, often crushing the spinal cord.

Helena touched the button on her receiver. "Greg?"

No response.

"Greg, come in!"

Nothing.

Kim's pretty face crumpled with distress. Greg was in serious trouble, and there was nothing they could do to help him. Helena felt useless and out of control, sick with worry. She stared at the radio in her hand, gripping it until her knuckles went white. She was frozen, struck by the strange urge to throw the device against the wall.

The sound of Josh's approaching golf cart broke through her paralysis. His driving was fast and erratic, but for good reason. She rose to her feet, her blood pumping with adrenaline. She spotted a hoof knife hanging on the wall. It was a sturdy tool with a long handle and a curved blade. Grabbing the knife, she strode out of the barn. Although Kim called her name, Helena didn't look back.

Josh parked the golf cart as close to the barn as possible. He exited the vehicle, his gaze narrowing on the impromptu weapon in her hand.

"Take me to the lion enclosure," she said.

"No."

She sputtered at his refusal. "Greg needs help."

"You can't help him."

Helena couldn't believe Josh wanted to follow the rules *now*, when a man was bleeding to death nearby. She dismissed him and continued toward the walkway. It was only a few hundred yards to the lion enclosure.

Josh had the nerve to jump in front of her, blocking her path. "Helena—"

"Step aside."

He surprised her by standing his ground. Although he wasn't armed, he carried pepper spray and a baton on his utility belt. He also had the distinction of being tall and well-built. There were some hard muscles beneath his official-looking uniform shirt. But he was just Josh Garrison, glorified security guard. She gave his chest a rude shove.

This move didn't faze him. Instead of stumbling back and letting her pass, he locked his big hands around her upper arms, holding her captive. When she tried to jerk free of his grasp, he tightened his grip.

Helena hadn't expected him to challenge her. She wasn't quite his size, but she was a physically imposing woman. She'd played basketball on the boys' varsity team in high school. To put it bluntly, she was a brute. Men rarely messed with her. And if there was one thing she knew how to do, it was push people away.

"You can't fight off a lion with a knife," he said, shaking her. "We need guns."

"He'll die before then!"

"He's already dead."

This awful probability gave her pause. She pictured Greg Patel's broken neck, his severed carotid artery. In the vast majority of lion attacks, death was instantaneous.

"He has kids," she whispered, her urgency fading into sorrow.

Josh's grip on her upper arms softened. Now his touch felt comforting, rather than cruel. She stared at his unmarred throat. It looked smooth and suntanned and unfairly healthy. A beat pulsed in his neck, proof of life.

Swallowing back tears, she lifted her gaze to his face. He was handsome in a gypsy-wanderer sort of way. His hair was tawny brown, long enough to curl at the edge of his collar. He had good bone structure and strong features. Lucky genetics, basically. His eyes were a warm gold color, framed by thick, dark lashes.

"Let's get Kim back to the staff building," he said. "Then we can see about Greg."

When she nodded, he released her. Going straight to the lion enclosure would have been foolish. Lions could protect a kill for hours. She needed tranquilizer guns from the weapons cabinet, and an organized team.

She followed him into the keeper area, her heart hammering in her chest. She felt so lost and confused, as if her entire world had been turned upside down. How else could she explain the fact that Josh Garrison was talking sense into her?

Inside the barn, he kneeled down beside Kim, brushing a tendril of hair off her forehead. "This is quite a goose egg. You smuggling the Hope Diamond under here?"

Kim hissed as he examined the tender lump. "I wish."

"How are your ears?" he asked.

"Fine."

"Nosebleed?"

Kim looked at Helena, uncertain.

"No," Helena said.

Josh brought Kim to her feet and lifted her easily, carrying her out of the barn. Although she insisted that she could walk, he didn't listen. Helena tucked the hoof knife into her back pocket, along with the bloody washcloth. She kept an eye out for lions as they walked toward the golf cart. Josh deposited Kim in the backseat, motioning for Helena to join her. Helena sat down and slipped an arm around Kim for support. There were no seat belts, and Kim was still woozy. Helena didn't want her to fall out of the cart.

"Whose arms do you prefer, Sleeping Beauty?" Josh asked. "Mine or Helena's?"

Kim smiled weakly. "Helena's."

"I don't blame you," Josh said, climbing behind the wheel. "She looks cozy."

Helena knew very well that Kim preferred Josh's arms, and his company. He was popular with all of the female employees— except Helena. His teasing seemed to put Kim at ease, which was odd. Helena had always felt self-conscious in his presence, unsure if he was mocking or flirting with her.

Maybe she'd been wrong about him. She'd ignored him whenever possible, so she could have missed out on the finer points of his personality. His calm, efficient response to the earthquake impressed her. She wasn't too stubborn to be grateful for his clear thinking just now. He'd prevented her from rushing into danger. He was smarter and more capable than she'd given him credit for.

As he drove away from Heart of Africa, Helena searched the elephant yard for Mbali. The calf was standing underneath her mother, nursing. The other cows had made a protective circle around them. Obi, the breeding male, guarded the herd.

Breathing a sigh of relief, Helena moved her gaze from her beloved elephants to the perimeter of the yard. It looked secure. No lions leapt out from the bushes as they passed by, but there were plenty of disturbing sights to behold on the way back to the front of the park. Some of the exhibits were wrecked. Others appeared empty. Meer cats peeped up from their burrows, afraid to venture above ground.

Somewhere in Lost Jungle, a rhesus monkey howled. They were loud, boisterous creatures, so the noise wasn't unusual in itself. The strange part was that she could hear it at this distance. All of the normal park activities had gone mute. There was no upbeat drum music, no birds chirping, no joyous splashing or movement of any kind. It was the sound of nothingness, of cowering anticipation.

Kim jostled against her side as they went over a bump. The concrete path, once flat, was now riddled with cracks and lifted sections. Helena tightened her arm around Kim and kept her eyes on the rear of the vehicle. Again, she thought of Greg Patel. His wife, Anya. Their teenage daughters, Nina and Trish.

The restaurants and souvenir shops at the front of the park had been hit hard. Glass crunched beneath the tires of the golf cart as they skirted past one of the ruined stores. Its windows were shattered, shelves knocked over. Stuffed animals and novelty items littered the floors. If the earthquake had struck during regular operating hours, there would have been children among the rubble.

The main staff building was still standing. It housed the employee lockers, break room and security center. When they arrived at the entrance, Michelle Lu, a veterinary technician, opened the door for them.

Josh parked the golf cart and got out. As he prepared to lift Kim, his eyes met Helena's. None of the usual mischief danced in them, only fear and anxiety. He might seem calm, even nonchalant, but only a very stupid man didn't have the sense to be afraid during the worst disaster of his lifetime. Josh wasn't stupid, apparently. He knew they were in serious trouble. And the worst was yet to come.

His fingertips brushed her breast and she went still. Although the contact was accidental, she shivered in awareness and his gaze darkened. Then he carried Kim away, and the spell was broken.

She got out of the cart, flushing. She didn't know what was wrong with her. The earthquake must have knocked a few screws loose. She'd never had this reaction to him before. Then again, she couldn't remember the last time he'd touched her. They might have shaken hands once or twice, years ago. She could still feel his strong grip on her upper arms, holding her captive.

Her pulse pounded with trepidation as she followed him into the staff lounge. It wasn't as chaotic as she'd feared, but there were several injured keepers in the room. Josh deposited Kim in an empty chair by the break table.

"I have to take care of these guys first," Michelle said. "Puncture wound from an antelope horn, and a snakebite."

"What kind of snake?" Helena asked.

"Malayan pit viper. But we have antivenin."

Luckily, the zoo's veterinarian kept antivenin and other basic first aid items in stock. There was a hospital and exam area in an adjoining building where they cared for sick animals and performed surgeries. Human patients were usually taken away in ambulances, but they'd just have to make do with the resources available.

After Michelle hurried away to gather medical supplies, Helena turned to Josh. "Are there other injured keepers?"

"Just Greg."

"What about Spears?"

"He's off-site," Josh said. "Management meeting."

Helena's stomach dropped. The director wasn't in the building. Neither was the curator or any of the zoo's other top officials. They had monthly meetings at the research facility in La Jolla. "Who else is here?"

Josh recited about a dozen names. The majority of the zoo's staff worked in sales and food service. Those employees hadn't arrived yet, and the maintenance crew had already left. They were running on a skeleton crew. "The keepers who aren't hurt are helping capture snakes at the reptile house or trying to fix the gorilla enclosure."

It dawned on Helena that the two of them were in charge. She outranked all of the other keepers on site, except for Greg. She was the animal expert, and Josh was the chief security officer. They were going to have to work together to restore order. Every living thing in the park was counting on them. The responsibility was enormous.

"How many code ones?" she asked, trying not to panic.

He rattled off a list of escaped animals so far. The cheetah and hyenas were among them. "None confirmed, just reported."

Helena wanted to make checking on Greg their top priority. He could be suffering, bleeding to death. They had to get the lion situation under control as soon as possible. Unfortunately, venomous snakes also posed a serious threat, and so did aggressive gorillas. Removing a keeper from those tasks could mean risking the safety of the rest of the crew. "Are the webcams working?"

"No. Everything is down."

"What about emergency services?"

Josh took a cell phone out of his pocket. He was allowed to carry one because he acted as a liaison between the park and local authorities. "I think they're overwhelmed, or communication systems have crashed. The park radios aren't picking up any police activity, and I haven't been able to get through on my cell phone."

"Let Kim try."

Josh handed Kim his phone. "Maybe you can reach someone outside the city."

While Kim attempted to send a text, Helena and Josh ducked into the security office to check the monitors. It was a mess inside, with papers and broken equipment all over the floor. The feeds were down, as Josh had reported, and the desk phone was dead.

"We turned off the water because of broken pipes," he said. "The gas has automatic shutoff valves, so we're fine there."

Helena was glad they didn't have to worry about blowing up, but the utilities were the least of her concerns. They needed to start prioritizing the code ones and securing the perimeter. Packs of predators could be roaming the park. If they escaped into the city streets, there was no telling how much damage they could do. Innocent lives were at stake, and she couldn't count on help from local law enforcement.

Although the zoo was surrounded by a sturdy twelve-foot fence, some animals could climb or even jump that high. Helena had no idea what she'd do about a code ten, which was an escaped animal *outside* the park. She was just a zookeeper. She didn't have the training to handle that kind of emergency.

As they left the office, she noticed an overturned vending machine in the hallway. Water bottles spilled across the floor. Opening one, she drank half of it and passed the rest to Josh, who looked thirsty. He emptied the bottle in three gulps, his throat working as he swallowed. His beige uniform shirt clung to his lean torso. He was sweating. So was she. The situation was incredibly stressful. Tearing her gaze away, she gathered several more bottles of water for the injured keepers and brought them to the break table.

Kim had good news. "I got a reply from my mom in Arizona," she said, tearful. "She heard from Steven. He's okay."

"Ask her to call 911," Josh said. "She can relay information for us."

Kim followed his instructions, reading the screen for a response. "She's on hold with them on her landline. They felt the earthquake there, too, so it might be a while. Is there anyone else you want to try?"

Helena didn't have time to contact more than one person, so she used the phone to send a short message to her mother. Then she extended it to Josh.

He shook his head. "I've already tried. My parents are on a cruise and my sister—"

Helena remembered meeting her a few months ago, right outside this building. The pretty blonde had been carrying a little girl in a princess party hat. Josh had introduced them as his niece and sister.

Helena had always wanted a sister. She'd been an only child, tall and reserved and slow to make friends. Her foreign accent hadn't helped. Instead of socializing with her classmates, she'd kept company with the animals on the farm where her mother worked. They'd been like family to her.

She couldn't imagine what Josh was going through, but the anguish in his eyes was clear. Without meaning to, she took a step toward him. "You haven't heard from her?"

"No."

"Where is she?"

"In Coronado, I hope," he said, clearing his throat. "She crosses the bridge for work every morning."

CHAPTER THREE

CHLOE GARRISON'S DAY was off to a great start.

The sun was shining, traffic was moving at full speed and Emma was singing silly songs in the backseat. Her daughter hadn't refused to eat breakfast or get dressed this morning. She'd also slept through the night, a minor miracle. Chloe had weaned her a few months ago, but Emma still sometimes woke up cranky and wanting to nurse. Maybe she'd finally gotten over that night-feeding habit.

Chloe felt deliciously free and light. Her breasts had shrunken back to pre-pregnancy, teacup size, but that was okay. She could wear sexy bras without worrying about leaks.

She could have *sex*, even.

Giggling at the thought, she ran her fingers through her newly shorn hair. She loved the short, asymmetrical layers. It was spring break. There were no classes this week. She had a perky haircut, a cute bra and time off.

Life was good.

"You want to go to the zoo this afternoon?" she asked Emma. Chloe was a housekeeper for three different families on Coronado Island. She worked mornings and attended community college in the afternoons.

"See monkeys," Emma said, kicking her little feet.

"We'll see the monkeys," Chloe said.

"Unco Josh."

"And Uncle Josh."

Her brother had bought them annual passes to the zoo with his employee discount, so they visited often. Emma wanted to go every day, but Chloe was too busy, and she tried to give Josh his space. They'd cramped his style enough by moving in with him last year. Although he never complained, she knew they were a major inconvenience. He didn't bring women home because of them.

The arrangement was temporary, of course. When she earned her degree and got a better-paying job, she'd find her own place. She couldn't wait. Josh was a wonderful uncle to Emma, and Chloe adored him, but he was a typical older brother. He liked stupid action movies and war video games. He hogged the remote. His babysitting skills left a lot to be desired. She did most of the cooking and cleaning instead of paying rent.

Living with her parents had been easier. Stifling, but easier.

Chloe was glad she'd made the change. It had been the most challenging year of her life—and by far the most rewarding. The struggle to balance work, school and motherhood consumed her days. She was too tired to worry about Emma's deadbeat dad, or any other boy. She hadn't been on a date in ages.

Which was why the thought of sex was funny. Only if a hot prospect dropped out of the sky and fell into her lap.

Shaking her head, she rolled down the window to feel the breeze in her hair. She was about to turn up the radio when she saw brake lights. Slow-and-go wasn't uncommon during morning rush hour, especially before the curve, but it was unwelcome. Her old Volkswagen handled zippy hills better than heavy traffic.

When she first moved to San Diego, she'd been nervous about driving across the bridge. It was two miles long and several hundred feet high. She'd read somewhere that it was the third most popular suicide bridge in the United States. There was no pedestrian access and nowhere to pull over, so she wasn't sure how jumpers accomplished the task. She imagined that they parked in the middle of the bridge and—

Bam!

Someone slammed into her bumper, sending the VW into a tailspin. Reality went flying out the window. Everything happened in a flash, as if they'd accelerated into warp speed. She couldn't make sense of the confusing blur. Then time switched to slow motion, maybe even reverse. She was vaguely aware that the danger wasn't limited to a minor accident. Cars and trucks were sliding all over the place. The entire bridge was hopping.

What the hell?

Her VW hit the guardrail on the passenger side and came to a grinding halt. She was facing the wrong direction, but that wasn't important, because traffic wasn't moving forward anymore. They were under siege. Sections of the bridge were lifting up and breaking apart. Vehicles went toppling over the edge. Chloe couldn't believe her eyes. She heard someone screaming and realized it was her. Emma was screaming, too.

"Mama!"

The rear of the car shifted and her heart jumped into her throat. She already had her foot on the brake. On instinct, she jerked up the emergency brake and twisted around, reaching out to Emma in the backseat. They grasped hands, as if that would prevent them from falling into the empty space behind the car. The section of the bridge they'd been about to pass over was gone. Inches from her bumper, there was a gaping abyss.

Chloe stared at Emma and held her breath.

Then the world stopped shaking. Chloe finally realized they hadn't been bombed or struck by an airplane.

"Earthquake," she gasped. "It was an earthquake."

Emma wasn't screaming anymore. She looked too terrified to cry. Chloe could relate. They might have survived the quake, but they were hardly in the clear. Her compact car was teetering on the edge of a broken section of bridge. She was afraid to move. If she leaned forward to retrieve Emma from her seat, they might plummet to their deaths.

There was a reason people jumped from this height: the fall was not survivable.

"You're okay," Chloe said to Emma. "Mama's got you."

Emma didn't know what an earthquake was. Chloe had grown up in San Luis Obispo, a coastal town north of L.A., so she'd felt small tremors before. Nothing like this. Pressure built behind her eyes as she thought of her parents and Josh. Her best friend, Marcy. Emma's father, Lyle, whom Chloe had wished destruction on a thousand times.

She hadn't meant it, apparently.

Smothering a sob, she glanced around with caution. Most of the bridge was still intact, but the section behind them appeared to have crumbled. She didn't want to upset the balance inside the car by craning her neck to look over her shoulder. Vehicles that hadn't careened into the bay were dispersing in the opposite direction. Waves churned beneath the bridge and smoke rose in the distance. She didn't see any people in her peripheral vision. If someone was getting out of their car and coming to rescue them, she couldn't tell. Chloe realized that they might be stuck here, frozen in place, for a long time.

That fear didn't materialize, however. Something worse did.

The shaking began anew, swelling like a monster under the water. Violent motion rocked the bridge's foundations and rattled the VW. Then the slab beneath them dropped in a stomach-curling jolt.

Chloe let go of Emma and faced forward, horrified. The broken section of bridge tilted at a sharp angle. Now they were perched at the top of a steep ramp, with the nose of the car pointed down. The few remaining vehicles tumbled off the far end. Her passenger side got hung up on the guardrail, but only for a moment. They began a sickening, near-vertical slide. Chloe released the emergency brake in a panicked attempt to avoid a rollover. The VW hurled toward the edge. At the last second, she pulled the emergency brake again and cranked the wheel to the left, desperate to slow their descent.

It didn't work. Or, it didn't stop them.

After a dizzying 360-degree turn, the car crashed into the opposite guardrail, which was the last remaining obstacle. Then it flipped over the side of the wrecked bridge and sailed into the bay.

They were only airborne for a second or two. Maybe the slab had fallen most of the distance to the water, or a rogue wave had swelled up to meet them. The details weren't important. Although she'd studied the laws of physics, she didn't have the wherewithal to calculate terminal velocity at the moment of death. She closed her eyes and prayed for a painless trip to heaven with Emma.

Once again, her expectations were thwarted. They landed with a hard splash. Her seat belt yanked tight and she knocked her head against the steering wheel. The impact stunned her, but it didn't kill her.

Black spots drifted across the front windshield like virtual checker pieces moving on a game board. She blinked at the fuzzy shapes, disoriented.

Emma was crying again. Water poured in through the engine, soaking the floorboards. The usually calm bay had transformed into a raging tumult. Although many cars had fallen, Chloe didn't see any of them on the surface.

They were sinking.

When the water reached her thighs, she snapped out of her stupor. It was freaking *cold*. Time to go.

First, Emma.

She turned to reach for her daughter but was impeded by the seat belt. Wincing, she fumbled for the release button with numb fingers. They came away wet. The water level was rising faster than she could function.

Shit!

Chloe shifted into high gear. She removed Emma from her car seat and pulled her into the front of the vehicle. Water swirled around Chloe's chest, robbing her breath. The car was getting sucked into a current, spinning as the bay swallowed them whole. Emma shrieked in terror. Her little arms clung to Chloe's neck, trembling. Another problem presented itself: the window was only halfway down. She didn't think she could open the door, and she couldn't fit through the space with Emma.

They were going to die in here.

No, her mind balked. Not like this.

She grabbed the handle and rolled down the window, grateful for all things manual. Her VW might be the oldest heap in San Diego. It didn't have air bags, power steering or air conditioning, but at least they could escape without breaking the glass. In theory. Water rushed through the opening at an alarming rate. She had to wait for the car to submerge.

"Can you blow bubbles for Mama?"

Emma's face crumpled. She was blonde and brown-eyed, like Chloe, with round cheeks and soft curls. Her cherub's countenance masked a stubborn disposition. Emma's temper tantrums were legendary.

Right now, that was a plus. Chloe needed her to be strong. To fight.

Chloe held her breath as the cold flood overcame them. Keeping one arm around Emma, she used the other to grip the jamb and push through the window. She kicked both legs and dog-paddled the short distance to the surface. It was shockingly difficult. Emma dragged her down and the chill robbed her breath. Her wet clothes hampered her movements. She broke through the surface and gasped for air, desperate to stay afloat.

Emma sputtered and screamed.

Jesus, God. Please help me.

Chloe should have taken off her shoes and sweater before exiting the vehicle. The price for that oversight might be their lives. Her skinny jeans, basic cardigan and canvas sneakers felt so heavy.

Emma only weighed twenty-five pounds, but it might as well have been two hundred.

Chloe couldn't swim like this. Not with one arm, fully clothed, in these conditions. She didn't have the upper body strength.

Emma's arms created a noose around Chloe's neck that added to her sense of doom. Pumping her legs furiously, she fought to stay above the surface. Her energy was already sapped. She looked around for something to grab hold of. They weren't directly under the bridge or anywhere near the shore. The bay stretched far and wide between downtown San Diego and Coronado Island. A powerful current threatened to sweep them out to sea.

It was hopeless.

"Help!" she yelled, to no one. "Help me!"

Then, as if conjured by her hoarse cry, a head popped up in the choppy waves. A dark-haired man was swimming toward them. He looked young and strong, though it was hard to tell with the glare on the water. Sunlight sluiced off his arms with every stroke, like the shining wings of a guardian angel.

When he reached her, Chloe realized that his sudden appearance was only half a miracle. He couldn't save them both.

"Dámela," he said, gesturing for Emma.

Emma clung to Chloe's neck, shivering. Her teeth were chattering, her lips blue. Chloe didn't understand what the man had said, but she knew what she had to do.

"Dame la niña," he panted. Then, in careful English, he said, "The baby."

Up close, the man resembled a warrior more than an angel. His hair was cropped short on the sides with a longer strip on top, Mohawk-style. Chloe assumed the language he spoke was Spanish, not some ancient Aztec tongue.

Sobbing, she gave up her daughter.

Emma howled a protest, stretching her arms out to Chloe. The man ignored Emma's frightened cries. *"Regreso por ti,"* he said, and took off. Unlike Chloe, he had no trouble swimming with a toddler in tow. He headed toward the closest shore, which was about a half-mile away.

Chloe tried to follow, but her limbs were useless, numb from cold and constricted by wet clothing. Hot tears poured down her face as she struggled to keep sight of them. Emma was her life, her love, her beating heart.

Chloe sank into the icy depths, praying the man would make it to land. A sharp object stabbed her thigh, giving her a rude prod, and saltwater flooded her nostrils. She shrugged out of her cardigan and clawed her way back to the surface.

After some wild thrashing and coughing, it occurred to her that she could tread water. Without Emma's extra weight and the cloying fabric on her arms, her range of movement was much improved. She could swim. Hope burst within her.

Paddling furiously, she attempted a basic crawl. Her shoes made it very difficult, almost impossible. She paused to take them off, her frozen fingers fumbling with the laces. Finally, she was free of them. Her skinny jeans were restrictive as hell, but there was no way she could remove them without drowning. It was hard enough to do it in her bedroom.

Chloe focused on Emma. Her pale curls clung to her sweet head. She kept screaming, bless her. The sound was music to Chloe's ears, guiding her onward. Her little girl had the lungs of an opera singer. Maybe Emma was her guardian angel.

They'd been swept north of the bridge, toward the embarcadero. It was a small peninsula between the international airport and the harbor. The park-like tourist area was near Seaside Village, and just a few blocks from the city's famous Gaslight District.

While Chloe paddled with grim determination, their foreign rescuer arrived at the shore with Emma. The embarcadero's grassy plateau was lined with trees and protected by clusters of large rocks, like a jetty. There was no gentle beach or gradual slope. The man scrambled over the jagged boulders, with some difficulty, and set Emma on dry land. Despite her obvious fear of him, he had to peel her arms away from his neck.

Then he came for Chloe.

Although she'd covered half the distance on her own, she was exhausted, and might have drowned without his help.

When he reached her, he tucked his forearm under her chin and towed her to shore. She didn't have the strength to pull herself onto the rocks once they arrived. He got out and grabbed her wrists, hauling her up like a dead fish. She let out a startled cry as her leg scraped along the uneven surface. Her jeans were ripped and bloody, exposing a gash on her upper thigh. The man released her arms and kneeled beside her, his brow furrowed in concern. Chloe could tell that the wound needed stitches.

"Mama!"

"Stay there," she choked out, terrified Emma would try to climb down to them. Wincing, she rested her hip on a rock and closed her hand over the laceration. Watery blood seeped between her fingers, staining the denim.

"*Te ayudo,*" the man said. He hooked her arm around his neck and lifted her up, supporting her on one side as they ascended the rocky embankment. With every step, pain radiated from her foot to her thigh. She ignored it, focusing on Emma. Finally, they were on the grass. The man set her down next to Emma. Chloe embraced her daughter with a strangled sob, forgetting her injury, disregarding the cold.

They were alive. Nothing else mattered.

After a long hug, she broke the contact to examine Emma's tearstained face. "Are you okay, baby?" Chloe inspected Emma's little arms and legs, her sturdy body. She was soaked and shivering, but unharmed.

"Thank God," Chloe whispered, hugging Emma again. "Thank God, thank God, thank God."

The man who'd saved them stood nearby. He was wearing a soccer uniform. Tall black socks, white shorts and a white shirt with the number *17* on the back. He took off the jersey and handed it to her.

Chloe accepted the garment with gratitude. Although damp, it was made of moisture-resistant fabric and felt pleasantly warm. She wrapped the jersey around Emma like a blanket, and then rocked her gently.

The stranger sat down beside them, silent. He appeared to be in his early twenties, and he was very fit. Not bulky or muscle-bound, but clearly a dedicated athlete. Bronze skin stretched taut over a sleek, sculpted torso.

"Mama," Emma said, patting her breast. "Milk."

Chloe flushed at the request, unable to comply. Emma didn't ask to nurse as often as she used to, but she still sought the comfort and closeness when she was upset. Weaning had been difficult for both of them.

The man waved his hand casually, gesturing for her to go ahead.

"I can't," Chloe said. "No more."

He glanced at her chest. Her thin tank top couldn't disguise her lack of...bounty. Making a noncommittal sound, he peeled off one of his long socks. There was a protective pad underneath that covered his shin. He wrapped the sock around her upper thigh with care. She made a sound of discomfort as he formed a snug knot.

"Lo siento."

She didn't know what that meant. "Thank you for saving us," she said, her leg still tingling from his touch.

"Por nada," he replied, flashing a smile.

Something about him took her breath away. Either she'd developed a serious case of hero worship, or he was handsome. The body was a ten all by itself. His face wasn't perfect, but it had character. She liked his dark eyes and white teeth, his fierce hair and hawkish nose. "Do you speak English?"

He shrugged, apologetic.

"I'm Chloe," she said. "This is Emma."

"Soy Mateo."

She wasn't sure she'd heard him correctly. "What?"

"Mateo," he said again, pointing at himself.

"Ma-tay-o," she repeated.

He nodded.

She wanted to ask him more questions but the horror of their surroundings distracted her. She couldn't believe this was happening. Had they really just survived a bridge collapse? Had anyone else made it? She searched the bay, which was calmer now. There were no boats nearby, no floating cars. Behind them, the park was empty. The broken bridge loomed in the distance, massive and surreal. Traffic had dispersed on either side. The air was thick with smoke from dozens of small fires.

And it was quiet. Unnaturally quiet.

She stared out at the water, her eyes filling with tears. An earthquake this size meant lots of human casualties. Dozens, maybe hundreds, had plummeted to their deaths. By some crazy stroke of luck, they were still alive.

She didn't know why they'd been spared. Or who else was left.

Her parents were on a Caribbean cruise. They'd set sail a week ago, so they were probably fine. Josh might not have fared so well. He worked in a densely populated area of San Diego, just a few miles away.

"Mama," Emma sobbed, wanting milk again.

Overwhelmed by the traumatic experience, unable to comfort her child, Chloe hung her head and cried.

CHAPTER FOUR

JOSH COULDN'T THINK about Chloe and Emma without his throat closing up.

He loved his sister, but he was more worried about Emma. She was just a baby. They'd celebrated her second birthday right here at the zoo, with pink cupcakes and princess party hats. Josh had donned his with pride.

Fuck.

If something had happened to them, he didn't know what he'd do. Jump off a bridge himself, maybe.

Pushing thoughts of Chloe and Emma aside, he focused on Helena. She was calm and in control, as usual. Dependability was her default mode. She approached every task with brisk efficiency. Shoulders straight, head high. A born leader. He was surprised he'd been able to stop her from charging into the lions' den. She struck him as the type of person who rarely changed course once she had her sights set. He liked that about her.

He liked a lot of things about her.

Unfortunately, she didn't hold him in the same regard. She'd formed a low opinion of him and he couldn't seem to shake it. He'd asked her out once, and she'd said no in a "not if he was the last man on earth" sort of way.

He hadn't meant any insult; on the contrary. But she'd kept her distance ever since, as if he'd offended her with his interest.

Before they raided the weapons cabinet, she collected a few more cell phones from the employee lockers. She gave one to Kim and returned Josh's. He tucked it away, hoping he'd hear from Chloe soon.

The guns were stashed in the director's office, which was next door, by the banquet hall. Although Josh had patrolled the area during the day, he'd never been inside. A private agency provided security for the swank events the zoo sponsored by night, and his pockets weren't deep enough to get invited the old-fashioned way. He wondered if Helena attended those parties, clad in strapless black velvet and long gloves.

Probably not. She wasn't much of a schmoozer.

There would be no charity galas here for anyone, anytime soon. The place was in shambles, with smashed bottles and a broken mirror behind the bar. Helena stepped around the glass and continued to a back office. Inside, there was a large desk, sleek leather furniture and an overturned bookshelf. No animal trophies, of course. A metal cabinet dominated one wall. When she opened it, he let out a low whistle.

They had an arsenal at their disposal. In addition to several shotguns, there was a lever-action Winchester and two Browning BLRs—big-game rifles with serious stopping power. Helena selected a tranquilizer gun and a set of slim darts with feathered ends. There were more types of darts than rifles.

Josh hadn't fired a gun in several years. He'd had a bad experience with a rifle, and he wasn't eager to repeat it. But he'd learned his lesson about hesitating, so he pushed aside his misgivings and took the Winchester off the rack. She watched him load it, a crease forming between her brows.

"You've had weapons training?" she asked.

"Of course."

She seemed surprised, as if she thought anyone off the street could do his job. He didn't carry a firearm for safety reasons, but he was certified in law enforcement. He'd also participated in several code one drills. His role was to evacuate the park and communicate with local authorities, not to take the kill shot.

"At a police academy?" she asked.

"No. I was in the navy for five years."

"I didn't know that."

He just shrugged. His stint in the military hadn't worked out the way he'd hoped, so he rarely mentioned it. There was nothing funny about watching his career aspirations go down in flames. On the bright side, he'd gained life experience and earned money for a college degree. And he was fairly accurate with a rifle.

She cocked her head to one side. "How old are you?"

"Twenty-nine."

He was pretty sure he looked his age, but she must have assumed he was younger. He figured she was about thirty. With her jet-black hair, pale blue eyes and statuesque height, she was striking.

His comic-book fantasy, come to life.

She returned her attention to the gun rack. "Why did you choose the Winchester?"

"It's better at long distances. You don't need an elephant gun to take down a lion, or any smaller predators we might see along the way."

"Shooting is a last resort," she said. "I want to use darts."

"I understand."

"Don't fire without my okay."

He couldn't make any promises. "If a lion jumps out at us, I'm not going to ask for permission."

"They charge as a warning, and don't always follow through."

Nodding, he loaded the rifle and put the strap over his shoulder. The weight felt familiar and comfortable, but he couldn't say he'd missed it. "How much time does it take the tranquilizers to work?"

"Depends on the animal. A few minutes, at least. They're more dangerous when cornered, and often attack after they've been darted."

"Great," he muttered.

"Are you sure you want to do this?"

He didn't, actually. It was his job to protect the park's human inhabitants, Helena included. Hunting lions was way beyond his pay grade. Code ones should be handled by top officials and a team of experts. They needed a half-dozen armed keepers casing the perimeter, and more crew members relaying information from webcam footage.

Instead, they were going in blind, just the two of them. He didn't like the odds, and he wasn't optimistic about Greg's chances for survival. Lions went for the jugular and didn't let go. Even if Greg was alive, they might not be able to reach him. Josh didn't want to shoot two healthy animals. He didn't want to shoot anything.

"I'd rather wait," he said.

"For what?"

"The other keepers. They can help after they're done rounding up snakes and securing the gorilla enclosure."

She contemplated his plan for about three seconds before shaking her head. "I have to drive by and check it out. Those lions might be loose. They could attack again. I'd never forgive myself if I waited and someone else got hurt."

He didn't argue with her. Driving by was a fair plan.

"You don't have to come with me," she added.

"You think I'd let you go alone?"

She adjusted the gun strap, not answering. On closer inspection, she wasn't as unruffled as she appeared. There was a smudge of dirt on her cheek and dried blood at the corner of her mouth. She also looked as if she'd been crying. These hints of vulnerability unsettled him. He wasn't used to seeing any chinks in her armor.

He wondered if she assumed he was untrustworthy, despite his military background. Maybe she was just too independent to trust anyone.

She wasn't an easy woman to read, and he'd been wrong about her before. After four years of working with her, the only thing he knew for certain was that she loved animals. Her face softened when she interacted with them, and her dedication to the job was undeniable.

She left the gun cabinet unlocked. They exited the banquet hall and approached the storage yard, where the maintenance vehicles were parked. His golf cart wouldn't protect them as well as a pickup truck with closed windows. Josh had the keys to one of the older trucks, so he unlocked it and climbed behind the wheel. Helena settled into the passenger seat, not protesting the arrangement. He started the engine and drove out of the yard.

It only took a minute to reach Heart of Africa. After they passed the elephant exhibit, he had to slam on the brakes. There was a huge rift in the middle of the road. The asphalt had lifted and separated, leaving an uneven section he couldn't go over. It was a major obstacle. They needed a ramp, and a couple of strong men to place it.

"Can we take Safari Street?" she asked.

"No. There's a tree down by the gorilla enclosure."

Both of the roads that encircled the zoo were blocked. Another path went straight up the middle, but it forked into a nature trail with stairs and a rustic footbridge. The second, wheelchair-accessible option was too narrow for the truck to squeeze through. Although his golf cart could fit, it would also leave them open to attack.

"We're almost there," she said, craning her neck to see around the corner. "Let's get out and walk."

He didn't think that was a good idea. There was five hundred yards of obstacle-filled space between them and the lion enclosure, with zero visibility. He surveyed their surroundings, searching for an alternative. Maybe he could get a better look from the roof of the vehicle, or the top of a building....

"The Skylift," he said, spotting one of the tall poles for the aerial tram. "We can see the enclosure from up there." It also had an excellent view of the downtown skyline and the San Diego Bay, including the Coronado Bridge.

"There's no electricity."

"We don't need it to climb the ladder to the top of the pole."

She followed his gaze to the tram pole, her expression wary. It occurred to him that she didn't ride the Skylift often. If ever. "What if there's another earthquake?"

Josh considered the pole. He'd seen service workers climb them before. There was a safety guard around the ladder. Compared to approaching the lion den without protection, it was a piece of cake. "You can go up first. I'll stay right under you."

"Why should I go first?"

"I don't want to fall on you. I'm heavier."

She studied his lean form. "Not by much."

He gave her an equal perusal. She had long legs and nice curves. He was no hefty bodybuilder, but neither was she. Had she forgotten that he'd overpowered her less than thirty minutes ago? "I'm always happy to be on top, if you insist."

Her eyes narrowed at his innuendo.

He regretted the joke as soon as it left his mouth. Suggestive humor wasn't appropriate at work, especially under these circumstances. Sure, he'd flirted with Kim, but Kim was friendly. They hadn't been alone together. And he didn't actually want to sleep with her. Those three details didn't apply to Helena.

He glanced away, heat rising up his neck. Instead of making them both more uncomfortable by dwelling on the awkward moment, he moved on. "You can stay here while I look."

"No. It's my responsibility."

Whatever. He backed up the truck a few feet and parked as close to the tram pole as possible. It was off the beaten path, disguised in a wooded area between exhibits. Although public access was prohibited, some people ignored the rules. That was where Josh came in. He'd removed a couple of boneheaded teenagers from the ladder before.

He'd also pulled an inebriated woman from the flamingo pond, and called 911 when a suicidal man jumped into the polar bear enclosure. A popular tourist attraction like the San Diego Wildlife Park drew its share of kooks.

He exited the truck with Helena, keeping his eyes peeled and his rifle ready. They approached a short redwood fence and stepped over it. He stuck close to Helena, his heartbeat thundering in his ears. She skirted around thick ferns, thorny ocotillos and birds of paradise. The park's exotic plants were well cared for, and almost as impressive as its collection of animals. He hoped there were no predators crouched in the bushes.

The tram pole was in a small clearing between exhibits. It had a built-in ladder with a safety guard on one side. Vertical bars followed the pole to the top and horizontal bars curved around the ladder at regular intervals, protecting it like a giant spinal column.

Josh stood watch at the base of the pole while she ascended. The clang of metal on metal startled him. The barrel of her gun had gotten caught on the first bar of the safety guard, which was about six feet up. He hadn't considered this complication. It was dangerous to climb with an unwieldy object, even more so to shoot while standing on a ladder. They'd have to leave the guns on the ground.

"Pass it down to me," he said, doing another sweep of the area.

She fumbled with the gun strap and lowered the weapon to him. He set it at the base of the pole, along with the rifle, and hurried to join her. The hairs at the nape of his neck prickled with awareness as he climbed the rungs. He didn't stop until he was inside the guard, his eyes level with her boots.

She glanced over her shoulder at him, seeming anxious.

"Okay," he said. "Let's go."

After a short hesitation, she started to climb. He went with her, staying right on her six in case another earthquake struck. Her butt was a pleasant diversion, as always. It looked firm and supple and perfect. Although her tan uniform pants weren't snug enough to reveal much, he enjoyed the view.

"Are you afraid of heights?" he asked.

She didn't answer his question, so he stopped staring at her ass and concentrated on the ladder rungs. He could take a hint. She didn't like him, she didn't think he was funny and she didn't want to share personal information.

This was nothing new.

"I have trouble with depths," he said anyway.

"What?"

"Depths," he said, a little louder. "Deep water."

"But you're a surfer."

He was surprised she knew that. "Yeah."

"And you were in the navy."

"Before I enlisted, I thought I was totally comfortable in the water. I starting surfing when I was ten, and I'm no stranger to cold temperatures or rough waves. But I struggled with the underwater rescue phase and I couldn't scuba worth a damn."

"Is that why you quit?"

"I didn't quit. I completed five years of active service. I just didn't reenlist."

She kept climbing without comment. He regretted bringing up the subject. Joining the navy's special combat forces had been his lifelong dream. He'd tried and failed. That wasn't the same as quitting.

But what did he expect from her, admiration? Yeah, right. He'd never been able to impress her. When they first met, he'd tripped all over himself trying to make her smile. She'd remained aloof, ignoring his efforts. Since he'd asked her out, she'd gone out of her way to avoid him.

He wasn't sure why he cared what she thought of him. Maybe her elusiveness was part of her appeal. That, and close proximity. He saw her almost every day. Sometimes his hands itched to strip away that cool facade and reveal the soft heat he sensed was underneath.

He'd accepted the fact that she wasn't interested. She wasn't the only beautiful woman in the world, or the only one who'd rejected him. He could take no for an answer. But he'd perked up a little when he heard that her boyfriend had moved away.

If she needed a man to warm her bed, Josh was ready.

He'd always enjoyed a challenge, and Helena certainly fit the bill. His sister had accused him of being a player, but he wasn't. Not really. He didn't have to lie or cheat to get lucky with women. It just came naturally to him, like telling jokes and goofing off.

Chloe had a negative view of men because of her ex-boyfriend, and Josh couldn't blame her. He was bitter about her situation, too. Emma's dad was a loser who'd shirked his responsibilities. If Josh saw Lyle on the street, he'd be hard-pressed not to kick his punk ass.

When they were about halfway up the ladder, Helena froze. Their radios sounded with employee chatter, but that wasn't what caught her attention. The metal rungs began to vibrate in his hands. Above them, tram cars swayed with motion.

Aftershock.

CHAPTER FIVE

HER WORST NIGHTMARE: heights *and* motion.

Helena could handle one or the other. She'd withstood the initial earthquake in the elephant yard and the first aftershock in the barn. She'd managed to set her fear aside and climb a tram pole that stood a hundred feet tall, even though she hadn't been more than ten feet off the ground in years. An aftershock at this dizzying altitude was too much for her. It rumbled closer and pressed in on all sides, trapping them in a crackling force field. Strange lights flashed in the smoky clouds at the edge of the horizon.

"Hang on," Josh shouted.

His advice was useless. What else was she going to do, jump off? She tightened her grip on the ladder rung, startled when it almost leaped out of her hands. Her boots slipped off the edge and flew wild, connecting with Josh's head. His grunt of pain was drowned out by her scream of terror as she dangled above him. Knowing that Josh was there to break her fall didn't help. Her already bruised knees slammed into the lower rungs and her cheek glanced off the side of the pole so hard she saw stars.

She clung to the ladder for dear life, trying not to kick Josh again.

Once again, childhood memories assailed her. She was five years old, paralyzed with panic in the back of her father's single-engine plane. Then she was in the audience at the air show, watching it spiral across the sky.

After the quake ended, those disturbing images lingered in her mind. She placed her feet on the rung and squeezed her eyes shut, enduring the heartache until it faded. Her biceps felt sore and her palms were raw. But other than a few new scrapes, she was fine. This aftershock had been shorter and less intense than the previous one.

"Are you okay?" Josh asked.

She nodded, glancing down at him. His left eyebrow was bleeding. "You?"

"Yeah," he said, wiping the blood off his face. The cut welled up and trickled a fresh streak down his jaw.

"Sorry."

"It's nothing."

It wasn't nothing; he needed a bandage, maybe even stitches. She descended a few rungs to take a better look. He gave her space by bracing his left foot and left hand on the safety guard. When she was close enough, she reached into her pocket for the rag she'd used on Kim earlier. "Put some pressure on it."

He held the cloth to his brow. "Thanks."

His proximity was oddly comforting. They were sandwiched together inside the guard, his bent elbow touching her hip. Her face heated as she remembered what he'd said about being on top.

The comment was inappropriate, even for him, but she'd let it slide. He was worried about his sister. They were both on edge. If she'd insisted on him climbing first, she might be the one with the bleeding head right now.

Their radios sounded with check-in requests. Josh had his hands full so she removed the radio at her belt to answer the call. "This is Helena. How is everyone?"

"We have a problem," Kim said. "A police officer stopped by just before the aftershock. They're evacuating the entire city, effective immediately, because of dangerous chemical spills and gas leaks."

Helena's stomach sank. "How much time do we have?"

"None. We're in a high-risk area for explosions."

She looked around, blinking rapidly. The park was populated with tall, leafy trees. She couldn't see over the canopy to assess the damage yet, but the smoky, empty sky appeared ominous. The fact that there were no planes or helicopters overhead didn't bode well. If San Diego had been declared a no-fly zone, they were in deep trouble.

Feeling dizzy, she closed her eyes and took a calming breath. "What are the evacuation orders?"

"Travel east, by foot."

"By foot?"

"The freeways are all messed up. People are gathering at the football stadium and riding buses to safety."

Jesus. The stadium was almost ten miles away. Getting there wouldn't be easy, but the employees couldn't stay here if the city was under evacuation. Helena didn't want to keep anyone at the park against their will, Josh included. It was unethical—not to mention illegal—to ask a staff member to risk injury or even death on the job. Although the zoo's animal collection was priceless, its human employees were more important. These people had families to reunite with, children to take care of.

"Okay," Helena said, swallowing hard. "Go ahead."

"Should we wait for you?"

She glanced at Josh. "Do you want to evacuate?" she asked him, taking her finger off the talk button.

"Do you?"

"I can't leave the animals."

"I can't leave the employees."

Helena accepted this answer. He was in charge of securing the park. She was responsible for the animals in it. They had to work together and hope for the best. Josh's commitment to safety seemed as strong as hers—and she was glad to have someone by her side.

"Don't wait for us," she said into the radio. "We're staying."

When Kim spoke again, her voice was strained. "The gorillas are locked away in the night house. Louis and Trent are still rounding up venomous snakes. The rest of us are leaving. We're taking wheelchairs for the injured."

"Be careful," Helena said.

"You, too," Kim choked out. "'Bye, Josh."

After Josh said goodbye to Kim and the others, Helena returned the radio to her belt.

Pulse pounding with trepidation, she contemplated the upper rungs of the ladder. They'd already come this far. Getting a view of the lion enclosure and the perimeter of the park was essential. "How do you feel about continuing?"

"Ready," he said, lifting the washcloth from his brow. The bleeding had slowed and an unsightly lump had formed. It wasn't a goose egg, like Kim's, but the swelling looked painful. Helena felt a twinge of sympathy.

"I am afraid of heights," she admitted suddenly.

Something lit in his eyes, a warm assessment she didn't want to like. He tucked the rag into his pocket. "I thought so."

"Why?"

"Just a hunch. You never ride the Skylift."

She shouldn't have been surprised that he'd noticed. He had a way of studying people and picking up on things. Necessary skills for dealing with the public. She didn't know why she'd told him. No one else knew about her phobia, not even Mitch. She hadn't explained her reluctance to fly out to Denver. Commercial jets didn't scare her as much as small planes, but she avoided both whenever possible.

Uncomfortable with her impulsive confession, she climbed up a few rungs, putting distance between them.

It wasn't like her to spill secrets, but this was an unusual situation. She felt bad about hurting him, and grateful for his presence.

That was all.

The space above the treetops was open to the sky, and therefore scarier. She couldn't bring herself to glance around while she ascended. Flames flickered in her peripheral vision and a layer of smoke shrouded the coastline. The lights she'd seen during the earthquake were gone, maybe a figment of her imagination or some freaky kinetic phenomenon. She focused on the ladder and tried to think positive.

Going up was easier than looking down. As long as she stayed in control, she'd be okay. Flying in a plane required her to depend on others—the pilot, mechanics, crew. On a ladder, she could climb at her own speed and take breaks if she needed to. The worst was probably over, as far as aftershocks. She didn't smell any fumes or chemicals.

The zoo had only been shut down twice in the ten years she'd worked here. Once for a fire hazard, once for a gas leak. Both evacuations had been precautionary, with no damages or injuries reported. They'd never had to relocate the animals. It was possible, even likely, that no further harm would come to them.

Boom!

The powerful explosion blew that theory out of the water. She cowered against the ladder, as if shrinking her body would protect her from hurtling shrapnel. Cringing, she snuck a peek at the fire cloud. It backlit a cluster of the city's tallest buildings.

"What do you see?" Josh demanded.

"Fire," she said.

"Where?"

She couldn't really tell. It looked like the ocean was burning, which didn't make sense. "In the bay, I think."

"Keep going."

Helena didn't move for fear of falling. Her pulse was racing, mind reeling. More eruptions followed the first. She swallowed a

scream as orange fireballs burst across the sky, sending plumes of
black smoke billowing into the air. Anyone near the explosions
would have been decimated. The majority of survivors must have
evacuated already. The slow, the weak, the injured—they were at
the most risk.

"Go up, or I'll pass you."

Bolstering her courage, she climbed the remaining ten rungs.
Her palms were sweaty, her heart pounding. When she reached the
top, her vision was blurred. She blinked to clear it, but she was too
terrified to glance around.

The peripheral chaos reminded her of the 9/11 terrorist attacks.
She'd been a high school senior at the time. School had been
canceled, and she'd watched the events unfold on live television.
Horrific images of ash clouds and debris. Bodies falling from the
towers. People jumping to avoid burning to death.

This was like 9/11. Only she wasn't watching it on TV. She was
living it.

While she clung to the ladder, trembling with fright, Josh
ascended to her level. He stood close behind her, invading her
space. His left foot was braced on the iron guard, his right hand
gripping the rung next to hers. His fingers were darkly tanned, the
knuckles scraped raw. The minor abrasions didn't look as out of
place as the lump on his brow. Maybe because he had a man's
hands, strong and capable and worn from use.

He had a man's body, too. She could sense his size and height,
the breadth of his shoulders and the deceptive power in his lean
muscles. She'd noticed that he was well-built and attractive on
numerous occasions, but she'd always dismissed him as boyish.
Twenty-one or so. Looking back, this almost seemed like a willful
underestimate. He'd been older than that when they'd met four
years ago.

He also had a man's presence. She'd felt it when he'd gripped
her upper arms earlier and she felt it now, larger than life behind
her. He was comfortable in his skin. He exuded confidence. She
was a tall woman, and she didn't feel small or diminished next to
him, but she liked his size. He could probably lift her up and carry
her. He had big hands.

She released a slow breath, trying to regroup. Her strange
reaction to Josh didn't mean anything. The earthquake must have
sent her hormones into overdrive. It was adrenaline, not attraction.
They were stuck with each other, and she needed his help. She was

relieved that he wasn't as careless or immature as he let on. That was it.

When she summoned up the nerve to take in a panoramic view, horror enveloped her. There was fire all around them, not just near the coast. Her gaze skimmed over leaning trees and crumbling rooftops. It looked like the apocalypse.

The zoo was nestled into a wooded area north of the Gaslight District. Museums, parks and historic landmarks flanked them on every side. She couldn't get a glimpse of the nearby streets or freeways from this vantage point, but it appeared that the city center had been hit hard. The modern skyscrapers were still standing. Older structures like Casa Del Prado and the California Bell Tower were gone.

Just…gone. Erased from the skyline.

Dismayed by the bigger picture, she narrowed her focus to their immediate surroundings. The zoo was divided into five sections: Heart of Africa, Copper Canyon, Rio Loco, Arctic Freeze and Lost Jungle. Leafy trees blocked her view of most of the area.

She turned her attention to the lion enclosure. It appeared empty, but that wasn't unusual. There were a number of shady nooks and crannies for the animals to retreat into when they wanted privacy or a nap. One of the enclosure's walls had cracked open, leaving a space large enough for the lions to slip through. Unfortunately, she couldn't see what was on the other side. Greg could be there, quietly bleeding to death.

After thirty seconds of looking around, she almost swooned from vertigo. Stomach lurching, she glanced over her shoulder at Josh. He wasn't studying the lion enclosure or any structure inside the park. His eyes were locked on something in the distance. She followed his gaze to the bay. Through a haze of black smoke and giant flames, she spotted the reason for his distraction: the Coronado Bridge.

It was…broken. A section in the middle had fallen apart.

The bridge was miles away, too far to see individual cars or people. But she could imagine them.

Josh covered his mouth with his left hand. The knuckles on this hand were scraped raw, just like his right. Veins stood out from his skin in harsh relief, snaking toward a point at the middle of his wrist. His eyes watered with the emotion he was trying to hold inside.

Helena knew he was worried about his sister. She supposed it would be more polite to look away and give him a moment of peace. Humans also needed privacy, and most men didn't like to show weakness. She could relate to that.

But instead of lowering her gaze, she held it steady. His tears didn't strike her as a sign of weakness. When they spilled over his hand, he wiped them away impatiently.

"She drives across that bridge with Emma every morning," he said.

Oh, God. Not the little girl, too. Helena couldn't imagine the pain of losing a child. She didn't know what to say.

He stared across the ravaged expanse, silent. The entire bay area was burning. His sister and niece might have survived the quake, the bridge collapse, the explosions and the raging fires. But they might not have. Helena couldn't bring herself to offer him any platitudes. She hated it when people lied and said everything would be fine.

After a long moment, he glanced at her. "Do you think I'd feel it if they were gone?"

"I don't know," she said, surprised by the question.

"Because I don't feel it."

She thought back to her childhood, remembering all of the times her father had performed in the air show. He'd done hundreds of daredevil stunts. She'd watched from the crowd, frozen with the certainty that he would fall from the sky. He never had.

Feelings were unreliable.

Josh picked up his radio to give Louis and Trent an update on the explosions. He stayed composed until he mentioned the bridge collapse. Then his voice sounded thin, as if he'd taken a hit off a joint and was holding in the smoke. Trent had to sign off because Louis needed help with one of the pythons. Josh returned the radio to his belt, clearing his throat.

"Can you check the perimeter?" she asked. "I would do it myself, but looking down makes me dizzy."

"Sure."

He examined the trees and structures below. He was thorough and deliberate, unbothered by their gut-churning distance from the ground.

While he searched the area, she contemplated the sunny yellow tram cars, dangling on heavy cables about ten feet away. They carried happy families over the park every single day. Mothers loaded squirming babies into those deathtraps all the time. She couldn't fathom it.

"I can't see all of the fence line," he said. "Most of it looks okay."

"Any sign of the lions or Greg?"

He shook his head. "What do you want to do?"

"Continue to the enclosure."

His jaw flexed in disapproval.

She knew that approaching the scene without Louis and Trent as backup would be dangerous, but she couldn't wait any longer. Greg might still be alive. The clock was ticking. "Do you have a better idea?"

Apparently not, because he started down the ladder. She turned and flattened her belly against the rungs to make more room for him. His body aligned with hers for a brief moment. The position felt unbearably intimate, like lovers entwined.

When his forearms touched her rib cage, she sucked in a sharp breath.

"Are you hurt?" he asked, pausing.

"No. I'm fine."

He seemed puzzled by her reaction, but he continued his descent. He had to skirt around her hips, which were wider than the ladder. She closed her eyes, aware that his face was inches from her bottom, his strong arms framing her thighs.

A pulse throbbed between her legs where she'd squeezed them together. She had to force herself not to squirm as he passed by. One false move could dislodge him.

This was an odd response to fear. It almost felt like arousal. Maybe her physical side had taken over because she was overwhelmed, mentally and emotionally. Or perhaps the traumatic experience had stripped away her natural defenses, leaving her more vulnerable to human contact.

Swallowing hard, she followed him down the ladder. The descent was even more harrowing than the climb. After about twenty rungs, she didn't have to worry about inappropriate tingles. She felt nothing but anxiety and cold sweat. It wasn't possible to move lower without looking down, over and over again.

Josh wasn't oblivious to her struggle. He went slow and murmured words of encouragement. It seemed to take forever. She was thirsty and tired, even though she was accustomed to strenuous activity.

"We're almost there," he said, his voice reassuring.

She wondered if he was suffering any ill effects from the blow to the temple. His knuckles had probably gotten scraped during the first quake. The impact must have knocked him off his feet, too.

As they reached the lower edge of the guard, Helena heard a subtle, ominous sound. It was the almost indiscernible whisper of padded footsteps. The vague impression of shifting molecules and stealthy motion; the soft *snick* of a single twig.

"Wait!" she cried out to Josh, just before the lion pounced.

CHAPTER SIX

CHLOE HELD HER daughter to her chest and wept for several moments.

It felt odd to have an emotional breakdown with a stranger sitting next to her. Mateo made no move to comfort her. When the moment passed, she rubbed her runny nose against her shoulder and took a deep breath. Emma stared up at her in concern, sucking the first two fingers on her right hand. She was a beautiful child. Golden-haired and brown-eyed, like Chloe, but with Lyle's signature features. His cruel mouth was a perfect cupid's bow on Emma. His winged brows gave her an elfish, Tinker Bell look.

Emma's angelic face fooled everyone. She was a handful. Her favorite word was *no*.

Chloe glanced at Mateo. He was staring out at the water, not at them. His chest rose and fell with labored breaths. The swim had exhausted them both, and he'd done all the work. Her blood was starting to cool. Soon she'd be shivering in her wet clothes.

It occurred to her that there were worse things than witnessing and surviving a disaster of this proportion. Dozens of people had just fallen to their deaths, and that was horrific, but she didn't know any of them. The same might not be true for Mateo. Had he lost a close friend or family member?

"Were you with someone?" she asked, sniffling.

He looked at her in confusion.

"Your family?"

"Mi familia?"

"Yes," she said. "Are they…out there?"

He followed her gaze to the bay. *"No familia. Solo mi equipo. Todos mis compañeros."*

She didn't follow.

"No family here," he said in stilted English. "Panamá."

He pronounced it with a heavy emphasis on the last syllable. She'd never heard it said that way before. Did his family live in Panama? It was a place in Latin America, if she remembered correctly. They had a canal.

"Y tú?" he asked.

"Me?"

"Tu familia," he said with patience.

"No," she said, shaking her head. "My parents and my brother—" She broke off, uneasy. She didn't know where her parents were, or if Josh was okay. "I wasn't with them."

Emma took her fingers out of her mouth. "Unco Josh."

Chloe was about to tell her daughter that they couldn't visit Uncle Josh yet when sirens started blaring. The sound was unfamiliar, and chilling. Not an ambulance or a police car, but short bleats at regular intervals.

Emma wailed in distress. "Mommy!"

"Tsunami," Chloe said, her heart in her throat. It was a tsunami warning.

Mateo needed no translation for this word. He leaped to his feet, studying the bay with trepidation. Some of the boats in the harbor had broken loose from their moorings. Other than that, the water was deserted.

So was the sky. They were less than a mile from the airport, so she imagined that flights had been canceled and planes grounded. But why were there no helicopters over the bridge? This was major news.

In the time it had taken Chloe and Mateo to swim to land, all of San Diego had fled. The embarcadero, a popular tourist destination, was deserted. They were alone on the grassy plateau. Normally there were joggers on the paths and people in the nearby park. Shops and restaurants lined Seaside Village, which was located on the other side of the peninsula. It was too far away to see much, but she imagined total devastation. The earthquake had been off the charts. If the Coronado Bridge had failed, the entire city must be in shambles. Smoke clouds obscured the tall buildings in the downtown area.

"Ya," Mateo said, offering her his hand. *"Vámanos."*

Chloe stood, with his help. Then she picked up Emma and propped her on one hip. Mateo put his arm around her. She grasped his slippery side and leaned on him heavily as they hobbled away from the shore, toward the concrete bike path.

Their progress was slow. They were both barefoot. Sharp pebbles dug into the soles of her feet and her thigh ached with every step. She couldn't run to save her life. Or her child's.

It was hopeless.

Mateo did his best to keep them moving. Although he was strong and well-built, he wasn't a big man, maybe five-ten to her five-eight. She didn't think he could carry her. There was no way he could carry them both. Emma could walk, of course, but Chloe was reluctant to let her go. In the event of an aftershock or killer waves, she wanted a firm grip on her daughter.

The sirens continued to blare. Emma clung to Chloe's neck and cried. Mateo's skin was slick and clammy beneath her fingertips, his hand hot on her waist. When he paused to rest, Chloe studied his face. He was breathing hard from exertion, his mouth grim.

It was on the tip of her tongue to beg him not to leave them. She didn't know why he hadn't run away already. Instead of sacrificing his life for two strangers, he could abandon them and save himself. With a sinking heart, she realized what she had to do. It was the same choice she'd made in the water. Agonizing, but necessary.

"Take Emma," she choked out. "Take her and get to high ground."

"Ay, mamita," he said, his voice chiding. *"No digas eso."*

"Please."

Ignoring her plea, he dragged them about twenty more yards down the path. The only business at this end of the peninsula was a tiny, half-destroyed gift shop called Surf Diego. Shards of glass littered the ground. The windows were broken and part of the roof had caved in.

Mateo released her near the entrance. He said something in Spanish. Goodbye, perhaps.

"Take Emma with you," she begged.

Emma shrieked in protest. "No, Mommy!"

He gestured toward the bay, which appeared calm. *"No hay olas. Estamos bien."*

She didn't understand.

Holding out his palm like a stop sign, he repeated what he'd said before. Then he pointed at the gift shop. She guessed that he wanted her to stay here with Emma while he went inside. He'd left her once before, in the water. And he'd come back for her. She nodded her acceptance, her pulse pounding.

He must have lost his shoes during the swim, just as she had. He put his bare foot next to hers, as if measuring the length. Then he adjusted his shin guards to cover his feet. Strapping them on like snowshoes, he entered the ravaged building.

While she waited, Chloe set Emma down on the sidewalk to check her over. Emma was wearing a red ladybug top with black leggings and her favorite red shoes. It was a miracle that the shoes had stayed on. They were wet and squishy, but still functional. Her diaper was saturated with seawater, however.

Chloe removed the diaper and tugged Emma's leggings back into place. Emma had started toilet training a few months ago. She wasn't perfect, but hopefully she wouldn't have an accident. Chloe wrapped Mateo's jersey around Emma like a cape and lifted her up again.

Although the bay was calm, the warning sirens hadn't let up, and her nerves were on edge. The air was heavy with smoke and gasoline and something that reminded her of Christmas. One year her dad had tossed some bows and gift paper into the fireplace. It made an awful, burning-chemical odor.

Mateo came out of the rubble with a beach bag. He was wearing a blue surf shirt and a pair of dockside loafers. There was another pair for her inside the bag. Not the right size, but close enough. She slipped them on, hoping they wouldn't be arrested for looting.

Properly shod, they prepared to leave again. Mateo put his right arm around Chloe, urging her forward. There was a park and a bike path at this end of the peninsula. Seaside Village, a shopping area, was on the other side. They needed to move past the shops to reach the mainland. It wasn't a long way, but their progress was slow.

Chloe struggled against a wave of despair. She wasn't sure they'd be able to reach safety or find help along the way. A bridge had collapsed. People were trapped in buildings. Neighborhoods were on fire.

Tsunami or no tsunami, they might not be able to escape this hellhole.

What if the embarcadero was safer than downtown? Maybe they should stay put and pray for rescue.

Mateo didn't appear to be suffering from any indecision. For a stranger in a strange land, he seemed rather confident. He stuck to his plan, whatever it was. They established a rhythm, loping across the park together. Without him, she couldn't have limped more than a hundred feet. He moved like a well-oiled machine, tireless and smooth. Sweat gathered on his forehead and snaked down his jaw. She wondered how old he was. He had the hard muscles of a man, but so did some teenagers.

The earth rumbled beneath them, threatening to break apart. Chloe pictured a huge rift opening up and swallowing them whole. She dropped to the grass with Emma, making a shield with her body. Mateo got down on his knees and threw his arms around them both.

Oh, God. This was the end.

It seemed too cruel to imagine they would survive the bridge, the submerged vehicle and the near drowning, only to get crushed by a falling tree or swept away in a tidal wave.

When the shaking subsided, Chloe lifted her head. Mateo stared at her, breathing hard. They were still alive. There was no tsunami. He stood, studying their surroundings. This quake hadn't felt as strong as the others.

"We're okay," she said, hugging Emma to her chest. "We're okay."

They kept moving away from the coast. Chloe's thigh ached. She was becoming numb to the pain. Instead of being alert and focused, she felt drowsy. Her mind couldn't handle sharp acuity. Her body wanted to quit.

Mateo stopped for a short rest, sharing a bottle of water that he must have picked up at the gift shop. Then he dug into his supplies for a little bag of magic: gummy bears. Emma accepted a handful with delight. Mateo was her new favorite person. The candy was a real lifesaver. He offered a few gummy bears to Chloe, who popped them into her mouth. The instant sugar rush lifted her spirits.

She could do this. She could keep going.

They continued their staggering journey toward the park at the end of the peninsula. Emma walked beside Chloe, holding her hand. The little girl was tired of being carried, and the extra weight on Chloe's injured side was uncomfortable. She hoped the tsunami warning was a false alarm.

Embarcadero Park was a grassy area interspersed with picnic tables and domed pavilions. It was on higher ground, so that was good. But also bad, because climbing would be difficult for Chloe.

Whoosh-boom.

Air sucked out and pressure slammed in as something exploded in the distance. It sounded as if a pile of fireworks had gone off, or the guys on the naval base had decided to test everything in their artillery at once.

She swooped up Emma and looked over her shoulder in dismay. The bay was on fire. The *water* in the bay was on fire.

Chloe was no science expert, but she understood the basics. Water didn't burn. So there was something on the surface, a type of fuel or chemical. More explosions followed the first. Huge clouds of fire burst on the shore like atomic bombs. There had been a major malfunction at the military base. Maybe the airport.

It didn't really matter. The important part was that a lot of stuff was on fire. Everywhere. Flaming debris was flying through the air, catching the branches of nearby trees. The earthquake had probably caused some pipelines to break, because the downtown area was going off like bottle rockets.

Forget the tsunami—they needed to escape the *fire*.

Mateo pulled her toward the only shelter available. It was some kind of heavy-duty storage shed made of concrete blocks. The roof might be flammable, but they didn't have much choice. They'd get incinerated if they stayed out in the open. The pavilions were already burning. Orange cinders were dancing on the wind and floating across the sky, like monarch butterflies. Her nostrils stung from chemical fumes.

The door must have been damaged in the quake, because it came right off the hinges. They scrambled inside, coughing. She squinted at the strange interior. There were fat blue pipes, wider than her waist in circumference, imbedded in the concrete floor.

"Are these gas pipes?" she gasped, horrified.

"Agua," Mateo said.

That meant water. Blue pipes. It made sense. She tried to shush a distraught Emma by pressing her lips to the little girl's forehead. To Chloe's left, there was a set of aluminum steps leading down to a second floor. Chloe was worried about the pipes exploding, but she was more worried about being able to breathe, and the main room was filling with smoke. They went down the steps, moving carefully. The lower section was similar to the upper, with blue pipes. It was dark and cramped, but the air was clean. For the time being, they were safe.

Her knees almost buckled with relief.

Mateo helped her sit down in the corner. When their eyes adjusted to the meager light, he supplied Emma with more gummy bears, chatting in a cheerful voice. Chloe could have kissed him. But she was tired, and suddenly cold. Her T-shirt and jeans were still damp. She touched the wet sock around her thigh, hoping the bleeding had slowed.

Mateo removed a hooded sweatshirt from his beach bag.

"Thank you," she said in a hoarse voice, putting it on.

He also had a child's T-shirt for Emma. Chloe took off her ladybug top first. She tucked the fabric under her bottom like a diaper, figuring any barrier was better than none. Then she helped Emma don the dry shirt.

"Flower," Emma said, touching the hibiscus decal on the front.

The firestorm raged on outside. Chloe could hear trees falling and wind blowing. Again, she wondered if the world was ending. It was a maudlin thought, but her mind often traveled that direction. She'd suffered from depression after Emma was born. Before, as well, although her parents had called it "teen angst." Getting involved with Lyle had fed her self-destructive tendencies. Breaking up with him sent her into a downward spiral.

Why was she alive?

She hadn't wanted to be, for months at a time. Her mother had taken care of Emma while Chloe slept all day. She hadn't gone to school or work. She hadn't even left the house. She'd done nothing but lay in bed.

It was difficult for her to believe she deserved to be here. Someone who'd tried to take her own life had been spared above others. For what? To witness the real end? Maybe this was the ultimate punishment for her carelessness and self-harm. Watching her child suffer and witnessing a fiery apocalypse.

She began to tremble, overwhelmed with emotion. They'd just survived another incredibly traumatic event. She didn't know if they'd make it out of this temporary hideaway. The city was burning down around them. People who'd been trapped inside their homes, who hadn't been able to escape fast enough, were now dying.

Chloe wasn't equipped to take this in stride. She didn't have the temperament to stay strong during a catastrophe. She couldn't handle seeing Emma in pain or in danger. Shrugging off death and destruction was beyond her.

Mateo gave Emma a keychain with a red penlight. She pointed it at the wall, making red dots dance across the surface.

Chloe kept shivering.

Mateo sat down beside her. After a short hesitation, he put his arm around her. He thought she was cold, and she was. The warmth of his body felt pleasant, but it was the basic human contact that soothed her. The same way his support had kept her going, and the candy revived her spirits, his touch lifted her up.

CHAPTER SEVEN

HELENA'S WARNING CAME a second too late.

She watched in horror as Josh froze on the ladder, midstep. The lower half of his body was beneath the safety guard, about four feet off the ground. He couldn't avoid Zuma's stealth attack. The lioness rushed from the shadows and leaped into the air, pouncing on Josh's dangling foot.

Helena swallowed a scream, expecting to see sharp teeth, gore and bits of flesh attached to a shinbone. Instead the lioness let out a playful growl and held his boot between her paws as if she'd just caught a mouse.

Josh made the high-pitched yelp of a man who'd been goosed. He jerked his foot back and forth, trying to shake loose from the big cat's paws. Zuma didn't put up much of a fight; she was just toying with him. He broke free and high-tailed it back up the ladder so fast Helena didn't have time to move to make room for him.

"Fuck," he said, crowding in behind her.

Directly below them, Zuma sniffed at the weapons and rubbed her cheek against the lowest ladder rungs. After circling the pole a few times, she batted a pile of leaves on the ground. Then she rolled in them.

Helena wasn't fooled; this was not a cute kitty.

Lions were social animals, even in captivity. Some were friendly with their handlers, docile at all times. Not Zuma. She was an aggressive member of the species, difficult to work with and picky about food. She could be gentle one minute and nasty the next. Her jowls were stained red with Greg's blood.

Helena pressed her forehead against the cool metal rung, her heart pounding. She pictured Josh kicking wildly and shooting up the ladder. His panicked whoop echoed in her ears. The scene played over and over in her mind like a Three Stooges reel. She imagined it set to a slapstick soundtrack, with a lively piano riff as he raced along the rungs.

There was nothing the least bit funny about a lion attack, or anything else they'd experienced today. But Josh's freak-out struck her as hilarious, and her attempts to smother the giggles didn't work. Maybe it was the stress of the situation. Maybe she was having a mental breakdown. She couldn't seem to get a grip on herself, so she just surrendered to the moment and laughed like a madwoman.

Josh seemed baffled by her outburst. He glanced down at Zuma, who was stretched out in the shade. Then he shifted his position on the ladder so he could examine Helena's face. It was probably red and splotchy. She was almost crying.

"Are you laughing?"

She nodded and laughed some more. Ugly laughing. Her nose was running.

"You're laughing at me. Witnessing my near-death amuses you."

"I'm sorry," she gasped, trying to get a hold of herself. "Are you hurt?"

"No, I'm not hurt. I almost pissed my pants, but I'm not hurt."

That set her off again. She giggled until she was out of breath. Then she sagged against the ladder, belly aching.

"Are you done?"

She blotted her eyes with the sleeve of her shirt. "Yes."

"You sure?"

"You must think I'm crazy."

"No."

"Weird, then."

"Not at all. I'm just glad we found your sense of humor. It went missing for a few years."

"Ha-ha," she said, rolling her eyes.

"You should laugh more often. It looks good on you."

She sobered at this statement, said in a warm tone. His gaze was admiring, even eager. He'd clearly enjoyed her loss of control, and not just because it broke the tension between them. There was a sexual element to his reaction. He liked seeing her flushed with pleasure.

She'd learned to be wary of male coworkers at her first job as a stable hand. Brusque tomboys weren't immune to crude advances. It was an unpleasant life lesson she'd never forgotten.

Some men preyed on vulnerable women. Others harassed the ones they felt the most threatened by. Helena placed herself in that second category. But Josh wasn't either type of man, despite his suggestive comments. His humor was good-natured and impulsive, not degrading. She'd been too busy avoiding him to acknowledge that.

She'd never acknowledged the chemistry between them, either. She hadn't been forced to confront it. The earthquake had shaken her up and busted down her guard, exposing a desire she'd been trying to suppress. She wasn't worried about Josh cornering her behind the vending machines or stealing a kiss. If anything, the idea excited her.

She *liked* him.

Well, maybe *like* wasn't the right word. Physical attraction didn't require her to like him. He might be smarter and more dependable than she'd given him credit for, but he wasn't her respected colleague. He wasn't best-buddy material. Josh Garrison was some other kind of material. One-night-stand material. Stumbling-home-from-the-bar material. Guilty-pleasure, mindless-hookup, shower-fantasy material.

Heat flooded her cheeks at the mental picture, which seemed twice as pornographic in his proximity. It was one thing to entertain dirty thoughts in private. Conjuring them while he was staring right at her was quite another.

Because of their respective positions on the ladder, his eyes were level with her mouth. His right foot was on a lower ladder rung, his left propped up on the guard. Their bodies were almost touching in several places. His chest rose and fell with steady breaths. She could feel the warmth of his hand next to hers and see beads of perspiration at his temple. A crease formed between his brows, as if he could read her mind.

Instead of teasing her further, he cleared his throat and glanced away. He looked a bit flushed himself. The temperature had risen between them. He smelled good, like ocean and clean sweat and salty male skin. She wondered how he would taste.

Time to move.

He couldn't go down; she had to go up. Feeling awkward, she ascended a few rungs. When her raging hormones subsided, she grabbed her radio to call Trent at the reptile house. "Trent, this is Helena. We've got a lion issue."

He didn't respond.

"The code one is confirmed," she said into the receiver. "We're on tram pole number three, in need of assistance."

Still nothing.

"Try yours," she said to Josh.

He lifted his radio and repeated the same information. With the same results. They spent the next few minutes trying to get through to Trent and Louis, to no avail. Josh sent a text on his cell phone. They waited. Zuma waited with them, napping in the shade.

"Maybe they left," Helena said.

"Without saying goodbye?"

It seemed unlikely. Trent and Louis were both dedicated herpetologists. They often traded pranks with Josh and Cordell, but the ongoing rivalry was grounded in friendship. The four of them were bros. "I hope they're okay," she said. Then a terrible thought occurred to her. "What about Tau?"

Josh looked down at Zuma. "I thought only female lions hunted."

"They hunt more often."

"Maybe I should make a grab for the gun."

"I wouldn't risk it," Helena said. "She could jump up and attack you in a flash. Lions can move incredibly fast."

"How fast?"

"Fifty miles an hour, in short sprints."

He touched one of the pouches on his belt. "I have pepper spray."

"How far does it go?"

"Ten feet."

Zuma was at least twenty feet away from the pole.

"I'll give you the spray," he said. "You keep an eye on her while I get the gun. If she comes at me, blast her."

Helena wasn't on board with this plan. "She might not stop. It's a deterrent, not a guarantee."

"So what do you want to do?" he asked, impatient.

"There's nothing we *can* do."

He fell silent for moment. "I have another idea."

"What?"

"I could mark my territory."

She smothered a laugh. "You want to pee on the pole?"

"Why not?"

"Because territorial instincts are triggered by competing members of the same species. Your urine won't scare off a lion."

"Aren't lions afraid of humans?"

"Some are, but Zuma's not threatened by the sight of you or even the guns. Peeing on the pole will only get it wet."

"Well, damn."

"Do you have to go?"

"I can hold it."

Helena was thirsty, hungry and tired. The sun shone directly overhead, indicating it was near lunchtime. She felt light-headed and claustrophobic, in addition to acrophobic. She didn't have to pee, though. Small favors.

"I know," he said. "I'll rig a lasso with my belt and pull up the tranquilizer gun."

"Your belt isn't long enough."

"I'll attach it to a sock."

She glanced over her shoulder at him. "It's not stiff enough, either."

He smiled at the unintentional double entendre, rubbing a hand over his jaw. The lump on his brow didn't detract from his good looks. It just gave him a manlier edge, like the scraped knuckles.

"You won't be able to pick up the gun without wire or a hook," she said. "Something prehensile, like a tail."

"Where are the flying monkeys when we need them?"

She grimaced at the mention. *The Wizard of Oz* had terrified her as a child. Iceland wasn't known for its gentle fairy tales, but she'd always been puzzled by the American affection for such a disturbing movie.

"Not a fan of flying monkeys, I take it," he said.

"No."

He took his cell phone out of his pocket. "Do you want to text someone?"

They were still pretty high off the ground, and her palms were sweaty.

"I'll do it for you," he offered.

"My mother's number should be there."

He scrolled with his thumb. "Kat Fjord?"

"Yes."

"What message?"

"Just tell her that I'm still at work, and I'm okay."

After sending the text, he glanced up at her. "Anyone else?"

Helena thought of Gwen, her best friend since childhood. She owned a tattoo parlor downtown, but it didn't open until noon. Helena hoped Gwen had been in a safe place during the earthquake. "You could try Gwen."

"Gwen?"

"She's a friend of mine."

"I remember her. Dark hair, tattoos."

It didn't surprise her that Josh had noticed Gwen. She was pretty and unusual. Sometimes she stopped by the zoo to do animal sketches or have lunch with Helena.

"What's her number?"

She started to recite it but drew a blank. "I don't have it memorized. All of my contacts are stored in my phone."

He accepted this answer, but he still seemed curious.

"What?"

"Nothing. I was just wondering why you thought of calling her before…"

Her boyfriend. Helena's stomach clenched with unease. Mitch was smart enough to contact her mother for news, but she felt guilty about not trying to reach out to him. Instead, she'd fantasized about touching Josh.

He put the phone away. "It's none of my business."

She agreed. The next few minutes passed in tense silence. Josh wasn't good at stillness. He shifted his weight back and forth, stretched his neck muscles, readjusted his grip. Either he had to pee really badly, or he was drumming up the nerve to say something.

She focused on the nearby tree branches, glancing down at Zuma every so often. The aviary must have collapsed, because there were exotic birds flitting around. Maybe one would land near Zuma and inspire a chase.

"For the record," Josh said, "I didn't know you had a boyfriend when I asked you out."

She closed her eyes, wishing he'd leave the subject alone.

"I'm not a poacher."

"Why are you bringing this up?"

"Because you've given me the cold shoulder ever since."

She'd given him the cold shoulder before, too. But he was so used to adoring women, he hadn't recognized it.

"I'm sorry I made you uncomfortable," he said. "I didn't mean to."

Helena steeled herself against those words. She didn't want to feel a connection to him. It was harder to resist a man who cried for his sister and apologized in earnest. "I'm not giving you the cold shoulder. This is just my personality."

"If you say so."

"You don't believe me?"

"I'd rather know what I did to offend you."

She clenched her fists around the metal rung, making a revving motion. He was using his sneaky conversational skills on her, and they were working. She couldn't deny him a simple answer. "I thought you asked me out as a joke."

"Why would I do that?"

"To make the other guys laugh."

"They did laugh," he admitted.

"I saw them." Later that afternoon, she'd spotted him with a group of male keepers. She'd walked by them on her way to the staff building, and they'd started guffawing like hyenas as soon as they thought she was out of earshot.

"Louis told me you didn't have a boyfriend. He set me up to get shot down, so yeah. They laughed their asses off."

She glanced over her shoulder at him again, evaluating his sincerity. It sounded like something Louis would do. Those guys loved to play pranks on each other, the dirtier the better. She should have considered this explanation before.

"They weren't laughing at you," he said. "And I would never ask out a woman as a joke. That's a dick move."

She flushed at his implication. She *had* assumed the worst of him. "I don't always know how to interpret people."

"What do you mean?"

"It doesn't come easily to me. I'm better with animals."

"I've gathered that."

"I'm also not a native English speaker."

"You're not?"

"I'm from Iceland. We speak Icelandic there."

"Huh."

"I wasn't fluent until the third or fourth grade. So I got teased for having a weird accent, among other things."

"Like what?"

"My height and lack of…good humor."

"Oh." Exactly the same things he ribbed her about.

"They called me Morticia Addams."

"Morticia Addams is sexy."

Her stomach fluttered with warmth. Her classmates hadn't meant it as a compliment, but Josh did. She believed that he found her attractive—and it felt good to be wanted. On the other hand, he was young and hot-blooded. Judging by the amount of flirting he did, he had a roving eye and an overactive libido.

"I tease you because I like you," he said. "That's why I asked you out, too."

"You like a lot of women."

"Is that why you said no?"

"You know why I said no."

"What if you didn't have a boyfriend?"

"I did, and I do, so let's drop it."

"Okay," he said, agreeable. "Tell me about Iceland."

"It's cold, and isolated, and surrounded by water."

He laughed at this terse description. "Why did you leave?"

"My dad sent for us when I was five."

"He came here first?"

"He was born here. He got stationed in Keflavík near the end of the Cold War."

"Navy?"

"Air force."

"How long was he there?"

"Long enough to get my mother pregnant."

"So you didn't meet him until you were five?"

"That's right."

"Did you like him?"

"I don't remember much about him," she said, which wasn't quite true. He'd been brash, and affectionate, and handsome. She hadn't understood what he was saying half the time, but she'd liked him. "He died when I was eight."

"Shit," he muttered. "I'm sorry."

She was sorry, too.

"Have you been back to Iceland since then?"

"Once, when I was sixteen. We went for my grandmother's funeral. By then I was so Americanized I could hardly speak Icelandic."

"Were you sad?"

She didn't know if he meant the loss of her grandmother or the loss of her language. "Yes," she said, to both.

"Where's your mom now?"

"She lives in Oregon."

"Are you still close?"

"Very close. She visits every Christmas."

"You don't go there?"

"No."

"Because you don't like flying," he ventured.

She made a noncommittal sound, reluctant to say more. He'd retrieved a shocking amount of personal information from her in a short time. He was a good listener, which probably put women at ease.

Josh seemed to get the message that she didn't want to talk and stopped trying to engage her, but he managed to be just as intrusive when he was quiet. He removed his belt and one of his shoelaces. Needing both hands free to work, he bent his forearm around the guard before securing a loop to the end of the belt. Then he reached into his pocket for a set of keys. He uncoiled one of the key rings and twisted the thin metal into a hook.

Once the hook was attached to the belt, he put the loop around his wrist. The contraption still wasn't long enough to reach the guns, so he added his tactical baton, using it like an extension of his arm.

"Give me the pepper spray," Helena said.

Josh handed it to her. They both moved down on the ladder and got into position at the bottom of the guard. They were vulnerable to attack here, guard or no guard. Zuma couldn't climb the pole, but she could jump at least ten or twelve feet high. With a well-placed swipe, she could do a lot of damage.

He lowered the hook while Helena watched Zuma. The big cat didn't seem interested in what they were doing. She yawned, displaying sharp incisors.

Josh's hook hovered above the strap of the tranquilizer gun, not quite touching it. He descended another step and tried again. It was a risky move, but this whole strategy was dangerous. Helena's pulse raced as the hook slid along the edge of the gun strap and almost caught.

Then a sandy-brown blur sailed across the space.

Zuma.

Helena let out a little squeak of panic and pressed the button on the spray canister, sending an arc of chemicals through the air. Some of the mist hit Zuma's torso and tail as she lunged for the belt. She bit into the leather with so much force that the baton flew out of Josh's hand. He nearly lost his balance. Helena moved her arm and took aim for a second shot, not realizing she was still holding down the button.

Josh got sprayed instead of Zuma.

Maybe the toxic cloud saved him from another attack, because Zuma fled the scene as quickly as she'd entered it. She retreated to the nearby bushes, where she paced back and forth in agitation.

Josh started coughing and spitting. His eyes watered from irritation and his face turned beet red. He looked as if he wanted to peel his own skin off. Although he didn't vomit, he gagged several times.

Helena felt terrible for him. Tucking the offending canister into her pocket, she rubbed his arm and made soothing sounds. It took him about five minutes to recover. He straightened, clearing his throat.

"I'm so sorry," she said.

"Why did you *do* that?"

"It was an accident! I missed the first time, and when I tried again, you were in the way."

He spat on the ground again. "Remind me not to stand next to you when you're holding an assault rifle. Christ."

"I'm sorry," she repeated, cringing.

"At least it wasn't a direct hit."

"It wasn't?"

"My head was turned. I can't imagine taking a full shot to the face."

"Most men can't."

He squinted at her blearily.

"Never mind. It's kind of a girl joke."

"I get it," he said. "I just can't believe you said it."

"I thought it would make you feel better."

They moved back to their higher perches. His belt contraption lay coiled on the ground next to the weapons. Zuma continued to pace, saliva dripping from her jowls. The chemicals had irritated her, too.

"Do you think she'll attack again?" he asked.

"I don't know. She might be afraid."

"Or she could be ready to rage."

"Yes."

He tried to radio Trent again, with no response. Zuma settled down in the shade and licked her paws. Helena had no idea how long the lion would guard the base of the pole. It could be minutes, hours, even days. She looked up at the sky. Dark smoke clouds marred the brilliant blue expanse. There were structure fires in the area, maybe entire neighborhoods engulfed.

"What now?" Josh asked, following her gaze.

"We wait."

CHAPTER EIGHT

Josh was miserable.

He'd learned about patience and lying in wait for the enemy during his stint in the navy. He'd endured countless hours on a narrow bunk in a tiny cabin on a huge ship. But he hadn't enjoyed those aspects of military service, or many others. He preferred the constant motion and varied challenges of his zoo security job. Working outdoors in San Diego was a beautiful thing. He loved the weather, the diversity, the upbeat energy…the women. Seeing hot women in short shorts was a hell of a perk.

He also liked kids. Kids were cool.

What he didn't like was inaction. They were in the middle of the worst disaster in the city's history. There were wild animals running loose and fires breaking out all over the place. Chloe and Emma might be injured or desperate for help, and he couldn't do a damned thing about any of it. He was stuck on this fucking pole, twenty feet off the ground. He was thirsty, hungry and sick with worry. His eyes were raw from the smoke and pepper spray. The lump on his brow ached, and his bladder was about to burst.

He looked up at Helena. She hadn't spoken in over an hour. Which was a pity, since he hung on every word she said. He was fascinated by her background, her no-nonsense attitude, her unexpected sense of humor. She'd made a dirty joke with a straight face. He didn't know whether to be intimidated or turned on.

That was part of the draw, though. She unsettled him and excited him at the same time. Something about her stern-taskmaster persona, combined with the enticing hint of softness underneath, struck him as erotic.

The afternoon stretched into infinity. Elephants trumpeted. Monkeys screeched. Smoke clouds drifted across the sky.

"I have to take a piss," he said finally.

"Go ahead."

"What about you?"

"I'm okay."

He descended a few rungs and stood on the safety guard with his back to her. Unzipping with one hand, he directed his aim and relieved himself quickly. It felt a little disconcerting, like peeing off the side of a mountain. Zuma was napping in the shade below. Not a care in the world. When he was finished, he tucked in and fumbled with his zipper.

Instead of staying on the lower rungs, he moved up to Helena's level and braced himself on the safety guard next to her. Invading her space was awkward, but he was tired of cranking his neck to look at her. "I'm going to climb to the top again."

"Why?"

"So I can yell for Trent and Louis. I'll bang on the metal with my keys, too. They should be able to hear me."

She glanced up the ladder, mouth trembling. Her lips were dry and pale pink. Delicate, unlike the rest of her. He felt a powerful urge to moisten them. "There might be another aftershock."

"Not as strong."

"You don't know that."

Her concern for his welfare surprised him. As much as he'd like to stay close to her and cater to her needs, he had to do something. It was getting late. When the sun went down, the temperature would drop. They couldn't sleep on the pole. "I have to try."

"Okay," she said, sighing. "Go ahead."

He was glad she didn't insist on accompanying him. She'd dealt with her phobia pretty well so far, but he could tell she was scared. It would be easier to climb without her, and he didn't like seeing her suffer.

Speaking of suffering…he felt a burning sensation beneath his zipper, as if someone had poured chili powder down his pants.

"Fuck," he said, realizing what it was.

"What's wrong?"

"I must have had pepper spray on my hands."

She frowned for a second, not following him. Then she glanced down at his crotch and started laughing. "Oh, no."

He shifted his weight on the safety guard, gritting his teeth. Although he was protective of his male parts, the minor irritation wasn't going to kill him. It was almost worth it to see her smile again. She wasn't a joyless person, clearly, but she didn't share this side of herself often. Her laughter was a rare gift. Intimate and revealing, sexier than a flash of skin. She didn't do this with everyone.

He'd always had a bit of a humor fetish. The only thing he enjoyed more than making a woman laugh was making her come.

And Helena wasn't just any woman. She was special. Different. Difficult. She had a stunner of a smile. He could tell a lot by a woman's smile, or so he imagined. Helena's suggested that she wasn't quite so reserved in bed. Her blue eyes sparkled with intelligence. In his experience, smart women were more creative partners.

Damn. He couldn't believe she'd misinterpreted his attempt to ask her out. No wonder she'd hated him all these years. Not that he'd ever had a chance with her, but still. It felt good to clear the air between them.

Her smile faltered, probably because he was ogling her. He couldn't help it. She was beautiful, and flustered, and thinking about his penis. He was thinking *with* his penis. It felt hot and heavy and in need of soothing. She moistened her lips with the tip of her tongue, and the nervous gesture almost blew the top of his head off. Jesus. He tore his gaze from her mouth, trying not to imagine those pretty lips stretched around him.

She has a boyfriend.

You have more important things to worry about. Chloe. Emma. Survival.

The second reminder cooled his libido much more than the first. He didn't give a damn about Helena's boyfriend at the moment, maybe because his dick was half-hard. Maybe because they were in a life-or-death situation, and it seemed like the two of them against the world. Maybe because he'd always wanted her. He *did* care about his sister and his niece, however. He cared about getting the hell off this pole.

She moved to one side of the ladder to make room for him to climb. Brushing by her was uncomfortable for them both. He didn't want to rub up on an unwilling woman. Her gaze flitted over the front of his pants as he ascended. Although he wasn't noticeably aroused, she flushed and looked away.

If he didn't know better, he'd think she was attracted to him.

He discarded that notion as wish fulfillment. He had no illusions about Mount Saint Helena. A smile wasn't an invitation. She'd glanced at his crotch because she felt sorry for him, not because she wanted to jump on his dick.

Get it together, Josh.

When he reached the top of the pole, his discomfort faded into the background and all of his inappropriate thoughts fled. The fires had spread through the downtown area. Coronado Bay looked like a war zone.

What if Chloe hadn't made it across the bridge?

Regret hit him like a ton of bricks. He should have insisted on helping her buy a new car. She drove an old rust bucket out of stubbornness. Maybe he should have refused to let Chloe and Emma move in with him, too. Their mother hadn't approved of the arrangement. She'd said Chloe was in a fragile state. She'd wanted to keep Emma close.

Josh had taken his sister's side. Chloe needed to get away from Lyle and escape the bad memories. Their mother meant well, but she didn't see Chloe as an adult who could take care of herself and her child. To be fair, Chloe had been a wild teenager, emotionally unstable. Josh blamed Lyle for her struggles. His sister was much happier without that loser dragging her down. She'd been doing a great job with Emma, too.

It wasn't a perfect situation. They argued, like most siblings. Emma had temper tantrums. Sometimes Josh missed the peace and quiet of his old bachelor pad. Just last night, he'd yelled at Emma for tearing up one of his favorite comic books. Chloe had intervened, picking up the crying toddler and carrying her away. She'd said a few choice words to Josh over her shoulder, which pissed him off.

He'd gone to bed angry and woken up early to go surfing. If something had happened to them...

Fuck.

Pressure built behind his eyes again, but he pushed the feeling aside. He had a job to do. When he trusted his voice, he started yelling for Trent and Louis at the top of his lungs. Then he banged his keys against the pole, making a loud clang. He couldn't see the reptile house from this vantage point, but he hoped they were there, and able to hear him.

All he got for his efforts was a sore throat. There was no returning shout, no response on the radio. After about ten minutes, Josh put away his keys and checked his cell phone. No new messages there, either.

He climbed back down the ladder, defeated. Instead of continuing past Helena, he stayed on the rungs above her. Yelling had made him thirsty. His mouth was dry, his tongue thick. He felt like he'd taken a hard slam against the sandbar and had gotten hit upside the head with his surfboard.

But he hadn't lost hope. He didn't believe that Chloe and Emma were dead. He didn't feel it in his heart. Greg, on the other hand, was another story. Josh was almost certain the lion keeper was gone.

"No luck?" Helena said.

"No luck."

Josh stared at Zuma with resentment. The big cat hadn't moved from her comfortable spot in the shade. Her ears flickered every so often, as if to ward off insects. "How long can lions go without water?"

"Four or five days, at least."

He hung his head in dejection.

"What did you see up there?"

"More fires."

"Getting closer?"

The flames appeared to be spreading, but not towards the park. "No."

"How's your…"

"It's fine," he said gruffly. He was surly and uncomfortable, his nerves on edge. Didn't she know that talking about his cock could stimulate it? His bad boy didn't need any more encouragement.

He wasn't usually this obsessed with sex. Sure, he thought about it. He thought about it as often as most guys did, if not more. But he was twenty-nine, not nineteen, and he knew how to control himself. Maybe his current preoccupation was his mind's attempt to shift focus from death to life, from pain to pleasure. He doubted he'd react the same way to another woman. He'd always been hot for Helena.

After a long stretch of silence, she spoke. "Why are you afraid of deep water?"

"I don't know."

"You didn't almost drown as a kid?"

"No. I had some close calls. Once I hit my head against the reef in Santa Cruz. Crawled onto the beach and passed out."

"How old were you?"

"Fourteen."

"Did that trigger your phobia?"

"I doubt it. I went surfing again two days later. I didn't have any trouble in the water until I got recruited for SWCC."

"SWCC?"

"Special warfare combatant-craft crewman. It's a division of the navy."

"Like SEALs?"

"Not that elite, but close."

"What happened?"

"I tapped out three times during the scuba training. I'm not sure if it was the gear or the depth or both, but I felt suffocated."

"Did that disqualify you?"

"No," he said, clearing his throat. "I might have been able to advance. The bigger problem was that I also failed underwater rescue."

"What's that?"

"Another training exercise. It's one of the most challenging requirements. You have to rescue another crewman from the bottom of a pool. His job is to fight and struggle, much like drowning victims do in real life."

Josh couldn't explain the panic he'd experienced during those sessions. His brain had stopped worked and his muscles had seized up. He hadn't remembered any of the strategies he'd learned from his instructors. He'd choked.

"So it's not just depths you have an issue with, it's being held down by a person or smothered by equipment."

"Deep water is the common denominator."

"Were there any women in the class?"

"No. The program isn't open to women."

"Hmm."

She didn't ask any more questions, and he was too parched to continue. The temperature had dropped over the past hour. They'd be shivering soon.

He was trying to find a more comfortable position on the safety guard when the earth started rumbling again. This aftershock was less powerful than the others, but the tremors damned near knocked him off balance. Underneath him, Helena gripped the ladder rungs until her knuckles went white.

Zuma lifted her head and roared. Tau answered her.

Chills traveled up his spine. He didn't believe in evil animals or sinister behavior, but it seemed as if the lions had claimed the entire park as their territory. Zuma knew who her enemies were, and she was willing to oust them.

"Helena and Josh, come in."

It was Trent! Josh had never been happier to hear another human voice. He glanced down at Helena, a smile breaking across his face.

Her eyes were alight with the same magic. She lifted the radio to her lips. "Trent?"

"You're still here," Trent said. "Thank God."

Josh picked up his radio. "What the fuck happened to you guys? We've been trying to call you all day."

"My radio was dead, and Louis's ended up in the flamingo pond. It's a long story."

"We need your help," Helena said. "We're stuck on tram pole number four with Zuma underneath us."

"What do you want us to do?" Trent asked.

"Do you know how to shoot a rifle?"

There was a moment of silence. "Louis says he can figure it out."

Helena exchanged a worried glance with Josh. It wasn't the answer she wanted to hear, but beggars couldn't be choosers. "Grab one of the rifles from the gun cabinet and drive over here in a maintenance vehicle. Park behind the truck, but stay inside the vehicle. Fire a warning shot in the air. I think that will scare her off."

Josh approved of her plan. Attempting to dart Zuma under these conditions would be very dangerous. It was getting late. They were all tired. Josh didn't trust Louis to hit the side of a barn, let alone a swift, deadly predator.

Trent responded with an affirmative and they located the weapons cabinet. Josh had to talk Louis through loading the rifle and releasing the safety mechanism. Trent had never even held a gun before, so he wasn't much help. Josh hoped Louis wouldn't blow his own foot off.

When they heard the sound of the approaching vehicle, Zuma lifted her head to investigate. The engine cut out. Seconds later, a warning shot echoed throughout the park. The lioness jumped up and tore through the trees.

Josh pumped his fist in the air. Victory.

Helena spoke into the radio. "Did you see her come out?"

"No," Trent said.

"You think she went to the enclosure?" Josh asked Helena.

"I hope so."

"We should go for it."

Helena raced down the ladder and picked up the tranquilizer gun. He dropped down beside her, grabbing the rifle. "Stay behind me."

They crept the short distance from the base of the pole to the fence line that separated the foliage from the road. Trent and Louis were parked behind the truck. Josh didn't see Zuma, so he vaulted the fence swiftly. Helena followed him. Her pale eyes glinted in the fading light, like a fierce nocturnal creature.

He wrenched open the door to the truck and shoved her inside. She scrambled across the seat in a hurry. Heart hammering in his chest, he climbed in after her and slammed the door shut. She placed the tranquilizer gun on the dash. He engaged the safety on the rifle and set it aside. Then his arms were around her, and her breasts were smashed against his chest, and her ragged breaths fanned his neck.

They were alive. Everything was alive, his senses heightened and his pulse racing. Blood rushed in his ears. His response wasn't sexual, exactly, but he liked the way she felt against him. He liked the way they fit together.

Their embrace was half relief, half triumph.

She broke the contact first, wiping the tears from her eyes. There was a bottle of water in the cup holder between them. She wrenched the cap off and drank in thirsty gulps, spilling down her chin. When she thrust the bottle at him, he drained it and wanted more. He wanted to kiss her now, to revel in her wet lips. He wanted a deeper connection, a harder touch. Groping, panting, life-affirming pleasure.

He didn't act on any of these urges, and his unrequited lust didn't make the moment any less satisfying. They were on the ground and safe again. He felt like a hero. She'd hugged him back without reservation. It was good.

Trent's voice on the radio interrupted the moment. "You guys okay?"

Helena fumbled for her radio while Josh took the keys out of his pocket. "We're okay," she said into the receiver, glancing at Josh. Her voice was kind of quaky and low-pitched, huskier than usual. He imagined it was the way she'd sound just before she had an orgasm, and he almost dropped the keys.

She looked through the back windshield, waving at Louis and Trent. Then she settled into the passenger seat. "Let's go."

CHAPTER NINE

THEY SPENT MOST of the day underground.

It was dark, and dank, and unpleasant. Chloe's leg ached every time she moved, and her butt was numb from sitting. She shivered off and on, more from fear than cold. The fire raged on outside, destroying part of the roof and triggering periodic explosions in the distance. Smoke permeated the upper level of the building.

Emma seemed aware of the danger and tension all around them. She asked about Mommy's ouchie, Uncle Josh and the earthquakes. She got bored with the penlight and wanted to go upstairs. She demanded more gummy bears.

Mateo had been a godsend, but he didn't have an endless supply of candy. When the gummy bears were gone, Emma started to cry. Chloe hugged the toddler tight, crooning lullabies and patting her back until her daughter fell into a fitful sleep, sucking her two fingers. It wasn't that much different from a normal day, as far as Emma's behavior.

Chloe tried to relax while Emma was quiet, but her mind refused to stop churning. How long would they have to stay down here? Would the fire burn out or rise higher, fed by broken gas lines and massive fuel spills?

They had no food. Very little water, unless she counted what was in the pipes. They'd have to venture back outside eventually.

Mateo's presence gave her a small measure of comfort. Being with him was almost like being alone because they didn't speak the same language, but it was nice to see another face in the dim light. His shoulder felt strong and solid against hers. He sat right beside her, as close as a boyfriend would get. Either he was trying to keep her warm, or he had a very casual sense of boundaries. She didn't mind. He hadn't put his arm around her again, nor had he lingered over the contact this morning.

Chloe was too tired and miserable to attempt a stilted conversation. He understood very little English, and she knew about ten words in Spanish. Emma had no reservations about engaging him, however. She chattered away, unconcerned by his inability to follow. He listened carefully and responded often, seeming amused by her. His interest was clear; Emma didn't need his full comprehension.

Chloe liked his voice. It was low-pitched and friendly. He spoke Spanish with an unusual accent, a sort of musical cadence that was unlike the rapid-fire exchanges she'd heard before. Maybe Panama was the Jamaica of Latin America.

The day dragged on. No tsunamis struck, and the warning alarms stopped blaring. Some of the smoke cleared. There were no more aftershocks. Emma awoke from her nap, hungry.

When Chloe's stomach growled, Mateo rose to his feet. He pointed at the stairs and made binoculars with his fists.

Emma had no trouble interpreting him. "I look, too!"

"No," Chloe said. "You can't go with him."

Mateo hurried up the stairs while Emma screamed and kicked in Chloe's lap. Her little foot glanced off Chloe's injured leg, making her gasp in pain.

"He'll be right back," Chloe said.

Emma wasn't good at waiting. Two seconds or two hours, it didn't matter to her. She had no real concept of time, like most toddlers. When Chloe tried to distract her with the penlight, Emma threw the item at the stairs. Luckily, Mateo was quick. He came down the stairs wearing an optimistic expression.

"Ya," he said, offering her his hand.

If he wanted to venture outside, Chloe wasn't going to argue. She was stiff and sore from sitting so long. She let go of Emma and hobbled to her feet. As soon as she rose, gravity took its toll. The blood drained from her head and an uncomfortable weight settled in her bladder. She winced, pressing her fingertips to the inseam of her jeans.

Mateo frowned at this action. *"Que pasa?"*

"Nothing," she said, jerking her hand away from her crotch.

He asked her another question, still concerned.

"I just have to pee."

"Yo también," he said with a nod. *"Vámanos."*

Getting up the stairs wasn't any easier than coming down them. She let Emma go first. The adults followed, with Mateo supporting her left side. Once they reached the main floor, the smell of charred wood assaulted her nostrils. Part of the roof was gone. She lifted Emma into her arms and shuffled forward, through the open door.

The destruction to their immediate surroundings wasn't as bad as Chloe had expected. There was a disturbing combination of untouched green grass, singed eucalyptus trees and smoldering ruins. The pavilions had burned to the ground. Seaside Village was flattened. Most of the restaurants and small businesses in the area had been decimated.

It looked post-apocalyptic, but not unrecognizable. Many of the city's large skyscrapers and major hotels were still standing. For now. The fires hadn't died down—they'd just spread inland. Everything that could burn here had already burned. Fresh, dark smoke clouds rose from the downtown neighborhoods in the distance.

Beyond the embarcadero, the bay was lit up like a roman candle. Flames had engulfed the naval weapons station and international airport, creating a thick black fog across the coast. She could barely see the setting sun through the hazy curtain. The western sky swirled with violent colors, deep pink and toxic orange. It was horrifically beautiful.

"Fire hot," Emma said.

Chloe tightened her grip on her daughter. She didn't know which direction to travel. The air quality was terrible, with strong chemical fumes and eye-irritating smoke. Bits of ash and debris floated on the wind.

"*Allá,*" Mateo said, pointing to a public restroom at the end of the bike path. Concrete walls had protected it from fire damage.

She limped alongside Mateo, eager to reach the structure. Her leg ached a little less than before, and she was able to put some weight on her foot. But the dock shoes were a loose fit, and carrying Emma was awkward. They needed a better mode of transportation. When they arrived at the restrooms, Chloe went inside with Emma. The basic fixtures appeared undamaged. Before she closed the door, Mateo rattled the handle and shook his head.

He didn't want her to lock it.

She accepted this condition easily. At least he wasn't trying to assist her.

Emma had to go, so Chloe perched her on the commode and held her there. This was one of the secret miseries of motherhood that no one talked about. Chloe couldn't eat, sleep, or use the toilet until her child had been taken care of.

Just once, she'd like to pee *first*.

When Emma was finished, Chloe set her aside. Wincing, she removed the sock that was tied around her thigh. The laceration underneath was about six inches across, and seeping blood.

She needed stitches, but she'd live. It was a superficial wound, not a shark bite.

"Owie," Emma said.

"Hold this," she said, giving Emma the wet sock.

"Go out."

"Don't you dare," she warned. The last time they were in a public restroom, Emma had opened the door and left the stall while Chloe was occupied.

So embarrassing.

She wrestled her jeans down her hips, holding her breath as the damp fabric dragged over her abraded flesh. Then she sat and relieved herself. Rising was a challenge, so she gripped the aluminum bar beside the toilet for balance. The flush worked, but the sink had no water. She secured the sock around her leg and grasped Emma's hand before exiting the restroom. Mateo was waiting by the door.

"Listas?"

They were ready. Together they stumbled across the green hills of the park, making slow progress. Although Chloe let Emma walk beside them, she kept her eye on the blackened palm trees nearby. They resembled giant torches, still burning.

Seaside Village had been reduced to ashes. They found a cobblestone path among the remains of quaint boutiques and quirky cafés. Chloe wasn't sure where they were going. She wanted to get away from the noxious smoke, and she couldn't bear the thought of returning to the cramped utility room.

Traveling inland meant entering the Gaslight District, which might offer no shelter whatsoever. And it would be getting dark soon.

Mateo paused in an empty parking lot as they left the embarcadero. There was a half-destroyed liquor store across the street. He urged her that direction. As they got closer, Chloe noticed the downed power lines at the end of the block. A driver had lost control of his vehicle and struck a telephone pole. The pole had fallen, crushing the SUV and obstructing the intersection. Everything had burned. There was a corpse slumped behind the wheel. Chloe could see bits of white skull beneath the blistered flesh.

She picked up Emma and hugged the child's head to her chest, determined to shield her from the macabre scene.

Mateo went inside the liquor store for more supplies. The place appeared to have been ransacked, but it was hard to tell. While he stepped over jagged shards of glass, Chloe edged away from the front window. She was chilled by the sight of the dead body at the intersection. There were more where that came from. Inside demolished buildings and crashed cars. They were all around here.

As she recoiled from the thought, her heel brushed something rubbery. She looked down at a man's discolored arm, sticking out from underneath a crumbled block wall. His hand was open, fingers slack with death.

Smothering a shriek, she lurched forward and covered Emma's eyes, horrified by the disembodied appendage.

Mateo came out of the store with his beach bag full. His eyes moved from Chloe's face to the arm and back again. The opposite intersection was blocked, so they had no choice but to skirt by the corpse and keep going.

At the corner, he looked east and said something that sounded like "hospital." He pronounced it without the *H*, and stressed the last syllable, so she wasn't sure.

"Hospital?" she asked.

"Sí."

The closest one she could think of was the naval hospital, near the wildlife park. Josh went there for exams and treatment. It was several miles inland, on the other side of the Gaslight District. A chaotic maze of fire and rubble awaited them. Injured, with a toddler, climbing over debris and inhaling smoke…it wouldn't be easy.

But what else could they do? Heading in that direction was as good a plan as any. Maybe they'd find help on the way. She pointed east and nodded.

Before setting off, they shared the snacks Mateo had gathered. He'd grabbed chips, chocolate cupcakes and soda. Emma was delighted by the contraband items. She'd never had so many unhealthy snacks in one sitting. Although Chloe was starving, the sight of charred flesh had killed her appetite. She ate a few chips and sipped soda, her skin crawling.

When they were finished, Mateo picked up Emma. She touched his jaw with chocolate-grubby fingers. Exploring, not protesting.

Chloe didn't argue the arrangement, either. It was easier for her to walk without Emma's added weight. They continued down

Harbor Drive. The streets were empty, which was bizarre in a city known for gridlock. Parked vehicles appeared unoccupied. Everyone must have fled the coast when the tsunami alarms sounded.

Ash and dust particles hung in the air as they reached the iconic sign at the entrance to the historic district. The massive arch hung drunkenly at one corner. The other end had fallen and smashed into the curb.

The Gaslight District was San Diego's party central. Chloe had never been to the bars or nightclubs here. She and Josh lived in Hillcrest, a lively neighborhood north of the zoo. She didn't date. After breaking up with Lyle, she'd sworn off drugs and alcohol. She had no reason to visit the trendy, touristy hotspots.

Many of the older buildings in the district were made of brick or stone, fire-resistant but not earthquake-proof. Although the structures had sustained considerable damage, they weren't engulfed in flames, and the air quality here was better. Maybe this was the best route to take through the city, after all.

As they shuffled past the creaking sign, the ground began to tremble. Another aftershock! It rumbled down the street like a gang of motorcycles, gaining strength and momentum.

She ducked under the eaves of a nearby building with Emma and Mateo. There was an ominous snapping sound, and then…

Crash.

The sign broke loose and slammed down on the sidewalk, very close to where they'd just been standing. Chloe put her arm around Emma and clung to Mateo, smothering a cry of distress. This quake was shorter than the others but it still packed a punch.

When it was over, Chloe glanced around warily. Twilight had crept over the city, bringing grainy dimness and a slight chill. They were only a block in, and she was already exhausted. The downtown area had never looked so deserted, or so menacing. She imagined a parade of zombies waking at dusk and emerging from the rubble.

Mateo asked if she was okay. At least, that's what she thought he said. Emma sucked her two fingers and stared at the broken sign with big brown eyes. Chloe did what she'd always done. She squared her shoulders and kept going.

It was the most unpleasant journey of her life. They encountered numerous obstacles. Huge rifts in the roads, downed power lines, abandoned vehicles. The only other people they saw were a group of young men looting a video store. One of them stood on the sidewalk with a baseball bat. Mateo put his arm around Chloe and kept his gaze forward as they skirted by, saying nothing.

Chloe followed his lead. She didn't want to mess with any criminals. This was no time to make a citizen's arrest.

After traveling several more blocks, Chloe had to admit defeat. It was getting dark. Her leg ached and her flimsy shoes weren't suited to the terrain. There was no way they could get through the entire district in one night. Mateo seemed to need a break just as much as Chloe did. He was sweating from exertion, breathing hard. His streamlined physique was built for speed, not for carrying heavy weight.

Although none of the gaslights were working, Chloe caught a glimpse of a promising shelter. It was a bar/restaurant that appeared to have been converted from a parking garage. The garage door was wide open, the brick walls were intact and the roof hadn't collapsed.

"Let's go in there," she said.

He nodded, veering that direction. When they arrived, he set Emma down on the sidewalk in front of the open garage door. Motioning for Chloe to stay put, he crept inside. He used a lighter he'd pilfered from the liquor store to inspect the interior. For zombies, perhaps. Or gang members. It must have been free of threats, undead or otherwise, because he returned with a lit candle and a smile.

Chloe limped forward, holding Emma's hand. The décor was basic. Industrial, even. Cement floors, brick walls and bare wooden tables. There was a social space on one side of the garage and a restaurant on the other. The aroma of spilled alcohol behind the bar was strong, but she didn't see any broken glass. Just a few overturned chairs.

Mateo led them to a cozy nook in the middle of the garage. It was a VIP section, separated by velvet ropes. There were a few small tables, some leather ottomans and a large, cushioned bench. She knew where they were sleeping tonight.

But first things first. "Bathroom?"

He continued past the swanky lounge, into a dark hallway. There was a ladies' room on the left side. After opening the door for her and Emma, he set the candle down on the sink. Then he gave them privacy.

Chloe took care of Emma and used the facilities quickly. There was no water, which was a shame, because they were both covered in soot. When she came out with the candle, he ushered them back to the VIP area. She sat down gladly. Emma started exploring the furniture, climbing over ottomans and square end tables. A small, new-age style fountain made of stone and copper stood in one corner.

Mateo had found a flashlight somewhere. He disappeared into the hall, returning with an armful of tablecloths and dish towels.

"Bless you," Chloe said, dipping one of the towels in the fountain. She used it to clean Emma's hands and face. Then she scrubbed her own skin. Mateo followed her lead and rinsed off his own grit.

"Quieres pizza?" he asked.

Hunger gnawed at her stomach. She hadn't eaten enough earlier. "Pizza?"

"I want candy," Emma said.

He laughed, clearly understanding these words. The candlelight flattered him, but so did his relaxed expression. His teeth were very white against his dark complexion. He had a wolfish smile. Fierce and gentle at the same time.

"No mas," he said to Emma, holding up his empty palms. Then he picked up the flashlight and wandered off again. What he came back with wasn't quite pizza. It was flatbread, mozzarella, tomatoes and olives.

Deconstructed pizza.

They devoured it, every morsel. For dessert, he presented a plate of fresh pears and candied walnuts.

"This is the fanciest date I've ever been on," she said honestly.

If he knew what that meant, he didn't reveal it. He stared at her for a long moment, his eyes gliding down to her injured leg. Then he rifled through his supplies and took out a Valentine's Day teddy bear. It was a small toy, cheaply made. He must have picked it up at the liquor store. Emma accepted this gift with delight. She wrapped her bear in a tablecloth blanket and rocked it like a baby.

Mateo also had something for Chloe: a first-aid kit. She paled at the sight of the box, feeling queasy. Did he plan to stitch her up?

He walked over to the bar and retrieved an unbroken bottle of whiskey, along with a shot glass. Now she was really queasy.

"Quieres?"

"No."

He frowned at her answer. She knew that treating her leg would hurt, but she couldn't drink alcohol ever again. Not even a little bit. She'd fought hard to stay sober, and even harder to overcome her depression.

"I can't," she said, moistening her lips. It was embarrassing to be confronted this way. Even though she knew it required more strength to tackle her problems than ignore them, she felt weak and abnormal. Most girls her age took shots with glee. They weren't single mothers. They didn't haphazardly attempt suicide, either.

She was...a buzzkill.

He came forward with the bottle, ignoring her protests. When he sat down across from her and gestured to her thigh, she realized that he intended to pour whiskey on the wound, not down her throat. There were disinfectant wipes in the first-aid kit, but maybe a quick splash would be less painful.

"A ver?"

She removed the sock with trembling fingers, uncertain what he'd asked. The wide rip in her jeans revealed an ugly laceration.

He cleared his throat and said something about *pantalones*.

Flushing, she stood and unfastened the top button of her jeans. She lowered the zipper, wiggling the denim down her hips, and sat quickly. Although the sweatshirt kept her panties covered, she felt naked.

He handed her a washcloth to put under her thigh. Then he uncapped the bottle and extended his arm, bathing her flesh with liquid fire.

Holy hell. It hurt so bad.

She bit back a cry and slammed a closed fist against her good leg. Tears gathered at the corners of her eyes. Blinking them away, she glanced at Emma. Her daughter was pretending to breast-feed the teddy bear, oblivious.

Chloe unclenched her hand and took a deep breath. Ready.

Mateo didn't drag it out. He applied some antibiotic ointment and a few butterfly bandages. Then he secured several squares of gauze over the area with tape. That was the most intimate part of the ordeal. He ran his fingertips along the tape, making sure it was stuck to her thigh, and her skin broke out in goose bumps.

When he was done, she felt better. The big, sturdy bandage was a definite improvement over a damp sock.

"Thank you," she said, pleased with the results.

He smiled at her. *"Por nada, mamita."*

She stood to drag her jeans up her hips. Although he hadn't seemed interested in her exposed areas before, he looked now. It was almost as if he'd forgotten her state of undress.

He jerked his gaze away, a muscle in his jaw flexing.

They were quiet for several moments. Emma scolded her teddy bear and sang it lullabies. Chloe's heart swelled with emotion. Her love for Emma was like nothing she'd ever felt before. It had overwhelmed her and terrified her, intensifying her worries about unworthiness. But that love had also saved her from herself.

Mateo studied Emma, contemplative. *"Y el papá?"*

Chloe understood this question. He was asking about Emma's father. "He's not...we're not together."

Instead of continuing the conversation, he put away the first-aid kit in silence. Maybe he couldn't find the right words, or he was too polite to inquire further. But she sensed that he'd like to know more about her, and she felt the same way about him.

Emma crawled onto the bench beside Chloe, who was hugging her baby bear. Chloe covered her with the tablecloths Mateo had provided. The washcloth stacks made soft pillows. She stretched out next to Emma, leaving some room for Mateo.

He didn't join them.

The lounge was about the size of a double bed, just large enough for three. It would be a tight squeeze, but he had nowhere else to sleep. She placed a washcloth stack and a tablecloth in the remaining space, scooting closer to Emma.

His brow furrowed at the sight of the pillow and blanket she'd set up for him.

Declining this unspoken invitation, he pushed an ottoman against the wall and sat down facing the open garage door. He'd tried to close it earlier, to no avail. Perhaps he planned to keep watch all night. Protect them from zombies.

Chloe closed her eyes and put her arm around Emma. She was too keyed up for a peaceful rest. When she finally drifted off, she dreamed of Josh.

CHAPTER TEN

HELENA'S BODY TINGLED from the brief contact with Josh's.

The way he'd stared at her mouth had given her hot flashes. She'd dribbled water down her chin, clumsy from thirst, and his eyes had darkened as if this was the sexiest move ever. She'd been convinced that he was going to kiss her.

And she'd have let him.

It wasn't just the intensity of the moment; she liked him. She couldn't deny it any longer. He was handsome and charismatic, even funny. After spending the past six months alone, she'd become more receptive to his charms.

She'd always been a physical person. Feelings weren't her strong suit. She was better at showing than telling. Matters of the heart confused her, but she understood anatomy and science. She liked to touch and be touched. Josh was a fellow hedonist. It took one to know one.

But so what? She was a 32-year-old woman in a longstanding, long-distance relationship. This wasn't the first time she'd looked at another man or felt a surge of lust. It didn't mean anything. Attraction wasn't action, and fantasy wasn't cheating.

Josh was just a distraction, a symptom of her unhappiness with Mitch.

Their problems had started last year, before he left for Denver. She needed to sit down with him and have the discussion they'd both been avoiding. Until then, she was perfectly capable of controlling herself around Josh.

Sure, he had a great physique. His personality was appealing. He had good hands, and he probably knew his way around the female body. If the bulge in his pants was any indication, he had the equipment to satisfy on that front as well.

She flushed at the wayward thought, smothering a groan. When he glanced at her, she coughed into her fist, embarrassed. Life experience had taught her that size and looks had no connection to skill in the bedroom. The same was true in the animal kingdom. Sometimes the showiest males were the biggest disappointments.

Pushing the almost kiss from her mind, she squared her shoulders. They'd survived a major earthquake and spent a harrowing day together, but they were safe now. This wasn't the end of the world. There was no reason to panic and let her hormones go wild. She wasn't going to play Noah's Ark with Josh Garrison.

He made a three-point turnaround and followed the other vehicle to the staff building. As soon as he parked, she hopped out and hurried inside, avoiding eye contact. There were a couple of flashlights on the break table. She picked one up and switched it on before walking down the hall to the women's restroom. It was a mess, with broken mirrors and water all over the floor, but the toilets were intact.

After using the facilities, she paused to study her reflection in the shards above the sink. Her eyes glittered with cool determination. The familiar sight calmed her. She had dirt smudges on her face and neck. Although the water was turned off, the faucet offered a tiny handful. She used it to wash up. Better.

When she returned to the main staff area, her guard was firmly in place. Josh was sitting at the table with Trent and Louis. There were snacks scattered across the surface. A lantern-style flashlight sat in the middle of the table, along with a battery-operated radio.

The only station that came in was based in Tijuana. According to Mexican officials, the entire city of San Diego was under evacuation. Residents had been urged to head east on foot. All major roads and freeways were closed. Emergency services personnel were working on recovery efforts, but access to damaged areas was limited. The National Guard had been called in to assist.

When the broadcast was over, Trent turned down the volume on the radio. Helena cracked open a soda and tore into a bag of white cheddar popcorn. Although she would have preferred real food, she was too hungry to complain. Josh leaned back in his chair nonchalantly and crunched on pretzels. Trent and Louis seemed tense. Or maybe they were just uncomfortable. They were both wet and splattered in mud.

Trent Fisher was the second most popular male employee at the wildlife park. For a herpetologist, he was friendly and accessible. He had longish hair and a scruffy beard, and he wore a sweatband around his forehead. Even Helena, who had no interest in fashion, recognized his lack of style. But it didn't matter to her, or any of the other women at the zoo, because Trent was hot. He resembled a Nordic Viking.

Louis Simms looked more like a stereotypical reptile enthusiast. He was pale and stout, with a soft chin and slender hands. He had a brilliant mind, if not a sparkling personality. Helena respected him as a colleague.

Louis and Trent were best friends who'd been working together for years. They were a bro-team, like Josh and his security partner, Cordell. Although she saw all four men on a regular basis, she hadn't given much thought to their ongoing rivalry. She wondered if Josh's ironic winter mustache had been a deliberate mockery of Trent.

Shrugging, she ate another handful of popcorn. The undercurrents between people were like the workings of a car engine. She didn't want to lift the hood and study either.

"So what happened to you guys?" she asked.

It was a long story, as promised. After rounding up the majority of the loose snakes and loading them in crates, Trent and Louis caught a glimpse of Sunny, the yellow python, slithering into the nearby flamingo pond. Louis jumped in after his favorite cold-blooded baby and ruined his radio. Trent didn't get his radio wet, but the batteries were dying and he didn't notice it until late in the day.

"Did you hear me yelling?" Josh asked.

Trent nodded. "That's why we decided to quit. We finally got Sunny under control and came to the office for another radio."

"Are there still some code ones?"

"There's a shitload of code ones," Louis said. He rattled off a list of frogs, centipedes and salamanders. "We couldn't catch King, either."

Helena glanced at Trent in dismay. King was the largest cobra in the reptile house, and he was incredibly aggressive.

"I milked him last week," Trent said.

"Does that mean he's safe?"

"No, but he'll probably just hide. I'm more worried about Bam."

"He's out?"

"And he hasn't eaten lately," Louis added.

Bambang was a Komodo dragon, the largest lizard species on earth. They were ambush predators, known to attack humans.

Despite this bad news, Helena was grateful to Louis and Trent. They'd gone above and beyond their duty—but she'd come to expect that from her coworkers. The primate keepers had secured their area before leaving. Greg had done his utmost to contain Zuma.

All of the park's employees should be commended, Josh included. The fact that there were still animals on the loose didn't mean anyone had been careless.

"Thanks for staying to help," she said.

"Of course," Trent said, frowning.

Louis puffed up at the praise. "No keeper worth his salt would do otherwise."

"What's your plan for tonight?" Trent asked.

She didn't have one. It was early evening already, and lions had excellent night vision. "Get some rest."

"And tomorrow?"

"I don't know." She'd only been sitting down for five minutes. Surviving until morning was the best idea she could manage.

"I have to go," Trent said.

Louis did a double take at this unexpected announcement. Traveling through the ravaged city after dark seemed unwise. The fires hadn't reached them, but they were burning elsewhere. "Right now?"

"I haven't heard from Melody."

Melody was Trent's on-again, off-again girlfriend.

"Dude," Louis said. "No one's heard from anyone."

Trent dragged a hand down his face. He looked exhausted. "She's pregnant," he said in a low voice.

A collective hush fell over the table. Helena wasn't sure how to respond to this news. Melody was a bit of a free spirit, evading Trent's attempts to tame her. An unplanned pregnancy was a tricky situation. Congratulations didn't seem appropriate under the circumstances, and Trent's expression invited none.

"We were keeping quiet about it because she hasn't decided what to do," he said, sounding grim.

"*She* hasn't decided?" Louis repeated, incredulous. "Don't you get a say?"

Trent shot his best friend a warning glare. "Shut the fuck up."

Louis put his palms up in surrender. "Whatever, man."

Helena wasn't so indifferent to human dynamics that she couldn't feel sympathy. Trent was worried about his pregnant girlfriend. Helena didn't blame him for wanting to leave. "We'll be okay here without you," she said. "Go on and do what you have to do."

Before he left, Trent tossed some supplies into a backpack. He grabbed one of the flashlights, several bottles of water and a few snacks.

"Take the rifle," Josh said flatly. "You might need it."

"I don't care," Trent replied. "I won't use it."

"I will," Louis said, picking up the rifle and slinging the strap over his shoulder. "You shouldn't go alone."

Trent turned to Helena, his brow furrowed.

"He's right," she said. "Safety in numbers."

"I don't want to leave you in the lurch, Helena."

"Josh is here."

"You won't try to catch King or Bam?"

She'd sooner wrestle alligators. "No."

"What about Zuma?"

That was a trickier issue. Zuma had already killed or seriously injured Greg. A roaming lioness was a more significant threat to human life, especially if she got out of the park and ventured into the downtown area.

"We're just going to hold down the fort for now," Josh said. "Maybe the fires will burn out by morning and the evacuation warnings will be lifted."

Helena murmured an agreement, though she wasn't sure help would arrive so soon. The park wasn't a nuclear reactor, threatening global meltdown. Even if the director was trying to get through, roads were blocked and access was limited. Emergency service workers had their hands full with other problems.

"I'll take care of Helena," Josh added.

She glanced his way, surprised by this claim. She didn't need anyone to take care of her. Trent nodded his approval. After shaking Josh's hand in an oddly antagonistic manner, he said goodbye to Helena with a crushing hug.

Although Helena was disconcerted by Trent's sudden embrace, she allowed it. These were special circumstances, and she couldn't deny him this small comfort. She'd always found him attractive. His body felt strong and masculine and pleasant against hers. At the same time, she noticed something missing. There was no heat between them.

"I hope everything works out with Melody," she said, releasing him.

Louis didn't get sentimental over the farewells, which came as no surprise to Helena. According to him, there were two types of zookeepers. "Bunny huggers" were affectionate, diehard animal lovers, usually women. They acted on emotion and instinct. Non-bunny huggers took a more scientific approach. They were detached and analytical, basing their decisions on data, not warm fuzzies.

Louis wasn't a bunny hugger, obviously. Neither was Helena. But some of the best keepers in the park were, Kim included, and Helena didn't like the term. It was sexist and derogatory.

"If you see a green frog with red spots, don't touch it," Louis said.

She promised that she wouldn't. Then they were off, walking through the employee exit and across the parking lot, disappearing like thieves in the night. When they were gone, she wrapped her arms around herself, frowning. She couldn't remember how Mitch's embrace felt. She knew one thing—he'd never stared at her mouth the way Josh had.

"That was interesting," Josh said.

"What?"

"The news about Melody," he said, giving her an odd look.

"Oh. Right."

"What else would I be talking about? Trent's passive-aggressive hug?"

She flinched at the question, unwilling to admit she'd been comparing Josh to other men in her mind. "I don't know what you mean."

He made a skeptical sound.

She'd picked up on Trent's protective attitude, and the weird vibe between him and Josh. The reasons behind it were a mystery to her. "I thought the two of you were friends."

"We are, but he's been a little bent out of shape lately."

"Over what?"

"I danced with Melody at a pub after the Christmas party."

Ah. Helena hadn't joined the revelers or heard about this minor scandal. "You said you weren't a poacher."

"I'm not," he said, scowling. "It was just a dance."

"You weren't trying to hook up with her?"

"Hell no. Trent was right there. Looking back, I think she wanted to make him jealous. I guess it worked."

"Why do you say that?"

"Obviously he laid it down. Maybe even that night."

She wrinkled her nose at the idea of using unprotected sex to stake a claim.

He laughed at her expression.

"You approve of his strategy?" she asked.

Shaking his head, he said, "I doubt there was any preplanning involved. People get carried away and make mistakes. It happens."

"It's happened to you?"

"No."

"Maybe she doesn't want kids."

"Maybe she doesn't."

Helena sat down across from him, contemplating a bag of cookies. Although she was still hungry, the conversation made her stomach tight. It hit too close to home. Children had been a divisive issue between her and Mitch. "Do you?"

His brows rose at the question. "Sure."

"How do you know?"

He shrugged, tearing open a candy bar. "I like kids, even little ones. It's been cool to hang out with Emma every day."

"You see her every day?"

"Pretty much," he said, chewing a bite of chocolate and nougat. "They live with me."

"Since when?"

"Last year."

Helena hadn't known that. With a start, she realized that she'd been grilling him about personal matters. His responses interested her. Everything he revealed about himself made her want to know more. This was worse than almost kissing him. Disturbed by the revelation, she shut up and ate cookies.

After refueling, Helena made a list of code ones by priority. Then she considered the needs of the secure animals, many of whom would be easy targets for a loose predator. The park required a staggering amount of daily care and upkeep. Without the staff, cages and enclosures couldn't be cleaned. Food couldn't be delivered.

The good news was that most of the exhibits had water features, and some species could go a long time without water. Animals often went hungry in the wild. Most were able to survive for extended periods on very little nourishment.

Her main concerns were the cheetah, the lions and the Komodo dragon. Cats were roamers and hunters, by nature. She imagined Zuma prowling the beaches at night. Komodo dragons, while less likely to attack a human, were attracted to carrion. Bambang might smell Greg and investigate.

Helena groaned, fisting her hands in her hair. The entire situation was a nightmare.

"I have an idea," Josh said.

She looked up from her list. He'd been bouncing a tennis ball off the wall for the past thirty minutes, like a hyperactive kid who couldn't sit still. "What?"

"There's meat in the fridge, right?"

"Right," she said, wondering if he wanted to fire up a grill.

"We can toss a side of beef off the Skylift and wait for the lions to take the bait."

"There's no electricity to run the Skylift."

"I'll roll out one of the portable generators. You can operate the controls while I'm in the tram car with the dart gun."

She considered his suggestion. It had potential. Zuma and Tau might be tempted by a choice cut of meat. Shooting from the Skylift was safer than shooting from the ground. The best thing about the plan was that Helena didn't have to ride the tram.

"Do you think you can hit a target from that distance?" she asked, tentative.

"What's the range for the gun?"

"About a hundred feet."

"I can do it."

They spent the next hour going through the contents of the earthquake kit, studying blueprints by lantern light. There were instructions for all of the park's machinery, including the Skylift. Helena had never operated the controls before, but it seemed fairly straightforward. Setting up the generator shouldn't be a problem. If the Skylift was functional, she could turn it on and wait at the landing while Josh rode the tram to an area near the lion enclosure.

"This could work," Helena said.

"You want to go for it?"

She nodded, folding the blueprints and stacking them in a neat pile. "First thing in the morning."

"Unless help arrives by then," he said, optimistic.

"Have you heard from anyone?"

"No," he said, checking his cell phone. "I'm not sure texts are going through anymore. I've had no bars since the third aftershock."

The park radios didn't have their usual range, either. The emergency channel that connected them to local authorities had been down all day. Helena imagined that cell phone towers and signal stations were in shambles.

"Where should we sleep?"

She glanced around the staff building. The wildlife park didn't encourage lounging, so no cozy couches or comfortable chairs graced the break room. The floor wasn't carpeted. "The hospital has a couple of fold-out cots," she said. "Sometimes keepers stay overnight in the intensive care unit."

"As long as I don't wake up with a cobra coiled next to me."

She rubbed her eyes, smiling wryly. "Snakes *are* attracted to heat sources."

"Don't tell me that. I'll think about it all night."

So would she. "It's almost nine," she said, glancing at her watch.

"I'm ready when you are."

She'd forgotten his habit of surfing before work; he'd probably been up since dawn. She gathered a bottle of water and the lantern. He brought the rifle, even though the hospital was in an adjoining building. They walked down the hall together and entered the ICU.

The hospital had sustained minor damage. There were no newborn babies or critical patients at the moment, so the cages were empty. Fluorescent lights and some panels had fallen from the ceiling. Josh cleared the heavy debris while Helena swept up the glass. When the floor was clear, she removed the folded cots from the closet.

"Let's set up in there," Josh said, gesturing to a large animal run. It was made of finely grated aluminum that no snake could slither through.

Although the space was tight, she agreed. She might feel awkward about sleeping so close to Josh, but she doubted peaceful rest was in the cards. At least they didn't have to worry about stray reptiles.

She retrieved two wool blankets and two travel-sized pillows. The disposable pillowcases crinkled under her arm as she carried them back to Josh. He was already inside the cage, sitting on the edge of the cot.

"You look like a convict," she said, handing him the pillow and blanket.

He accepted the items with a smile. His eyes were bloodshot, his brow still swollen. "You're a prettier cellmate than I imagined."

⟜ She couldn't help but smile back at him. "You want me to put a bandage on your head?"

"Does it look bad?" he asked, touching the cut.

"It doesn't look *good*."

"Pamper me, if you must."

She went to the cabinets, which were in disarray. After she found a box of bandages and some alcohol wipes, she returned to his side. Sitting next to him, she tore open the square package and removed the moist wipe. He winced as she cleaned the area gingerly. Then she applied a single bandage.

"There," she said, smoothing the adhesive strips. When his gaze tangled with hers, she realized how close she'd gotten. Her lips were inches from his jaw, and her right breast was pressed against his shoulder. She lowered her arms and scooted back, flushing.

"Thanks," he said simply.

She studied him for a long moment. He looked the same as always, if a little roughed up. Handsome face, tawny hair, warm brown eyes. He had the relaxed attitude and tanned complexion of an avid surfer. His skin was more weathered than she'd realized, and there were other qualities she hadn't seen before. Hints of maturity and intelligence.

He wasn't so evolved that he wouldn't dance with Trent's girlfriend on a lark, or describe Trent's contraceptive blunder as "laying it down." But he had a sense of honor, along with a penchant for mischief. He was a good man to have around.

She put away the bandages and stretched out on her bunk, willing her heart to stop racing. He made her feel alive.

No, scratch that.

The situation made her feel alive. They weren't soul mates. They were just...cellmates. Trapped in a zoo like animals, forced to bond and coexist.

He turned off the lantern to save batteries, casting them into darkness. She closed her eyes and thought of Mitch.

Last year, their relationship had hit a rough spot. Around the same time, he'd lost his job at the engineering company. His education level and experience made it difficult for him to find suitable work. The months dragged on and his self-esteem plummeted. He'd become frustrated and withdrawn.

When he landed the new position, she'd been happy for him. And for herself, if she was being honest.

She hadn't asked him not to leave. He hadn't asked her to come along. Neither of them wanted to talk about calling it quits. They'd been together for six years, and they still had feelings for each other. It was hard to let go.

Just as she was drifting off, another aftershock struck. She reached out on instinct, grasping for Josh in the dark. His hand met hers, strong and secure. Their fingers linked together and held.

CHAPTER ELEVEN

JOSH WOKE AT DAWN, his cock hard and his pulse racing.

In his dreams, Helena had stripped naked and climbed on top of him. It was dark inside the animal cage, so he could barely make out the details of her body. She had some kind of markings or tattoos, like cheetah spots. It was bizarre.

Not so bizarre that it wasn't *hot*, of course. As she'd writhed against him, his hands had itched to touch her decorated skin, to cup her breasts and grip her curvy hips. But when he'd tried to lift his arms, he realized he was tied down. He pulled against the bonds in annoyance, and they'd constricted tightly.

It was a cobra. He'd had a fucking cobra wrapped around his wrist. The snake sank its fangs into the fleshy pad of his thumb.

He inhaled a sharp breath, jerking his hand toward his body. It was tingling from lack of circulation, not neurotoxic venom. He'd fallen asleep with his arm outstretched, fingers entwined with Helena's. She must have let go in the middle of the night. Now she was lying on her side with her back to him.

Straightening abruptly, he pumped his fist a few times to get the blood going.

He didn't want to offend Helena with the sight of his raging hard-on, so he got up and left the cage, carrying his boots in one hand.

Twenty minutes later, he had his arousal under control. He'd retrieved one of the generators from the storage yard and wheeled it into the employee lounge. He'd plugged in his cell phone charger, along with the radio port and the microwave. When Helena shuffled in, he was listening to the news. She looked sleep-rumpled and vulnerable. Not at all like the feral creature from his sex dream.

He pondered the Morticia Addams comparison. She had the same dramatic coloring, cool attitude and statuesque figure. She'd always reminded him of another character, however. His comic-book fantasy, the object of his geeky teenage affections, the ultimate superheroine: Wonder Woman.

She definitely resembled the female icon. Tall, strong, black hair, blue eyes. She had a take-charge attitude. He pictured her with her hands on her hips, chin high. Ready to save the world and stomp some ass.

"Good morning," he said, smiling.

She made a zombie noise and continued down the hall, toward the restrooms. Clearly not a cheerful riser. Shrugging, he heated up some water in a foam cup. He hadn't been able to find sugar or creamer, so he drank his instant coffee black. When she returned to the table, she did the same. They ate granola bars in silence.

"I could go for some bacon and eggs," he said.

She nodded her agreement, seeming more awake now. "When you mentioned raw meat last night, I thought you wanted to grill."

"Is there a grill?"

"The director keeps one behind the clubhouse."

He pictured the two of them sitting at a romantic table, eating steaks by candlelight. It would be almost like a date. A date in an abandoned zoo. After a devastating natural disaster. With a woman who hated him.

Well, maybe *hate* was too strong a word. She'd warmed up to him over the past twenty-four hours. They'd hugged and held hands. Last night, when she'd bandaged his forehead, he'd sensed that the attraction between them wasn't one-sided. What she felt for him might not be affection, but it wasn't hate. Not by a long shot.

After breakfast, she rifled through the mess of personal items on the floor of the locker area. She found a hairbrush and some toothpaste. Although he didn't bother with the brush, he cleaned his teeth in the men's room, rinsing with a mouthful of bottled water. He also took off his shirt and splashed his armpits. Despite being stranded at the zoo, there was no reason for him to smell like an animal.

Refreshed, if not exactly fresh, he put his shirt back on and joined Helena in the staffroom. Her hair was tidy now. She never wore makeup, as far as he could tell. Her lips weren't lush or color-rich, but he liked the shape of them.

He liked the subtle curve of her mouth, the only hint of softness in her face.

Their first stop was the kitchen, which was on the other side of the animal hospital. Josh brought the rifle with him as they toured the pantry. Many of the animals ate something called browse, leaves and twigs. Others subsisted on hay and dry pellets. But there was also a staggering amount of fresh produce required, along with perishable meats and fish. Some of the stock had already gone bad.

Helena removed a slab of meat from the freezer. It must have weighed thirty pounds, but she didn't have any trouble. "We should stick a hook in this and dangle it from the tram. That way the lions can't drag it away before you get the chance to dart them."

"Good idea," he said, inspecting the rest of the meat in the freezer. Most of it was still frozen solid. If they wanted steaks, they could have them.

There was also a mountain of vegetables in the pantry bins, and bananas for days. Helena grabbed one for herself and tossed him another. After they located a meat hook and a rope, they went back to the staff area. She carried the meat in a metal tray. He followed close behind, keeping an eye out for cobras.

Before setting out, he checked his cell phone. There was no internet access and no new messages. The handheld radio's emergency channel was still dead. Pocketing the phone, he attached a fully charged radio to his belt, just in case. The Spanish-language station repeated the same information as last night: head east to evacuation centers, be careful, avoid fires.

He said a quick prayer for Chloe and Emma.

The generator was too heavy to lift into the pickup, so they walked to the loading dock, rolling it along. Visitors could board the tram at the front of the park and ride it to the opposite end, or vice versa. The main dock was near the remains of the reptile house. After they arrived, Josh initiated the bypass system, and the controls lit up with life.

Victory.

Helena high-fived him with a smile. He climbed into the tram car with the tranquilizer gun and the bait. She made sure the hook was secure and gave him some extra darts. They went over the plan again. Then it was go time.

As she stepped away from the car and approached the control panel, he grew anxious. They should be heading east, like the radio recommended. He doubted that Helena would leave the zoo willingly, however. She was captain of this ship. The damned place could be on fire and she'd stay here, throwing buckets of water on elephants.

Even so, they'd decided on a very aggressive strategy. He'd rather stay in the staff area all day, playing cards and grilling steaks. It would be a hell of a lot safer. He hadn't thought about the fact that she'd be out here in the open next to the destroyed reptile house. His hand tingled from the phantom cobra bite. He had a bad feeling.

He didn't like bad feelings.

Instead of voicing his reservations, he swallowed them. Intuition told him that she wouldn't listen, and she'd brought the rifle with her. The loading dock was protected on three sides, so she only had to watch the front.

"Be careful," he said, his throat tight.

She hit the button with the heel of her palm.

He rode the tram about halfway across the park, noting that the fires had spread. The smoke was worse than yesterday. Entire neighborhoods were smoldering, and the flames at the coast were sky-high. There were helicopters in the distance today. He didn't know if that was a good sign or not. They needed boots on the ground. Dropping in rescue workers by air was dangerous, not to mention inefficient. But maybe that was the only option when the freeways were damaged and the sea was ablaze.

Christ.

When Heart of Africa came into view, Josh grabbed his radio. "Almost there," he said, waiting until his car was above the road. "Okay, pull the stop."

The tram shuddered to a halt.

He couldn't see the lion enclosure from this vantage point, but it was the best location to drop the bait. There was an open stretch of asphalt, without leafy ground cover or heavy trees blocking his shot.

One end of the rope was tied to the safety bar. The other was attached to the plastic hook lodged inside the side of beef. He lowered it carefully over the side. Before it reached the ground, he swung the rope like a pendulum. He deposited the meat in the open area, rather than directly underneath him.

The stage had been set. Now he aimed the tranquilizer gun and waited. It felt like second nature. He'd spent so many hours in this stance. Uneventful hours. Harrowing hours. The first time he'd been called on to actually pull the trigger, he'd hesitated. That split second had cost the life of one of his crew members.

Helena's voice broke the silence. "Anything?"

"Nope," he said into his receiver.

"Keep me posted."

He replayed a thread of yesterday's conversation. Sitting in a tram car against the backdrop of a devastated city, ready to shoot a lion…it was a fitting occasion to think about fear. "You asked me if something happened to me in deep water, like a near-drowning."

"So?"

"I was just wondering if you had a bad experience with heights."

No response.

"Might help to talk about it."

"Okay, Dr. Phil."

He laughed softly at her caustic tone. "Scared?"

The goading worked. "I got sick on the way here from Iceland. I don't remember being afraid, but it was a long, uncomfortable flight."

"What else?" he asked, sensing there was more to the story.

She sighed into the receiver. "My dad was a stunt pilot."

He hadn't been expecting that. "Really."

"About a week after we arrived, my mother and I went to see his show. It was a combination of things, I guess. Getting airsick. Not understanding the language. Then watching the planes spinning through the sky…"

"Was there a crash?"

"No, but I never got over the fear of one. He took me up in his Cessna once, hoping that would help. It didn't. I was terrified until we landed." She paused for a moment, as if collecting her thoughts. "Every time he left for work, I begged him not to go. I was convinced that he wouldn't come back."

"What happened to him?"

"He was killed in a drunk driving accident," she said, her voice hard. "Funny how I worried about the wrong thing."

He didn't think it was funny at all. "I'm sorry."

"Sorry you asked?"

"Sorry he died."

"Yeah, well. I hardly knew him."

His chest twisted at the obvious lie. She might have convinced herself this was true, but no little girl begged a stranger not to leave her. Josh remembered her saying she'd been five when she met him, and eight when he died. Three years.

He'd bonded with Emma in about three minutes. After three days, she had him wrapped around her finger.

"Good thing we had this talk," she said. "I'm cured."

He ignored the sarcasm. "It's my magic ear," he said. "Now you have to ask me something."

She was quiet for so long he thought she wasn't going to bother. Finally she said, "Why did you join the navy?"

"I always wanted to be in the special forces, and it seemed like a good deal. See the world, earn some college money."

"Did you see the world?"

"I saw the inside of a ship."

"Where did you go?"

"The Persian Gulf."

"How was it?"

"Unpleasant, for the most part. The confinement was difficult and the work was backbreaking."

"What about college?"

"What about it?"

"Why didn't you go?"

"I did go. I took some classes before I joined the navy. Then I moved here and worked part-time until I graduated from the University of San Diego."

"You graduated?"

"They gave me a diploma and everything."

"What field?"

"Environmental studies."

"You have a bachelor's degree in environmental studies?"

"I do."

"Why are you working as a security officer?"

She asked this question as if she thought a monkey could do his job. Maybe he wasn't solving crimes or saving lives, but he knew how to handle himself in a fight and he did CPR on a regular basis. Half the calls he responded to were medical. It wasn't all sunshine, short shorts and golf cart cruising. He'd applied at the wildlife park because he'd wanted to do something *fun*, after serving his country for five years. Something peaceful.

Now he was armed and ready for ambush, surrounded by what looked more like Iraq than downtown San Diego. Pretty ironic.

"It's a great job," he said. "Outdoor setting, interesting people."

"Beautiful women."

"Can't argue that."

"Speaking of women, I haven't seen you with anyone lately."

"Keeping tabs?"

"Hardly."

Living with Emma and Chloe had curbed his dating habits, to some degree. He'd been surfing more and going out less. He was getting too old for the bar scene, anyway. "Maybe I'm in the market for a steady girlfriend."

"Since when?"

Since your boyfriend left town.

He didn't say that, of course. He hadn't really been pining away for her. But he had taken note of Mitch's departure and considered its implications. "Cordell's married now. Most of my friends are starting families."

She went quiet at the mention of families.

"How's Mitch these days?"

"Busy."

"What's the status between you two?"

"Why are you so curious about it?"

"Just wondering."

"I think we should save batteries," she said, ending the conversation.

He clipped the radio to his belt and shrugged. It sounded like her relationship with Mitch was on shaky ground. She loved the zoo too much to leave it. Unless her boyfriend came back to San Diego, they were toast.

Josh settled back into his ready stance, trigger finger poised, barrel aimed at the target. Male intuition told him that he could be her rebound guy. He'd seen her eyes darken last night, watched the color wash over her pale skin. They'd be good together. She didn't have to *respect* him for a down-and-dirty hookup. A weight settled in his gut as he realized that wasn't enough. He wanted a real connection with her.

Okay, rewind.

He'd taken a little detour into fantasyland. She hadn't broken up with her boyfriend. Nor had she hinted to Josh that she was on the rebound.

If by some off-chance she *did* want to use him for sex—yeah, right—did he really believe he'd have the strength to say no? Because he'd suddenly developed a prerequisite for hearts and flowers, after bedding a number of women whose names he couldn't remember?

He needed a reality check.

Focusing on the bait, he waited for his target. The minutes stretched into an hour. He started to feel claustrophobic, as though he was stuck on the pole again. Or stuck in the cabin of his tiny bunk. Stuck on guard duty above decks. Stuck with the body of his fallen comrade, a sailor he'd failed to protect.

The morning sun sizzled on his forearms, relentless. His mouth was dry, palms sweaty. He'd rather be surfing.

Then there was movement in the bushes.

His gaze sharpened and his shoulders tensed. After yesterday, he didn't know what to expect. Zuma could move in a flash or pounce playfully. This lion did neither. He emerged from the glossy ferns at a slow pace, thick ruff around his neck. It was Tau, and he was immense. Four hundred pounds of power and grace. He made Zuma look petite.

Apparently both lions were out.

Josh didn't see Zuma, but his gaze was locked on Tau. The big cat glanced up at Josh, well aware of his presence. Although he had a clear shot, Josh didn't take it. Tau opened his jaws and rumbled out a staccato vocalization as he strolled up to the meat. He sniffed it. Then he hunkered down and started feasting. Josh aimed at his left flank, aware that he might only get one chance. If he missed, and Tau bolted, they'd be back to square one.

Very carefully, he squeezed the trigger.

Bull's-eye.

Tau flinched when the dart struck his hind quarters. His muscles twitched at the discomfort, but he didn't run. He stayed right where he was and kept eating.

Josh's pulse raced with triumph. It was a huge adrenaline rush, bigger than catching a crusher wave. He held his ready position, not taking his eyes off the lion. Helena had told him that the tranquilizers wouldn't work right away. If Tau tried to flee, or if the drugs didn't knock him out after twenty minutes, Josh was supposed to tag him again.

About five minutes passed, maybe less. Tau stopped chewing and started drooling. His head weaved back and forth, like he was seeing double. A moment later, he was out. Facedown in the side of beef.

Josh set aside the tranquilizer gun, pumping his fist. Yes! He realized that he had to do something with the rope before the cart started moving again. They might need to reuse the bait, so he pulled it up. This process took several more minutes. By the time he spoke into the radio, he was sweating heavily.

"I got him," he said, breathless with excitement. "Tau is unconscious."

No answer.

"Helena? You can bring me back now."

Still nothing. His pulse kicked up another notch. He wondered if she was pissed off at him for asking about her boyfriend. Maybe her radio wasn't fully charged. Or maybe she was lying on the floor of the loading dock, bleeding to death.

CHAPTER TWELVE

HELENA REVISED HER opinion of Josh again: He was just as dumb as she'd always figured.

He had a college education from a quality school. With his degree in environmental studies, he could be an animal keeper. He could have a career in a number of important fields. Instead he tooled around the park in his golf cart, smiling at pretty women and pulling pranks. His military experience was wasted here, as well. The park wasn't a hotbed of criminal activity. He carried pepper spray instead of a gun.

At twenty-nine, he'd already accomplished more than a lot of other men. San Diego was full of beach bums and party boys with no skills whatsoever. Working security wasn't flipping burgers. He might even make decent money. Keeper wages were low, so she couldn't judge on that front. What bothered her was the fact that he'd given up after one setback. He'd been accepted to an elite special ops training program, which was impressive in itself. When that hadn't panned out, he'd veered off to Easy Street.

Maybe he was running from something. She'd opened up to him about the connection between her fear of heights and her father's death, but he hadn't told her much in return. Then he'd had the nerve to press her about Mitch.

What a jerk.

Josh's smug voice broke through her mental tirade. "I got him," he said on the radio. "Tau is unconscious."

Tau instead of Zuma? The lioness was the bigger threat, but this was better than nothing. Josh sounded as if he'd conquered the world. Helena rolled her eyes in annoyance. Tau was so mellow he probably didn't need tranquilizers.

"Helena?"

Not bothering to answer, she disengaged the emergency stop mechanism and pressed the go button. Nothing happened. After a moment of confusion, she realized that she had to turn on the generator again. Josh repeated her name in a demanding tone. She restarted the generator and hit the go switch. The tram whirred to life.

As she reached for the radio on her belt, a strange noise gave her pause. She hadn't been keeping watch for predators. In her distracted state, she'd been complacent. She'd turned her back on the entryway to the loading dock while she messed with the generator and the controls. Instead of staying vigilant, she'd been cranky and careless. Big mistake.

The gun strap was lying across her chest, the rifle resting against the small of her back. In one not-so-smooth motion, she whirled around and grabbed the barrel of the rifle, bringing the gun forward.

Bambang was in the loading dock. Ten feet away.

"Oh, fuck," she breathed, retreating a few steps.

The Komodo dragon weighed more than she did, and he was a formidable foe. Quick-moving and bulky, with long talons that scraped the concrete as he scuttled forward. He was dark gray, scaly and tough as nails. He had razor-sharp teeth and a forked tongue.

As a bonus, Komodos were venomous.

It was long believed that bacteria from the lizard's saliva weakened prey. Zoo researchers, Trent and Louis included, had recently discovered otherwise. Komodos and many other lizard species had venom ducts that released when the animals bit down. The new information was groundbreaking.

All of these details flew through Helena's mind in a split second. She thought of Gwen, her mother, her coworkers…Josh and Mitch. Again, she felt an emptiness inside her, a blank space where something else should be.

The rifle strap hampered her movements, and terror made her clumsy. Her trembling fingers found the lever action instead of the trigger guard. She couldn't glance down at the gun to get situated. Not when a giant lizard was coming at her.

She stumbled back another step and bumped into a tram car. This was the opening Bam needed. He rushed forward on sturdy legs, claws scratching the smooth cement, head tilting as he zeroed in on her ankle.

Helena forgot about the rifle and grabbed the only other thing in reach—the safety bar on the tram car behind her.

She held on and lifted her legs, swinging out of harm's way. Although she tried to climb into the cab, she wasn't successful.

The door was on the other side.

She clung to the bar in horror as the tram car traveled through the horseshoe-shaped dock, taking her farther away from the predator. And higher off the ground.

She was faced with an awful choice: drop down and battle the lizard, or stay up and fight her own fear. Her hands clenched around the bar, knuckles white. She left the loading dock, dangling ten feet above the ground.

Twenty feet. Thirty feet.

Oh, Jesus. It was too late now. If she let go, she'd break her leg.

Forty feet came, followed by fifty. The fall would be fatal at this distance. She stared at her hands, willing them to stay strong. Her palms were sweaty from panic, her arm muscles sore from yesterday's debacle.

She considered trying to swing her leg over the side, but terror kept her frozen in place. The rifle might get hung up. She might slip and die. Better to stay still. Squeeze her eyes shut and endure this, the most harrowing moment of her life.

Josh continued to say things on the radio, but she couldn't hear above the blood pounding in her ears. She could only imagine.

Are you there, Helena? Come in, Helena.

When the tram car reached the first pole, it stuttered over the pulley mechanism. Her stomach dropped to her knees and her heart lodged in her throat. If her weight threw the car off balance, it might get stuck. Then she'd be *really* screwed.

But the car continued forward, and her hands stayed clenched. This process repeated several times. She heard Josh again. Not on the radio, but across from her in another car. He sounded like a raving lunatic. Her shoulders burned and her hands felt numb.

She was slipping.

Almost there.

She didn't know if Josh said it, or if it was a voice in her head. But she managed to hold on for ten more seconds, counting them like a lifeline. The second loading dock came into view. She gritted her teeth against the need to let go.

Almost there.

The ground rose up to greet her in slow motion. Then there was concrete beneath her feet, but her legs didn't work. As much as she wanted to let go, she couldn't relax her clawlike grip. The soles of her boots dragged along the floor of the loading dock. She sobbed out loud, picturing herself going around the turnstile and climbing in height again.

She finally released the bar, rolling into a pitiful heap on the concrete.

"Helena, come in! Fuck!"

Josh had to be at the other end by now. If she could move her arms, she'd pick up the radio to warn him.

"I see Bambang," he said, calmer now. "I'm assuming you're okay. I'll be there soon."

She managed to crawl to the side of the dock with the rifle. Trembling, she sat forward and hugged her knees to her chest. When the feeling returned to her hands, she planted them on the rifle. Logic told her that Bambang couldn't be in two places at once, but there were a number of other loose predators. The cheetah, hyenas…Zuma.

Josh continued to clock his progress. He said he was in Heart of Africa. A moment later, his tram car appeared. She stood to help him, but he had no trouble opening the door and leaping out while it was moving.

"Christ," he said, gripping her shoulders. "You took twenty years off my life!"

She stared back at him in silence, unable to form a response. She couldn't remember why she'd been mad at him. He looked frantic. His hair was damp and disheveled, as if he'd been tearing it out. The bandage must have fallen off his forehead. He had crazy eyes. Crazy, caring, warm gold eyes.

She felt it again, that missing piece inside her. The empty place.

When he set down their guns and drew her into his arms, she realized she'd been numb all over. His body heat suffused her, enlivening her senses. He smelled like sweat and sunshine and pepper spray. She pressed her nose to his neck and touched his back, where his uniform shirt clung damply to his skin.

A thrill vibrated through her at the feel of his hard muscles. Her fingers spread across the masculine expanse.

He went still.

She inhaled his scent, wanting to wallow in it. To slide her palms under his shirt and dig in her fingernails.

He didn't seem opposed, despite his inaction. His heart hammered against her chest and his arms stayed locked around her, biceps flexed. They fit together nicely, though the radios on their belts prevented full contact. He lifted his head to study her. She didn't know what he was searching for; some indication that she was thinking clearly, perhaps.

Well, forget that. Thinking clearly wasn't her top priority right now. She needed to be in her body, not in her head. Josh was an excellent candidate for mindless pleasure.

He looked even more like a hooligan today, with his bruised brow and rumpled clothes. The stubble on his jaw was patchy. It grew thicker on his chin and upper lip, where tawny bristles mixed with darker browns. She imagined the rasp of that facial hair on her throat, brushing her tight nipples, nuzzling her inner thighs.

God.

He studied her mouth the same way he had yesterday. She wondered if he was imagining it trailing down his stomach. His gaze had a hypnotic effect, dripping over her like slow honey. Her eyelids grew heavy and her lips parted in anticipation.

He glanced toward the front of the loading dock, checking for predators. Then he pushed her back against the wall, buried his hand in her hair and crushed his mouth over hers. The situation called for intensity, and he gave it to her. His kiss was breath-stealing, life-affirming, heart-twisting. It was exactly what she wanted. A hint of roughness and desperation. His tongue plundering her mouth, his stubble scraping her lips.

He tasted indescribably good. Not quite salty, like the ocean. Not like bitter coffee or minty toothpaste or any other recognizable flavor. It was something less definite but more appealing, the intoxicating combination of compatible pheromones and strong sexual chemistry. His mouth was the perfect texture, the perfect temperature. He also knew how to kiss, in bold, hungry strokes. She couldn't get enough of him. It was a feast of slippery tongues and delicious pressure.

His hands roamed over her body, groping her bottom. She threaded her fingers through his hair, adding to the disarray. Then she tugged at the roots, making him kiss harder. He groaned his compliance, switching to a different angle. Heat exploded between them. The radios were in the way of what she wanted—his erection against the cleft of her thighs. The empty place inside her was there now. She ached for him to fill it.

Tearing her mouth from his, she reached down to unfasten his belt. It wouldn't cooperate, and she couldn't wait.

Panting, she smoothed her palm over the front of his pants, exploring the rigid length of his erection.

Wow.

He trapped her hand with his. Her eyes flew up to his face. He was breathing heavily, his jaw tense. After glancing around the dock again, he gave her a hesitant look. Regret washed over his flushed features.

Helena couldn't believe it. His cock was burning into her palm, stiff and hot, and he was calling a halt.

"It's not safe here," he murmured.

She jerked her hand from his grasp, stricken.

He swore under his breath. Stepping away from her, he raked his fingers through his hair. "I don't suppose we can take a rain check?"

This outrageous question, more than anything else, broke through the haze of lust and adrenaline surrounding her brain. What was she thinking? There were wild animals on the loose. She'd just been attacked by a Komodo dragon at the other dock. What was *he* thinking, for that matter? They'd been crazy to start kissing in the first place. There was no way they were finishing.

"That's what I was afraid of," he said.

She fumbled for some excuse for her behavior, and found none. "I'm sorry," she said, gesturing toward the tram cars. "I shouldn't have…it was just…"

"Don't," he said, his gaze hardening.

"Don't what?"

"Don't bullshit me about what happened. That—" he pointed at the tram "—didn't make us want to fuck."

She flinched at the accusation.

"This—" he indicated the space between them "—has been here all along. I've felt it more than once. I know you have, too."

"I just had a near-death experience," she said, flattening her palm over her racing heart. "What I felt was terror."

"That's it?"

"Yes."

"And if Kim had been here instead of me, you'd have had the same reaction?"

"Maybe."

He actually laughed. "I'd love to see that."

She swallowed hard, knowing he was right. The combination of fear and attraction had caused her to lose control. "It was an accident. If you think I have feelings for you, you're imagining things."

"I'm imagining things?" His gaze moved from her parted lips to the rise and fall of her chest. He moved closer, invading her personal space. Challenging her with his directness. "I'm imagining that if I hadn't stopped, you'd be up against the wall right now. Your legs would be locked around my waist and I'd be buried inside you."

Her knees went weak at the mental image.

"Tell me you don't want that."

She looked away, refusing to answer. It wasn't fair for him to press her like this when her body was still tingling with arousal. The tram cars continued to arrive and depart the station in a methodical row.

"You want it," he said, putting his mouth close to her ear. "I want it. I'll make it good, Helena. I'll do you right."

She forced herself to speak. "I can't."

"Because of Mitch?"

"We're still together."

"Are you?"

She wasn't sure where their relationship stood, but she couldn't say that to Josh. It would only encourage him, and he was hard enough to resist. Either way, she'd betrayed Mitch. Even if it was over between them, they hadn't ended things officially. She was about to shove Josh away in self-disgust when he retreated on his own.

"Here comes my car," Josh said, picking up the guns.

"What?"

"Here comes my tram car. We should take the same one back. It has the meat in it."

Helena was stuck. It was too dangerous to walk, and they couldn't get a vehicle to this location. She had to ride the Skylift again.

There was no time to second-guess this decision. They boarded the tram car as soon as it entered the station. She took the seat opposite him, gripping the safety bar for dear life.

Her hands felt raw, her senses reeling. The half-chewed side of beef was on the floor between them, along with a coiled length of rope.

The tram car began its sickening climb. Her tension rose with it.

"I thought you were cured," Josh said.

She didn't smile at his joke.

"How'd you hang on for so long?"

"I couldn't let go."

"I'm glad you didn't."

There was something in her eyes, like dust. She blinked a few times to clear her vision. They passed by Tau, who looked fine. Sailing over the park in the tram wasn't as bad as she'd anticipated. It was a hell of a lot better than dangling on the outside.

"What happened?" he asked.

She returned her attention to Josh. It was difficult to look at him. It would be even more difficult to look in the mirror. But he didn't seem ashamed. His expression was neither nonchalant nor smug. If she could take a guess, she'd say he was concerned about her. "I had to restart the generator, and I turned my back to the entrance. Bambang came out of nowhere."

"Why didn't you shoot him?"

"I wasn't ready. It's harder than it looks in the movies."

"I know."

"Did you shoot people, in the navy?"

"Yes."

"What's it like?"

"It sucks."

Helena wondered if she was capable of killing a person. It would be difficult enough for her to put down a dangerous animal. Despite the traumatic experience, she was glad Bambang hadn't been injured.

"The first time I was ordered to fire my weapon, I hesitated," he said. "I couldn't tell if my target was armed. That was my mistake."

"Why?"

"Because he *was* armed. He lifted his weapon and killed the guy right next to me."

Her throat closed up. "I'm sorry."

"So am I," he said, meeting her gaze.

CHAPTER THIRTEEN

CHLOE WOKE FROM a fitful sleep, disoriented.

She'd been dreaming about a tsunami. Emma had been ripped from her arms and swept away in the tumbling waves. Chloe had somersaulted through the water, bubbles rising from her throat as she screamed for her daughter.

Now she was in a strange, but cozy, place. Judging by the sparse light, it was early morning. Emma was cradled against her stomach, warm and secure. There was another heat source behind her. A sleeping man, snoring softly against her nape. Mateo must have gotten cold last night and decided to join them. The front of his body was molded to her back, and his hand was underneath her sweatshirt—under her tank top—cupping her right breast. He made a drowsy sound and flexed his fingers.

Her nipple hardened into a tight bead in his palm, jutting at the lacy cup of her bra. She was acutely aware of the inseam of her jeans, which had ridden up while she slept. Her vulva tingled with a mixture of discomfort and arousal.

She knew she should disengage herself from his embrace…but it felt good. He murmured something in Spanish and flicked his thumb over her nipple, wrenching a soft gasp from her lips.

The hairs on her neck stood on end. His erection swelled against her bottom, the silky fabric of his soccer shorts gliding over worn denim.

Then he froze, seeming to wake fully. *"Hijo de puta,"* he muttered, yanking his hand away from her breast.

Chloe tried to pretend she was asleep, but he was so clumsy in his panic to stop touching her that he fell off the bench with his hand still caught in her tank top. She was pulled backward with him. They landed in a tangled pile of limbs and tablecloths on the floor. Her injured thigh came down between his legs.

"Sorry," he choked, grimacing in pain.

When he finally got his hand out of her cookie jar, she straightened her clothes and eased away from him. This was so embarrassing. Emma was still asleep on the cushioned bench, hugging her teddy bear.

Mateo said a bunch of things she didn't understand. He was trying to apologize, but he hadn't done anything wrong. She'd practically been purring with pleasure, arching against him. It was an accident. Nobody's fault. There was no way for her to tell him this, and she didn't think he'd believe her, anyway. So she showed him. When he went quiet, she leaned forward and brushed her lips over his, very gently.

He stared at her as if she'd lost her mind.

She smothered a laugh, her pulse racing with excitement. If she had a little more confidence in her appeal, not to mention her breath, she might have tried a lingering kiss. He looked confused, but not disinterested.

"I have to go to the bathroom," she said, using the bench to boost herself up. He helped her stand, chivalrous as ever. She tested the strength of her injured leg and deemed it acceptable. The dull ache didn't stop her from limping forward. He followed her down the hall, propping open the door for her.

"Thanks," she said, skirting by him.

The corner of his mouth tipped up. He seemed to have processed the fact that she wasn't offended. She ducked inside the bathroom, giddy as a schoolgirl. She wanted to doodle his name in a journal and like all of his pictures on Facebook. Did he have a page for his soccer team? A shirtless photo, taken after the championship game?

Swoon.

She peeled down her jeans and used the restroom. Her thigh was discolored above the edge of the bandage. Underneath, her skin was probably black and blue. It felt bruised to the bone. When she was finished, she tugged the denim into place and returned to the lounge, rinsing her hands in the fountain. She covered Emma with the extra tablecloth.

Mateo was in the kitchen at the back of the restaurant. He'd found a dry salami and was cutting it into thin slices. *"Quieres?"*

Chloe was hungry, but not that hungry. "I'm a vegetarian."

He gave her a blank stare.

"I don't eat meat."

"Ah," he said, popping a slice into his mouth. He gestured to a large refrigerator, indicating other options.

She opened the door with trepidation. The interior was room temperature, so she ignored anything that could spoil. There were more pears and candied nuts, along with a container of crumbled blue cheese. When Mateo saw the cheese, he frowned at her in disapproval. He shook his head, pointing at the color.

She realized that he thought it was bad. They must not have blue cheese in Panama. She ate some of the cheese to demonstrate its safety. Delicious. Then she offered him a crumble, raising it to his lips. He allowed her to feed him.

She could tell he didn't like the taste when he grimaced and reached for a bottle of water. After washing it down, he said something uncomplimentary, maybe accusing her of trying to poison him.

Giggling at his reaction, she opened the fridge again. There was a round pan at the bottom of the fridge that looked promising. She uncovered it, revealing what appeared to be a pear tart. Mateo cut a slice for her and watched while she took a bite.

"Oh, my God," she said. "Yum."

He wasn't as wary of the tart. Chewing carefully, he nodded his approval. *"Eso,"* he said, finishing the slice. But then he went back to his salami, as if he preferred savory over sweet. Josh was the same way.

Chloe woke up Emma for breakfast. She liked the salami *and* the tart. After she ate her fill, they got ready to leave the restaurant. Mateo packed some snacks and water in his beach bag. Chloe tucked a washcloth into Emma's pants like a diaper, just in case she had an accident. They had a long journey ahead.

The smoke at the coast was still heavy, and there were fires burning in various locations. Chloe wanted to continue east as far as possible. When they reached Park Street, they could follow it north to the naval hospital. She figured the total distance was about three miles. An easy walk, under normal circumstances. With roads blocked and piles of rubble everywhere, it was a challenging maze.

Once again, the area was quiet and deserted. The earthquake had struck before operating hours for most local businesses. Schools were on spring break. But many residents had been in their cars, en route to work. She couldn't imagine the number of fatalities. There must have been hundreds on the bridge alone.

Emma refused to be carried by Mateo or Chloe, which slowed their progress. Chloe's leg felt better, but not good. The ill-fitting docksides didn't help. They slid up and down her heel as she limped along, causing friction. The shoes weren't comfortable for a stroll around the mall, let alone a hike through a ravaged city.

About an hour later, she was about to cry uncle when she spotted a Goodwill sign across the street. The front window was broken, but the interior looked safe. There was merchandize all over the floor.

"I need better shoes," she said, pointing at the store. "Boots."

He glanced down at her feet, and then toward the Goodwill. "Boots. *Sí.*"

They entered the space with caution. It was a large area, full of awesome junk. Chloe went straight to the shoe racks, which were overturned. She set Emma down with a book that made animal sounds and began digging through the pile while Mateo looked for *pantalones*. She found a pair of black combat boots first. They were too big, so she saved them for Mateo and settled on a pair of brown leather half boots for herself.

She needed socks, too. There was a plastic bin behind Emma. Chloe sorted through them and selected two pairs, blue for her and black for Mateo. She pulled on the socks with the boots, which were a perfect fit.

Mateo returned with a backpack instead of his beach bag. He was wearing a long-sleeved shirt and worn Levi's, which he appeared to have pulled on over his shorts. She presented the combat boots and socks to him, admiring his well-muscled thighs.

Emma hit the button to make the tiger growl. *Mrowr.*

Chloe rose to her feet, with his help. Leaving him with the boots, she browsed around, grabbing an extra outfit for Emma. She also searched through the ladies' garments, selecting cropped yoga pants and a soft T-shirt. They might have to spend the night on the floor of the hospital, or who knew where.

Mateo tucked his jeans into the boots and stood, testing their comfort. She smiled at his utilitarian fashion choices. Lyle's slouching rocker style and skinny frame paled in comparison. "Do they fit?"

"Sí, mamita."

"What does that mean?"

He laughed at the question. Instead of answering, he just shrugged. She put her extra clothes in his backpack, along with Emma's book. Before they left the store, he paused at the dusty front counter to scribble on scrap paper. *"Cuántos cuestan?"* he asked, referring to the items they'd gathered. "How much?"

"Forty dollars," she guessed. The note read:

Mateo Calderón Torres
Ave. Redonda No. 14
Cuidad Panamá, Panamá
Te debo 50 dólares

"Mateo Calderón Torres," she said, arching a brow. "That's a mouthful."

He didn't appear to understand, but he stared at her lips in a way that reminded her of this morning's kiss. Feeling self-conscious, she took the pen from him, adding "Chloe Garrison" and her own phone number to the bottom. He didn't protest.

On the way out, he almost tripped over a cane lying on the floor. It was serendipity. He handed her the cane, which was smooth wood with a rubber grip. She brandished it with ease, hobbling forward. The little bit of help made a lot of difference.

Chloe felt good as they stepped out together. She had new shoes, a better way to get around and a fresh outlook. Emma wanted to be carried, and she even allowed Mateo to put her on his shoulders. Unless they encountered an insurmountable obstacle, they were going to make it to the hospital today.

They hit a stretch of unblemished road and made excellent time, reaching Park Street without incident. The weather shifted from cool and misty to sunny and hot, which didn't help the air quality. She removed her hooded sweatshirt and tied it around her waist. She should have picked up hats and sunglasses at the thrift shop.

They only saw a handful of people that day. There was a mumbling homeless man pushing a grocery cart, and a roving band of young men, armed with impromptu weapons. Mateo ignored the vagrant, not the gang. He directed Chloe and Emma into a hiding place and put his arms around them until the men passed. Chloe was grateful for his protection. She didn't want to know what the men would do with a lone woman.

At midmorning, they came upon a large structure fire. It was blocks in the distance, involving what appeared to be an apartment complex and several industrial buildings. They'd have to find a way around.

Chloe pointed east with her old-man cane. It was uphill, so maybe they could get a better view of the area.

Two blocks later, at the top of the slope, she caught a glimpse of the freeway. And halted dead in her tracks.

Interstate 5 was a parking lot.

Looking north, the direction they were headed, there was a major accident. Not just another fire, but some kind of structure collapse and a huge pileup. Although she couldn't see clearly through the smoke, she got the impression of hundreds of vehicles. She imagined charred flesh and burning bodies. There were news helicopters in the sky, miles away. But no organized rescue effort, as far as she could tell.

No end in sight.

She glanced at Mateo, distraught. They would have to turn back and approach the naval hospital from the west side. It meant adding many extra blocks to their route. He took Emma off his shoulders and pointed to a bus bench under a shady tree. This was a quiet street, and the surrounding area looked safe. Chloe nodded her agreement.

When she arrived at the bench, she lowered herself to a sitting position with a groan. She hadn't realized how sore her muscles were. The cane was helpful, but her good leg ached from overcompensating. They drank water and ate pieces of flatbread. The bland meal was perfect for her uneasy stomach.

Emma explored the area under the tree, gathering the spiky green seed balls that had fallen from the branches.

Mateo picked up a pointy stick from below the bench. Chloe watched as he drew lazy circles in the flat dirt at their feet. She wanted to connect with him, but the language barrier made it difficult. Then an idea occurred to her. Even though he didn't *speak* English, he often understood what she was saying. They could communicate another way.

"How old are you?" she asked, gesturing to the stick.

He stopped making circles and wrote *21*. Chloe smiled at his quick comprehension, as well as the number. She was glad he was close to her age.

"Y tú?" he asked, handing her the stick.

She wrote *23*.

He smiled, too. Maybe he liked older women.

"Tell me about your family. Do you have brothers or sisters?" She returned the stick.

He smoothed the dirt with the sole of his boot and drew three triangles with circle heads. *"Tres hermanas."*

"Three sisters?"

"Sí."

"Older or younger?"

He wrote a *24* next to the first girl figure. Then *17* and *15*. Two younger, one older. Drawing a line from the older sister, he made two more triangle shapes. *"Mis sobrinas."*

"Your nieces?"

He nodded and wrote *3* next to both shapes. *"Gemelas."*

"Twins?"

"Sí," he said. Then a crease formed between his brows, and he started over. He drew two boy figures and two number *21*s. He crossed one out. *"Mi hermano. Se murió."*

She studied his face, interpreting the sadness in his eyes as well as the marks in the dirt. Two brothers, both 21. They had to be twins, as well. He had a twin brother...who was dead. "I'm so sorry," she said, touching his shoulder.

He gave back the stick.

Chloe glanced at Emma, who was still playing with spike balls. Then she drew her own boy figure, and *29*. "My brother, Josh."

He waited, as if expecting her to add more.

"That's all," she said. "One brother."

His gaze traveled up the length of her bare arm. Reaching out, he grasped her wrist and tilted it gently. *"Que te pasó?"*

She tried to pull her arm back, but he wouldn't let go. He was talking about her scars. The faint white lines were barely visible, more self-harm than hesitation marks. She hadn't been brave enough to cut deep or open up a vein. "It's nothing."

He asked another question, but she didn't understand. She looked at Emma again, tears filling her eyes. During her darkest days, Chloe had been convinced that her daughter would be better off without her. She didn't know how to tell Mateo that, when she didn't understand it herself. She'd do anything for Emma, even die.

He leaned forward and put his other arm around her. She rested her head on his shoulder, accepting the comfort. It wasn't easy to interpret his reaction, but he seemed more concerned than disapproving. His embrace was warm and quiet. He wasn't frowning, like her mother had. He wasn't frantic.

Emma climbed into her lap, inserting herself between them. She had a spikey ball clutched in her chubby little fist. Chloe could smell the saltwater in her hair and detect the faint, stale scent of saliva on her fingers.

Chloe had cried when she found out she was pregnant. She hadn't been ready for motherhood. Her parents wouldn't have objected if she'd had an abortion. But she'd been in love with Lyle, and he'd promised to take care of them.

What bullshit.

Lyle had only pretended to clean up his act. Her pregnancy had made it very easy for him to sneak around. While she'd stayed home, nauseous and tired, he'd been out late every night. He claimed to be working at a fast-food place. In reality, he was partying with his boys, attending band practice and selling drugs on the side.

She'd known this about him before the contraception fail. She'd partied *with* him.

He hadn't slowed down for Emma's sake. He hadn't seemed affected by fatherhood at all.

Lyle's disinterest in Emma had broken Chloe's heart. She wanted to be a good mother, so she'd changed for the better. He'd gone the opposite direction. A month after Emma was born, Chloe caught him snorting coke in the bathroom at her parents' house. She told him it was over on the spot.

He'd stolen the money from her purse and left, high as a kite. He hadn't called her since then or attempted to visit Emma. Not once in the past two years. At the time, she'd been devastated by his apathy. A combination of postpartum depression and breakup blues had brought her low. She'd cut her arm one afternoon and taken a handful of pills the next.

In the aftermath of this incident, her mother had been awarded temporary custody of Emma. Chloe had continued to live at home with Emma, but she didn't get her full rights back for several months.

She was glad she'd fought her way out of that dark period, with the help of medication. Now she was strong again, and she had the tools to stay healthy. But she also recognized her potential for slipping. During an experience like this, it was hard to think positive. Having a supportive person beside her made all the difference.

"Thank you," she said to Mateo, lifting her head. He might never know how much his help meant to her.

"Por nada, mamita," he said. *"Por nada."*

CHAPTER FOURTEEN

JOSH STUDIED HELENA as they rode the Skylift back to the front of the park.

She appeared conflicted, even nauseated by what they'd done, which wasn't very flattering. Her fear of heights probably factored into the equation, but so did guilt. She hadn't lied to him about her relationship with Mitch.

Josh curled his hand around the safety bar, uneasy. He *wasn't* a poacher. Dancing with Melody to get Trent's goat was a far cry from actively pursuing another man's girlfriend. He'd crossed the line with Helena and then some. What happened to his principles? Not only had he been eager for her to use him, he'd demanded a rain check.

He didn't think Mitch was right for her. His opinion was clouded by his own desire, of course, but now he was more certain than ever. Their chemistry was off the charts. He knew she'd felt it. She'd tried to *unbuckle his belt*. He could have had her right then. They'd both been primed and ready. Danger had heightened their emotions, exposing the attraction between them. It hadn't created the heat, just the intensity.

Even so, she clearly still had feelings for Mitch. Josh should back off. Give her the space she needed to figure things out.

He didn't want to, though. He wanted to finish what they'd started. He wanted her wet and hot and trembling. Legs spread, bare tits against his chest, nails digging into his shoulders. Lips parted in ecstasy as she came.

He tore his gaze away from her, willing his cock not to get hard again. They were almost to the loading dock. It would be awkward to jump out of the tram car with a boner. Bambang might be there, ready to bite any protruding body part.

Josh didn't see the Komodo dragon in the station. He exited the car first and turned off the generator. Then Helena handed him the meat and stepped out with the rope. "If Bam comes at us, throw it down," she said. "He's probably just hungry."

They didn't encounter the Komodo dragon on their way to the truck. He set the meat down in the back, and they retrieved a portable crate from the storage yard. It was a large, heavy-duty cage with steel bars.

"Do you think we can dart Zuma the same way?" he asked.

"I doubt it. She's sneakier than Tau, and she probably knows what happened to him." Mulling it over, she said, "Let's drug the meat and leave it by his cage. She might come to investigate tonight, when she thinks the coast is clear."

"Good plan," he said, impressed by her strategy. Maybe it took one fierce, cunning female to catch another.

They stopped by the hospital for the appropriate narcotics and continued to the lion enclosure. This was the riskiest part of the plan. They had to leave the safety of the truck, carry the crate to Tau and shove him in it. He was a huge animal, so it wouldn't be easy. They would also be vulnerable to attack, should Zuma decide to interfere.

Josh parked at the rift in the road and got out with the rifle. He helped Helena unload the crate and carry it past the broken section of asphalt. Then he stood guard while she retrieved a burlap blanket and the hunk of meat from the back end of the truck, placing both on top of the crate. She wheeled the crate the short distance to the sleeping lion.

Tau had looked big from a distance. Up close, he was a monster. His head was enormous. His furry neck appeared larger than the circle of Josh's arms. Josh didn't want to get anywhere near this massive beast. He glanced around for Zuma with his rifle poised, blood pumping with adrenaline.

"How are we going to get him in the crate?" he asked in a shaky voice.

Helena didn't seem afraid of Tau. But she'd always been fearless—on the ground. "It won't be easy," she said. Setting the meat aside, she bent to adjust the crate's wheels, securing it in place. Then she opened the gate and grabbed the burlap blanket, spreading it out next to Tau. "We have to roll him over and drag him inside."

She grabbed the big cat by the scruff like a kitten. Josh lowered the rifle and crouched down to take the other end. Tau didn't object to their clumsy efforts. When the lion was in the middle of the blanket, tongue lolling out, Josh lifted his side. Helena backed into the crate, crab-walking. It wasn't easy to move four hundred pounds of solid muscle, but she was a very strong woman, and he was no slouch. They managed, inch by inch.

Every second felt like an eternity. The hairs on the back of his neck prickled and his ears were attuned to the slightest sound. He hoped Zuma wasn't watching them, waiting for another opportunity to strike.

By the time they were done, he was sweating buckets again. Josh did a clockwork sweep of the area while Helena pulled the burlap free from Tau and crawled out of the crate. She secured the front gate with a padlock.

Josh was ready to hightail it back to the truck, but Helena had other ideas. "Let's go check on Greg."

"What?"

"I need to know," she said quietly. "Maybe we can drag him to shelter. I can't stand the thought of Bambang getting to him."

Josh swore under his breath. He knew Komodo dragons ate carrion.

"At the very least, we can cover him up. Please."

"Fine," he said, against his better judgment. He'd never been able to say no to women, and this one was his special kryptonite.

They hurried toward the lion enclosure. Josh went first, rifle raised. Helena followed close behind, staying right on his six. They found Greg facedown on the ground, just outside the barrier wall. A section of the wall had crumbled, leaving a wide crack. The keeper had probably been trying to block the escape route when Zuma attacked.

Josh didn't see any sign of the lioness, but that didn't mean she wasn't hiding nearby. There was a storage shed about twenty feet from the crumbled wall. Helena approached the shed, opening the door to check the interior. Her nod indicated it was clear. They crept toward Greg, moving with caution.

Helena laid the blanket on the ground next to him. With Josh's help, she rolled Greg over. The lion keeper was definitely dead. His skin was gray, dark eyes foggy. There was a circle of dried blood underneath him. Flies crawled in and out of his open mouth.

There was no time for shock, or grief, or even a respectful silence. They dragged Greg the same way they'd dragged Tau. His weight was easier to handle. When they reached the storage shed, she covered his body with the burlap.

Josh stood outside the door, rifle poised.

"Should we pray?" she asked.

"I don't know. I'm not religious."

"Neither am I."

She said something that sounded like "fray-oo" and rose to her feet.

"What does that mean?"

"Peace."

She shut the door and they walked back to the truck, eyes peeled for Zuma. Josh didn't relax until they were inside the vehicle again, safe and sound. He hesitated before starting the engine. Helena wasn't big on sharing feelings, but she looked choked up, and for good reason. Greg had been her immediate supervisor. Maybe even a father figure.

"Do you want to talk about it?" he asked.

She rubbed her cheek against her shoulder. "About what?"

He didn't press. He'd done enough of that earlier. She needed someone to do it, to push back at her and engage her emotions. Josh recognized that, even if she didn't. But a lot of people needed things he couldn't give them. His niece needed a better father. Josh couldn't force Lyle to get his act together, and he couldn't make Helena to open up to him.

It wasn't his place.

Saying nothing, he did a three-point turnaround and headed back to the front of the park. They hadn't gone far when she touched his arm.

"Stop here," she said. "Just for a minute."

He parked next to the fence to the elephant enclosure, aware that she wanted to check on the herd. They were in an open area at least a hundred yards from the lion enclosure.

Josh figured it was safe enough, as long as they stayed close to the truck, so he didn't protest when she climbed out. He just followed her.

The fence was made of sturdy blonde wood, smooth and polished. The posts were gripped by thousands of hands every day. Beyond this fence lay electric wires, currently not charged, and a dry moat. Both kept elephants in and humans out. Even the keepers had very little contact with the animals. The wildlife park wasn't a circus. The elephants didn't perform tricks for an audience or give rides to children.

The herd looked happy enough, though. They had a whole pond full of water, and some leftover hay. He followed Helena's gaze to

Mbali, the herd's most recent addition. Josh had to admit, baby elephants were cute.

"Mbali's getting big," he said. "How old is she now?"

"Fourteen months."

"Do you ever wish you could get closer to them?"

"I get close to trim their feet," she said. "Sometimes they reach out with their trunks and touch my hand."

"But the bars are always there."

"Yes."

"Why is that?"

"Because they kill people. More keepers have been killed by elephants than by any other wild animal."

"Even lions?"

"Lions, tigers and bears combined."

He hadn't known that. "They look so gentle."

"They are, most of the time. But it only takes once. They're like great white sharks. An exploratory bite is often fatal. Same with a careless swing of the trunk."

Glancing around for Zuma, he pondered her words. As friendly as the elephants appeared, he wasn't eager to climb into their enclosure. But he surfed in the Pacific Ocean with sharks almost every day. He just couldn't *see* them.

"They kill on purpose, too," she said. "They're temperamental."

"In the wild, or in captivity?"

"Both. Anyone in close contact is at risk. They need space to roam and distance from people. Greg always taught us not to project our emotions onto them or build unhealthy attachments. Too much human interference is damaging for animals. It can create a whole slew of problems, including species confusion. There are documented cases of chimps that seem to think they're people and won't take mates."

"Really?"

She nodded, still staring at Mbali. "And when you treat them like family members instead of wild animals, you stop believing they're capable of crushing you."

This pragmatic approach wasn't an unusual attitude for a keeper, in his experience. Helena wasn't a "bunny hugger," to borrow Louis's term. And yet, Josh still found it sad. He could see very clearly that she loved these elephants. Maybe it was foolish to imagine that they returned her feelings.

As if on cue, Mbali noticed Helena standing there. She trumpeted in greeting, running closer to the fence line. She raced back and forth, her trunk curled up jauntily. Then she scampered back to her mother.

Helena's face crumpled at the display. She pressed the back of her hand to her nose. So much for maintaining an emotional distance.

"If I didn't know better, I'd think you were a bunny hugger," Josh said.

She shook her head in denial.

"A deeply closeted bunny hugger."

"It's professional pride," she insisted, blinking the tears away. "Successful elephant births are rare in captivity."

"Why is that?"

"The mating process is difficult, for one."

"I'll bet. I've seen Obi's penis."

She gave him a wobbly smile. "Males don't actually penetrate the female during sex."

"You're kidding."

"No. The vaginal opening is too small, and it's kind of hard to get to."

"How do they mate, then?"

"There's a lot of rubbing and mounting involved. Then he sprays semen into her, like a fire hose."

He shook his head in wonder. "Wow."

"It can take years to conceive. The gestation period is long and the birth has to be carefully monitored. Sometimes mother elephants panic and trample their young. Calves have a high mortality rate." Her expression grew troubled. "The first few months were very stressful. I was here around the clock."

"I remember."

She glanced at him in surprise. He'd always watched her from afar. He noticed when she was having a hard time. She'd lost weight after Mbali was born. He'd wondered if there was something going on in her personal life.

Her gaze became shuttered. "We should go."

They drove back to the front of the park and entered the staff building in silence. It was past noon. Despite the disturbing events of the morning, he was hungry. "Have a seat," he said. "I'll forage for food."

She sank into a chair, burying her head in her hands.

He visited the men's room and washed up with bottled water. There were stocked vending machines all over the park, so they wouldn't run out of food or drinks. Instead of relying on snacks, he searched the kitchen for a real meal. He found some apples and several cans of tuna in oil. Grabbing both, along with a couple of forks, he returned to Helena. She glanced up when he set the items in front of her.

"Is this okay?" he asked.

She regarded the food without much interest.

"Do you want a soda?"

"No."

There was already water on the table. He took a seat and opened a bottle, drinking in thirsty gulps. She murmured something about the restroom and walked down the hall.

Josh popped open one of the cans of tuna and dug in. It was bland, but edible. He alternated between forkfuls and crisp bites of apple.

When Helena came back and sat down again, she seemed distant. She opened a can and chewed methodically. He pictured the way she'd looked at the elephant yard, her eyes vibrant. She had a different energy with animals. She'd always been passionate about her work, whether she was assisting a birth or describing the mechanics of pachyderm sex. Now she was quiet and withdrawn, avoiding his gaze.

He figured that she was uncomfortable for several reasons. Greg's death. The close call on the Skylift. Their tawdry make-out session. He couldn't help with the first two, but maybe he could put her mind at ease about the last.

"You don't have to worry about me making a move on you," he said, finishing his apple. "I can control myself."

Her mouth twisted at those words. He hadn't meant to offend her by suggesting that *she* was out of control. Sure, she'd lost her grip for a moment. It had been the most erotic moment of his life, and he'd participated with relish, so who was he to judge? He loved the fact that she'd gotten carried away. She should get carried away more often.

He drummed his fingertips against the edge of the table. "I won't touch you again. Unless you ask me to."

"Don't count on it."

"I won't tell anyone what happened, either."

"There's nothing to tell," she said, eyes flashing.

Her capacity for denial was astonishing. Strong woman, strong delusions. "Is Mitch coming back?"

She tilted the can of tuna to search its contents. It was empty.

He hoped she wasn't thinking about leaving. This job was her entire world. After what he'd seen between her and Mbali, relocation would be a heartbreaking option. "When you get tired of waiting for him, I'll be here."

"Why?"

"Why not?"

"Aren't there any more tourists or college girls you can sleep with?"

"I'm sure there are a few."

She gave him a pointed glance.

"Maybe I'm ready to settle down."

"You're just bored with easy pickings," she said. "Women fall at your feet, so you're chasing after the ones you can't have."

"The hell I am."

"Melody?"

"I didn't chase after Melody."

She took a sip of water, shrugging. "Whatever you say."

Josh tamped down his annoyance. He knew what she was doing. She didn't like showing emotions or needing anyone. She was afraid of letting him in. "I'm not chasing after you, either. Didn't I say I'd back off?"

"You issued an open invitation for sex in the same breath."

He conceded her point. He should've quit while he was ahead. "I was trying to tell you how I felt. It's called sharing."

"Well, cut it out."

The pricklier she got, the more he wanted to strip down her defenses. He liked sparring with her, and he could imagine how good it would feel to explore that energy in bed. Maybe she was right about him being bored. *Unfulfilled* was a better word.

Women didn't fall at his feet, however. Not the ones he went for. He preferred sober, self-aware partners. He enjoyed giving pleasure as much as receiving it. Anyone worth doing was worth doing right. That was his motto. And it wasn't as if he'd taken home a different girl every night. He'd dated some for weeks or months at a time.

Obviously, none of those relationships had stuck. If the perfect woman had come along, he'd have moved heaven and earth to keep her.

"Have you always wanted to work with animals?" he asked, changing the subject.

"Pretty much."

"Since when?"

"Childhood."

"Did you have a lot of pets?"

"Not really," she said, picking up an apple. "My mom worked on a small farm a few miles east of the city, and we lived there for a few years after my dad died. There were goats and cows and barn cats with kittens."

"And they were your friends," he mused.

She took a bite of apple, not responding.

He figured that a little girl who got teased for her funny accent and serious face might feel more at home with a group of animals than a pack of kids. Josh could relate. He'd been clumsy and skinny in high school. Humor had been his crutch. "You said you're more comfortable with them."

"I am."

"Because they're better listeners?"

"And they don't require responses."

He laughed at this, aware that she was getting annoyed with his questions. They didn't have to talk, as far as he was concerned. He wouldn't mind chilling out here in the staff area for the rest of the afternoon. They could grill a few steaks later. It was a hell of lot better than trying to capture wild animals.

That reminded him of something. "I saw a hyena outside the fence line."

She paused, midchew. "Where?"

"Birdie Trail." It was a popular jogging path in a wooded area between the zoo and the naval hospital.

"When was this?"

"Earlier today, from the Skylift."

"Are you sure?"

"Positive."

"Why didn't you say anything?"

"You were dangling in midair at the time. Then we…it slipped my mind."

She rose to her feet, leaving her apple on the table. "Shit!"

"Do you think he jumped the fence?"

"Hyenas can't jump that high. The fence must be damaged. We have to check the perimeter right now. If there's a broken section, all of the code ones could be roaming the city, attacking survivors."

She picked up the tranquilizer gun and he slung the rifle over his shoulder, following her back to the truck.

So much for relaxing.

CHAPTER FIFTEEN

THEY FOUND THE washed-out section of fence at the edge of Copper Canyon.

As soon as Josh slowed to a stop, Helena jumped out of the truck and approached the fence line. Her stomach sank as she saw the extent of the damage. Copper River had rerouted during the initial quake, pouring thousands of gallons of water across the dry earth. Now the ground was damp, riveted with huge cracks. About ten feet of chain link lay flat, half-buried in debris that the rushing river left behind.

She curled her hands into fists, wanting to cry. Hyenas traveled in packs, so it was likely that more than one animal had escaped. The others could follow.

This was too big a problem for her to handle. Dealing with a single code one inside zoo boundaries was a group effort. A wildlife situation of this magnitude was unprecedented. The lack of officials and authority figures didn't help. There was no communication, no law enforcement assistance. No guidance.

Helena didn't even know the procedure for a perimeter breach. It was a city-wide emergency. She needed dozens, if not hundreds, of helpers. Teams of keepers combing the park. More on the streets, with police backup. Maintenance crews for fence repair. Skilled construction workers to fix the compromised enclosures.

Instead, she had...Josh Garrison. Whose experience in hunting was limited to the human female variety.

She smothered a groan at the thought, still mortified by her behavior at the loading dock. The sequence of events was too overwhelming to contemplate. Bambang, the aerial tram, her runaway lust, Greg's dead face.

It was all too much. Too disturbing. She couldn't breathe under the weight of her stress and sorrow. Pressure coiled inside her, constricting her chest. When Josh put his hand on her elbow, she sprung away from him. He lifted his palm up in a peace gesture, his brows raised. She wasn't usually so agitated.

"What are we going to do?" she exploded.

"Repair it," he said simply.

"They're already out!"

"One is."

"More than one, I'll wager. That's why we haven't seen them around the park."

"We saw Bambang."

She rubbed her aching temple. "Don't remind me."

"We've already got Tau, and he's the biggest threat."

"You're wrong about that. Zuma might be smaller, but she's ten times as aggressive. And a pack of hyenas will feast on corpses. They might even attack the living. Hyenas target any kind of easy prey."

He stared into the distance, absorbing her words. "Do you want to track them?"

"I don't know how to track them. In an urban area, over concrete and asphalt, it's probably not even possible."

"Then we have to let it go."

"Let it go?"

"Yes," he said, decisive. "We've got more than enough to take care of inside the park. What happens out there can't be our top priority."

"Public safety is always the top priority."

"And the best way to protect people is with containment. Not by wandering around a deserted city and accomplishing nothing."

She swallowed hard. "What if Zuma got out?"

"Is she more inclined to explore the unknown, or stay and defend her territory?"

"The second."

"And she's not a scavenger, like the hyenas. She didn't disturb Greg."

Helena walked away a few steps, her stomach roiling. She pictured Greg's serious face, so unfairly defiled by death. His gray skin and the dried blood on his neck. When his wife and daughters found out, they'd be devastated.

"I'm sorry," Josh said. "I know he meant a lot to you."

"We worked together for ten years," she said, taking a deep breath.

"Longer than you knew your father."

This observation poked at a tender place inside her—and she snapped. Whirling around, she shoved at Josh's chest with all of the force she could muster. He stumbled backward but kept his footing, which wasn't very satisfying. Then he had the nerve to laugh at her failed attempt. So she curled her hand into a fist and let it fly. Instead of sinking it into stomach, she connected with the center of his palm. He blocked the blow neatly, harnessing her fury.

Damn him.

Tears pricked her eyes, but she didn't want to cry on his shoulder. She wanted to punch his too-handsome face. Wrestle him to the ground and make him hurt. Make him hurt *her*. Maybe some rough pleasure would ease her pain.

He didn't draw her closer. Letting go of her hand, he stood there, arms at his sides. Giving her a clean shot.

It was her move. Take what she needed. Hit him or hug him.

He must have meant what he'd said about backing off. He wasn't going to be goaded into crossing the line with her again. She'd lashed out at him in anger, not desire, but her mind had jumped from there to sex quickly. What other physical altercation could they have, after all? She knew how he'd respond if she initiated contact. He wouldn't strike back, but he'd touch her— with permission. Her cheeks heated at the realization.

She cradled her fist in her own palm and reconsidered his father comment. He probably hadn't been trying to needle her. He seemed intent on "sharing feelings." Which was a swing-worthy offense, but forgivable.

"It's a sensitive subject," he said in an even tone.

"I don't need you to tell me that I didn't have a dad in my life. I'm well aware."

"That's not what I was doing."

"Greg wasn't a father figure to me, either, so you can give it a rest with the comparisons. He was very professional. He treated animals like animals and employees like employees. Not family members."

Josh didn't argue, but he appeared doubtful.

She pointed at the ruined fence. "Let's focus on this. One clusterfuck at a time."

"Okay."

"I don't see how we can fix it, just the two of us. We'll have to move a ton of debris and dig out the chain link."

"We can put up a temporary section."

"Is there material for that?"

"Maybe in the storage yard."

She had to give him credit for thinking of an alternate solution. He was good at that, taking the easy road. She resented it a little. Maybe because she'd always done things the hard way, and she was too stubborn to change.

Waving him back to the truck, she took the passenger seat while he got behind the wheel. Although she'd cooled down some, she still felt sick. "I'm sorry."

"For what?"

"Trying to hit you."

"Don't worry about it."

"I could have hurt you."

"Only if I let you."

She watched him shift gears, a muscle in his forearm flexing. "You're a bit overconfident, aren't you?"

"No. I'm just the right amount of confident."

Closing her eyes, she shut out his appealing visage. His casual self-assurance should have bothered her, but it didn't. She was tense enough for the both of them. He was easygoing and reliable, if cocky. That was comforting. They'd managed to get a lot done so far. As much as it pained her to admit, they made a good team.

She wasn't pushing him away because he disgusted her. She was doing it because she couldn't resist him. Without even meaning to, he was breaking down her walls and chipping away layers, getting too close for comfort.

"I've had close-quarters combat training," he reminded her. "I'm sure you can hold your own against the average guy, though."

"Yes," she said, bitter. "I can."

"You've had to?"

She was continually surprised by his perceptiveness. "A long time ago."

"What happened?"

"I worked at a stable one summer," she said, staring out the window. "There was an older guy on the staff, another hand who exercised the horses. He used to call me 'Legs.' I think he was intimidated by my height, and wanted to make me feel small. He tried to grope me once while I was mucking out stalls."

"What did you do?"

"I elbowed him in the gut and he fell into a pile of manure."

Josh didn't appear amused by her story. "Did you complain?"

"No. I just never turned my back on him again."

He parked by an equipment shed and turned off the engine. His jaw was clenched, his hands still locked around the wheel. "Is that what you thought when I teased you? That I wanted to hurt you or make you feel small?"

She hesitated, uncertain of her answer. She knew it wasn't fair to compare him to that old stable hand.

"I don't," he said, meeting her eyes. "I like you the way you are. I like you tall."

She believed him. But she didn't *want* to believe him, because it stirred something inside her. Something stronger than desire. But she wasn't the kind of person who could deny the plainspoken truth, said straight to her face.

His sincere compliments didn't lessen her discomfort in his presence, however. He'd said he wouldn't make the first move, and she trusted him. The person she didn't trust was herself.

She wanted him. He wanted her. Over the past two days, her defenses had crumbled. She didn't know how she was going to keep her distance. He wasn't even trying to seduce her, and she *still* didn't have any self-control.

She got out of the truck, determined to stay strong. Lust, she could handle. The real killer was their emotional connection. She didn't have to worry about him touching her body; her heart was in far greater jeopardy.

They found fencing material and the tools they needed among the construction supplies. While they were loading the truck, she spotted a stack of orange cones and a can of spray paint. "We should make an SOS sign."

His eyes lit up at the suggestion. "Okay."

They'd be busy with the fence until nightfall, maybe longer. In the meantime, a plane or helicopter might fly over and see the warning. Helena would feel better if they made an attempt to communicate with officials. There were wild animals on the loose. Notifying the public was essential.

They added the cones to their pile of supplies. She brought the spray paint, along with some orange flags and a sidewalk sign. On the way back to the entrance, she stopped by the staff building to collect a radio and a few more items.

Josh drove to the front of the park and stopped next to the gate, which Helena unlocked. He set up the cones in a large SOS formation in the open area near the ticket booths, while she wrote a message on the sandwich board in black marker.

WARNING

She made a list of possible escaped animals and noted the hyena sighting beyond the zoo's borders. Then she wrote her name at the bottom and left instructions to communicate with her via radio. She put the radio in a plastic bag, hanging it on the corner of the sign. The orange flags fluttered at each corner.

Josh came back to study her work. "Where's my name?"

She added it under hers. There was hardly any room, so she had to squeeze the letters in. "This reminds me of a Stephen King book."

"*The Stand*," he said immediately.

"You've read it?"

"A long time ago."

"We're like Fran and Harold, the only survivors in the town, painting information on the side of a barn."

His brows drew together. "You're a good match for Fran, but I'm no Harold."

"Who are you?"

"I'm Stu."

"You're not Stu."

"Okay, I'm Larry. And you're Nadine."

She picked up the can of spray paint, shaking her head. "Nadine, the virgin? Please."

Walking away from the sign, she used the can of spray paint to write another message in huge letters on the sidewalk next to the orange cones: CODE 10. This code indicated a wild animal outside the park boundaries. There were helicopters in the smoky sky overhead. She hoped a pilot would get close enough to notice the SOS, and relay the message to the authorities. With any luck, zoo officials were standing by, and help would arrive soon.

"Are you sure you want to stay?" Josh asked. "We could get in trouble for ignoring the warnings."

"I'm not going anywhere."

"They might order us to evacuate as soon as they see the sign."

"Who's 'they'?"

"The National Guard."

"They'll have to come in and get me."

He smiled at her stubbornness.

"Do you want to go?" she asked.

"No."

She was glad for his company, irritating attraction aside. He wasn't useless or lazy. He hadn't tried to take over, which she appreciated. Most men, Trent included, would have assumed the leadership role. Josh seemed happy to share it with her.

"If we don't hear from anyone by tomorrow morning, we should walk down to the naval hospital and check it out."

"You think other people are there?"

"I wouldn't be surprised. They perform surgeries and do emergency treatment. If there are a bunch of patients who can't be moved easily, some of the staff would stay. They might have a better radio system, too."

They passed through the gate and hopped in the truck, traveling to their next task. She was calmer now. When the new section of fence was up, she'd breathe another sigh of relief. The code ten was still a major concern, but she couldn't be everywhere at once. Josh was right; they had to focus on containment.

Preparing the ground for the fence was a challenge. They had to fill the rifts in the earth and create a solid surface so animals couldn't slip under the barrier.

They both did a fair amount of digging, shoveling heavy piles of dirt into a wheelbarrow. The foundation they built wasn't flat or impenetrable by a long shot, but Josh said they could solve this problem with sandbags. They set the poles first, bracing them with metal stakes that had to be hammered deep into the ground.

The chain link was trickier to work with. After attaching one end to the pole using metal clamps, they tried to stretch the remaining material across the space. It wouldn't pull taut enough to create a strong barrier. Neither of them knew much about construction or how to achieve the necessary tension.

"There's got to be a tool for this," Josh said, panting from exertion. He had gloves on, like her. His forearms were streaked with dirt and his shirt was damp with sweat. On him, it looked sexy.

"What tool?"

"I wouldn't recognize it if I saw it."

"We could use the truck to pull it."

He agreed, securing a rope between the chain link and the bumper. She got behind the wheel, edging the vehicle forward slowly. When he called out for her to stop, she turned off the engine, but left the truck in gear and engaged the brake. It worked. They used the remaining clamps to secure the fence in place. Josh added barbed wire to the top, and ended up with a couple of nasty scratches for his trouble.

The final step was sandbagging. They returned to the storage yard for sandbags, loaded them and unloaded them along the fence line. It was exhausting. By the time they were done, the sun had dipped low on the horizon.

Josh surveyed their handiwork with pride. "Not bad, for a couple of amateurs."

She was just glad they were finished, and hadn't been attacked in the process. There was no sign of the hyenas, or any of the other code ones, but most wild animals were shy. They wouldn't be strolling through the middle of the park in broad daylight.

"How about those steaks?" he asked as they climbed into the truck.

Her stomach growled with hunger, but she was filthy. She had to wash up first. "I'd kill for a hot shower."

"There's water in the greenhouse," he said, giving her a canny look. "It has a rain cache system and solar heating."

"How do you know that?"

"I helped install it."

"Really?"

"They asked for volunteers, and I studied rainwater collection methods in one of my environmental science classes."

She'd had no idea.

"If you want to clean up, we should do it now, before dark."

"I need some fresh clothes," she said.

"So do I."

They stopped at a tourist shop called the Lion's Share. Although the place was in shambles, they were able to find T-shirts and pajama pants. She picked up some towels and soap. There was even zoo-themed novelty underwear. Josh selected a pair of giraffe boxer shorts. Helena grabbed the zebra-striped panties.

As they left with the loot, a strange noise alerted them to an animal presence. She froze next to Josh, listening. The plaintive yowl repeated.

"Next door," he said in a low voice.

There was a candy shop in the neighboring space. They set down the supplies on the hood of the truck. He crept forward and entered the rubble, rifle raised. She tiptoed after him, searching for an animal in the deepening gloom.

When she saw the honey badger, Helena gripped Josh's arm in warning. The animals were ferocious for their size, known to attack lions and eat cobras. This one was caught up in something, like string or rope. She inched closer to get a better look. It was a twisted piece of wire, maybe from a damaged enclosure. One end was stuck under an overturned shelf. The other was coiled around the animal's rear foot.

Honey badgers liked all kinds of sweets, so this little gal had probably wandered in here to feast. Then she'd knocked over the shelf and gotten trapped. She appeared to have chewed her foot raw in an attempt to get free. Poor thing. Helena clucked her tongue in sympathy. The cornered animal bared her teeth, revealing sharp canines.

"Do you still have those wire cutters?" she asked Josh. They'd been using them all afternoon on the fence repair.

He unclipped the tool from his belt and passed it to her. "You don't want to get a cage?"

Honey badgers stressed easily, and they were fierce. Helena didn't want to mess with her too much. "I'll just cut her free."

"She's going to take your hand off."

Helena glanced around for an appropriate treat. Chocolate was toxic to many animals, and she needed a stickier substance. She grabbed a package of salted caramel squares. The honey badger sniffed the air. Helena offered her a tiny piece, which she consumed greedily. Josh chuckled as the animal licked her chops.

Helena passed the caramels to Josh. "Give her half a square while I cut the wire. She might try to bite you, so watch out."

He agreed to the plan, crouching down in front of the badger while Helena snuck around the overturned shelf. She waited until he placed the caramel on the ground. When the badger went for the bait, Helena reached out to snip the wire.

The release tug on the animal's back foot must have hurt, because she whirled around, leaving the caramel untouched. Helena jumped back just in time. For some reason, Josh decided to intervene. He grabbed the honey badger with his bare hands.

She went nuts.

Helena saw a flash of white teeth and black fur as the animal attacked, flying around Josh's upper body like a feral tornado. He yelled and tried to shake her off. She was biting the hell out of his arms.

Helena didn't know what else to do, so she picked up the overturned shelf and heaved it at the animal-on-human melee. They both went down. The badger let out a surprised yip and scampered away, hissing. Josh watched her go from his prone position under the shelf. When the badger was out of sight, he rested his head against the floor and just lay there.

Helena stepped forward, lifting the shelves off him gently. He had badger spit, dirt and blood all over his arms. At least there were no bite wounds on his neck or face. Badgers could disfigure a person.

"She slimed me," he said, lying there with his arms outspread.

Helena smothered a laugh. Only Josh would make a *Ghostbusters* joke at a time like this. "Are you okay?"

"I think so."

Helena extended her hand to help him up. He rose to his feet with a groan. "I told you to watch out, not *dive in.*"

Before responding, he did what any man in his position would do: he cupped his fly to check his most important parts. Finding them unharmed, he moved on, wincing as he touched a spot on his side. "I thought she was going to attack you."

Helena lifted the hem of his shirt to investigate the wounds. He had minor scratches along his rib cage and several punctures on his arms. "You're all torn up," she said in a scolding tone. "You're lucky you don't need stitches. Or facial reconstruction surgery."

"I was saving you."

She lifted her gaze, startled.

"I saw her go after you, and I just...reacted."

What he was saying finally sank in. He'd put himself between her and harm's way on purpose. It was foolish, because she was the expert, not him. Laying hands on a honey badger without protective gear was insane. Greg wouldn't have approved of the sacrifice; keepers were trained to intervene safely or not at all. Josh's bravery could have gotten them both hurt. But she couldn't fault him for trying to protect her.

She also refused to examine his motives too closely. He'd acted on impulse. It wasn't evidence of strong feelings on his part.

It was natural instinct. That was all.

CHAPTER SIXTEEN

FOR THE REST of the day, they encountered nothing but obstacles.

Chloe had her first argument with Mateo after their morning rest. He didn't want to backtrack and couldn't understand why she did. They were able to communicate about some things without speaking. This wasn't one of them. She had to stop at a convenience store for a city map and show him the alternate route. Even then, it wasn't easy. She wondered if he had that stubborn-man affliction about asking for directions.

Then they were underway again, returning to the neighborhood with the huge fire. Going around it took hours. The outskirts of the Gaslight District were seedier than the center. A lot of the old buildings were in ruins. Most of the streets were blocked by rubble, rather than flames. There were abandoned cars everywhere, and stores appeared to have been looted. Chloe saw a few corpses and smelled plenty more. It was obvious that emergency services hadn't reached the epicenter. If there were other survivors, they were holed up indoors, not roaming around like vagabonds. It wasn't safe on the streets with criminals. Those who could evacuate already had. Chloe was starting to believe they'd never get out.

They finally reached El Cortez, a hotel marking the north end of the district. The historic site had fallen into disrepair before the earthquake hit. Now it was just fallen. The giant sign, which had once been visible throughout the city, had toppled hundreds of feet. It lay broken on a mountain of rubble. EL COR on one side, TEZ on the other.

After they passed that landmark, the streets began to clear. So did the smoke-clogged air. They walked through quiet neighborhoods that were free of marauders. Chloe's injured leg was screaming for relief, so she kept her fingers crossed that the final stretch would be unobstructed. Emma rode on Mateo's shoulders, clinging to him drowsily. She'd walked many blocks on her own and was in desperate need of a nap.

Chloe followed behind them, limping along. She ignored the pain and focused on taking one step at a time. Mateo suddenly lifted Emma off his shoulders, making a sound of distress. As he set Emma down, the trouble was obvious. Her pants were wet. So was his neck.

"Oh, no," Chloe said, clapping a hand over her mouth.

He didn't seem fazed by the accident. Laughing, he wiped the back of his neck with his shirt sleeve. Emma sucked on her fingers, also not concerned. Luckily, Chloe had picked up some diapers at the convenience store. She changed Emma and they kept going.

Mateo let Emma walk on her own for a while, holding her little hand. The sight made Chloe's heart twist in her chest. Emma had gripped Lyle's finger once when she was a newborn. He'd commented on her strength and smiled.

Chloe wondered if Lyle ever thought of that moment. When he woke up in the morning, before he smoked himself into a stupor, did he remember Emma fondly? Or were the memories so guilt-inducing that he pushed them aside, reaching for his drugs instead? Maybe he'd scrambled his brain to the point that he no longer had a picture of Emma in it.

Chloe needed a break, so they stopped for lunch at a health food store. There were carrot sticks, wheat bread and organic peanut butter. Mateo ate more of the salami he'd brought. Chloe gave Emma some all-natural licorice twists for being a good girl. She studied the map again, double-checking the route. It looked so much shorter on paper.

An hour later, they reached Cabrillo Bridge, and her spirits sank. The structure had collapsed across the busy freeway underneath. Dozens of cars were half-buried in the rubble. Many more were submerged. Once again, Chloe could see corpses behind the wheels of vehicles. It was horrific and disheartening.

"Crash," Emma said, pointing at the cars.

Chloe didn't bother to shield her daughter's eyes this time. They'd encountered too many bodies to ignore them all.

She wasn't sure Emma understood what they were looking at. Chloe hoped Emma wasn't traumatized, but how could she not be?

"Unco Josh," Emma said. "Gramma, Grampa."

"Grandma and Grandpa are fine," Chloe said, lifting Emma for a hug. She needed it as much as Emma did, if not more.

There were several ways to enter Balboa Park, where both the zoo and the naval hospital were located. The south route was blocked by a huge disaster. The west side was obstructed by a bridge collapse. They couldn't get through.

Mateo referred to the map. They could continue five more blocks and try to cross over into the northernmost edge of the park. Even if that route was passable, it was still about a mile to the naval hospital from there. Chloe knew her leg wouldn't make it that far. She couldn't stand the thought of another block, let alone another mile. It was getting late. As soon as the sun set, they'd be stumbling around in the dark.

"I can't go on," she said.

Mateo folded the map and put it in his pocket. They both studied their immediate surroundings, as if a magic carpet might sweep in and take them for a ride.

"*Allá,*" he said.

She followed his gaze to a place called Terrace Inn. It was a brick building that appeared to have sustained very little damage. Chloe imagined comfortable suites with cozy beds. Her knees weakened with longing. "Do you want to stop here and rest?"

"*Sí.*"

He didn't have to ask her twice. She put down Emma and they all walked across the street together. The inn's front door was locked, so they searched the side of the building and found an employee entrance. There was a service window with a cracked pane by the door. Mateo used his elbow to knock the glass aside. Then he opened the window and climbed in. A moment later, they were standing inside the lobby.

Mateo looked for room keys behind the front desk, but found only electronic cards. Leaving them there, he headed up a set of stairs to investigate. Chloe stayed behind, strolling by a café area. She discovered a path leading to an outdoor swimming pool. The surface of the water was littered with a small amount of ash and debris. All of the rooms had terraces overlooking the pool. Mateo appeared on one of the patios on the second floor.

"Swim!" Emma said to him.

He laughed and nodded his agreement. "Okay. We swim."

Chloe glanced beyond the edge of the pool, spotting a spa and gazebo on the other side. She doubted the water would be hot after two days without power, but the thought of soaking her sore muscles was so appealing that she walked toward it. The spa was protected by a thick cover. She crouched down to nudge it aside, testing the water with her fingertips.

Warm.

Not piping hot, or even bathwater-cozy, but comfortable enough to tempt her. Emma's face and hands were dirty again. Their clothes were filthy. Chloe felt like a limp rag, her hair stinking of smoke. She wanted to wash her entire body.

Mateo called down at her from the terrace. He was holding up a pair of towels. *"Quieres?"*

"Sí," she said, answering in Spanish without thinking. "Soap?"

He shook his head in confusion.

She set down Emma and rubbed her hands together. When that didn't work, she mimed washing her armpits. "Soap," she said again. "Bath."

He must have gotten the message, because he left the patio and joined them a moment later with beauty products. Shampoo, soap, towels. He uncovered the spa completely and stuck his hand in the water, his eyes sparkling.

"Swim," Emma insisted. "Me swim!"

"Sí, mamita," Mateo said, laughing again. It was the same endearment he'd used for Chloe, so it must not mean anything sexy.

Damn.

He sat down to remove his boots and socks. Chloe followed suit, wondering how she was going to bathe in front of him. He clearly wasn't suffering from shyness, because he tugged off his shirt and unbuttoned his pants, dropping them in a flash. But then, he was still wearing his soccer shorts underneath.

Instead of easing into the spa, he took a running leap toward the big pool, did a flip in midair and landed with a terrific splash. He didn't even test the water first. When he surfaced, grinning at Emma, she squealed in delight.

She was enthralled by him. Chloe knew exactly how she felt.

"Ven," he said, extending his arms to Emma.

Chloe took off Emma's shoes and checked her diaper, which was clean. Then she let Emma go toward the pool in her clothes. Both could get clean at once. She watched as Mateo grasped Emma under the arms and lowered her into the water. It must have been cold, but she didn't scream. He dipped her up and down, making her giggle.

They cruised around the pool for a couple of minutes, no more. Chloe watched them from the edge. When Emma started to shiver, he sent her back to Chloe, despite her protests. Chloe pointed Emma to the spa instead. She brought the soap and towels along. Emma got in and splashed around. Chloe longed to join her.

While she contemplated removing her jeans, Mateo pushed off the side and climbed out of the pool. She tried not to stare at his wet muscles, or notice the way his soaked white soccer shorts clung to his...thighs. She failed on both counts. What was he wearing under those shorts, a jock strap?

He grabbed a towel and looped it around his neck, asking her a question in Spanish.

She dragged her gaze up to his face, with difficulty. He gestured toward the spa, repeating himself. Was she going in?

Chloe looked down at her jeans, uncertain.

It must have dawned on him that she needed privacy. He strode over to a nearby lounge chair and stretched out on his back. Tucking his hands beneath his head, he closed his eyes. His torso was smooth and sleek, his skin bronzed. Chloe peeked at him for another few seconds, studying the dark tufts of hair under his arms.

Pulse racing, she fumbled with her zipper. Why was she checking out his armpits? He was a man. He had body hair. There was nothing noteworthy about it. Armpit hair wasn't supposed to be sexy. It was just...there.

She stood to wiggle out of her jeans, wincing at the ache in her leg. While she was struggling with the fabric, distracted by her strange fascination with Mateo, Emma slipped underwater. Chloe jumped into the spa with her pants around her ankles and grabbed Emma by the back of the shirt. Emma came up, sputtering.

"Están bien?" Mateo asked.

Chloe hugged Emma to her chest while Emma cried. "We're fine," Chloe called out, waving off his concerns. She was lucky she hadn't fallen in and broken her other leg. Emma calmed quickly and squirmed to be released.

"Be careful," Chloe said, setting her on the underwater bench. "Hold on to the side."

"I hold on," Emma promised.

Chloe sat down and finished peeling off her jeans. She decided to bathe Emma first. Singing her bathtime song, Chloe removed Emma's wet clothes and shampooed her hair. When Emma was clean, Chloe glanced toward Mateo again. He was soaking up the last rays of the setting sun, eyes closed.

It was now or never. She stripped down to her underwear and sank into the water. Her bandage was already soaked, so she submerged fully. She soaped her armpits, which weren't sexy in the least, and washed between her legs. On impulse, she whisked off her panties and gave them a scrub. She was working shampoo into her hair when Emma climbed over the edge and went streaking across the patio, giggling.

Chloe couldn't run after her—she had no panties on! "Come back here right now," she said in a stern voice, which Emma ignored.

Mateo grabbed a towel and chased after her, scooping her up easily. Then he pretended to nibble on her bare arms, monsterlike. Smiling, he carried her toward the spa. Chloe sank deeper into the water, which felt lukewarm now. Lukewarm and transparent.

His gaze moved from Chloe's sudsy hair and wet bra to the wadded-up ball of panties on the side of the spa. He didn't come closer. He just wrapped Emma up in the towel and kept her, waiting as Chloe hastily rinsed her hair.

She scrambled to put on her panties under the water, face flaming. Then she held a towel to the front of her body as she stepped out of the spa. Mateo seemed amused by her modesty. Maybe everyone in Panama was a free-spirit nudist. Tucking the terry cloth around her chest, she went to retrieve Emma.

"Thank you," Chloe said, embarrassed.

"No problem."

God, his accent. His smile. His *body*. Flustered, she glanced around for the backpack with their extra clothes. He must have left it in the room, because she didn't see it. She wondered if he wanted to go in the spa to wash up. He probably didn't care that much. The dip in the pool had looked refreshing enough, and he seemed content. So did Emma. She sucked her fingers and rested her head against his shoulder. Not reaching for Chloe.

An hour earlier, Chloe had been touched by the sight of Emma holding Mateo's hand. Now their easy bond disturbed her.

Emma had never been shy around people. She'd grown close to Josh in a short time, and she often chatted with strangers. But this situation was different. Chloe's feelings for Mateo weren't brotherly.

She hadn't dated since her breakup with Lyle, for good reason. Over the past year, she'd been focused on healing herself and taking care of Emma. She didn't know if she wanted her daughter to get attached to a strange man.

Especially a man Chloe knew nothing about. One who wasn't from here, and might not stick around.

Mateo carried Emma to the lounge chair and set her down. He said something in Spanish and pointed to the second-floor terrace. Chloe clutched the towel to her chest, shivering. As he walked away in his wet shorts, she identified his underwear as basic white briefs. Both layers were soaked to near transparency.

Goodness.

Chloe had never seen a man in tighty whiteys before. The few boys she'd been with before Lyle had worn baggy boxers. Lyle preferred skinny jeans with no underwear at all, which was pretty gross. Maybe Mateo's briefs offered more support for athletic activities. Soccer had apparently developed his butt into a work of art.

She sat down with Emma, remembering how his body had felt against hers this morning. His erection nudging her bottom. His thumb brushing her nipple.

"Milk," Emma said, patting Chloe's chest.

This request extinguished all of her sexy thoughts like a cold splash. "No milk."

"Hungwy."

"We'll have a snack as soon as we get dressed."

Mateo reappeared with the backpack and handed it to Chloe. She found the teddy bear, which Emma threw down on the ground in a fit of pique. Chloe wrestled Emma into a diaper and a clean T-shirt while Mateo stood nearby.

Emma wasn't very cooperative, and Chloe's towel slipped down to her waist. To her surprise, Mateo stepped in to take the squirming child off Chloe's hands. He picked up the teddy bear and tried to distract her.

Emma flung it into the pool. He laughed at her antics and retrieved it.

Shaking her head, Chloe donned the yoga pants and T-shirt she'd tucked away for herself. She offered him his soccer jersey. He thanked her and put it on. After she laid out their wet clothes to dry, they went inside to raid the café. There was bread with butter, canned corn and garbanzo beans. It wasn't a gourmet meal, and the kitchen smelled sour, but the chocolate chip cookies they ate for dessert were very tasty.

After dinner, Emma got cranky again, which was typical tired-toddler behavior. Chloe hobbled upstairs with her cane to put Emma to bed. The room was a double, with snowy white pillows and plump comforters. Emma crawled into the blankets with her damp teddy bear. Chloe stroked her daughter's hair until she fell asleep.

Chloe straightened to study Emma, who looked so sweet and angelic in repose. Her little mouth was pursed, curly hair in disarray. Even on bad days, Chloe's love for her daughter grew. The tantrums and trials brought them closer together. She tucked a blanket around Emma and kissed her chubby cheek. When Chloe rose, she found Mateo watching her. He'd put the first-aid supplies on the table.

She crossed her arms over her chest, anxious. Her bandage needed to be changed, but she wasn't eager for him to do it. His doctoring skills left a lot to be desired.

She lowered her yoga pants carefully and sat down in a chair by the table. He didn't insist on helping her take off the old bandage. She put it aside, noting the stained material. Her thigh was discolored with bruises, the laceration ugly. It needed more than a Band-Aid, but she'd have to make do. She smeared some antibiotic ointment on squares of gauze and secured it to her leg with heavy white tape.

When she was finished, Mateo gestured to the clock radio beside the bed. She nodded her permission. Emma was a very sound sleeper. He fidgeted with the channels at a low volume until he found a clear station. Chloe listened to the emergency information with interest. The entire city was under evacuation. Survivors had been advised to head east on foot. Recovery efforts were underway, but access to the affected areas was limited. The closest shelter was the football stadium, miles beyond Balboa Park.

Chloe's heart sank at the news. What if the naval hospital was deserted? They'd have an even longer journey tomorrow.

Mateo put away the first-aid supplies and took out the map, spreading it across the table. She pointed to the football stadium. He put his finger on the hospital first, and then moved it to the stadium. She agreed to this plan.

The radio station switched from harsh warnings to soft music, as if playing nostalgic songs might ease some of the world's suffering.

Mateo folded the map, staring at the remnants of the sunset through the open patio doors. The sky was brilliant again, a rapidly fading haze of orange fire and salmon pink. *"Regreso,"* he said, leaving the room.

He came back with a surprise: two candles, two wineglasses and a bottle. Her stomach fluttered with a mixture of delight and dismay. She was thrilled by the thoughtful gesture, disappointed she couldn't partake.

When he set the glasses and candles on the table, she shook her head. "I'm sorry. I don't drink wine."

"No?"

"No."

He muttered something under his breath, maybe a mild criticism of her failure to enjoy the finer things in life, such as red meat and fine liquor. Before she could tell him to go ahead and drink the wine, he left again, returning with Perrier.

She lifted her glass and smiled.

He poured sparkling water into both glasses. It wasn't cold, and it didn't taste that great, but she felt classy. He lit the candles and took the seat across from her. Slow, melancholy music continued to play on the radio. Songs of unrequited love, she imagined. Last night she'd joked that she'd never been on such a fancy date. This topped it. Drinking tepid Perrier by candlelight with an apocalypse view.

She should have felt letdown by the realization that this was her most romantic moment. Somehow, she didn't.

"I need a fancy dress," she said lightly.

His face brightened with an idea. Standing, he walked over to the closet and opened it, as if he'd forgotten something inside. There was a dark suit hanging on the rack, along with a garment bag. The room's inhabitants must have left the items behind. Chloe rose from the table to join him, smothering a giggle. He unzipped the garment bag. It contained a gorgeous champagne-colored gown, several sizes too large for her.

Mateo grabbed the suit and held it up to his body, wagging his brows. It wasn't his size, either, but he didn't appear to care.

"Should we try them on?" she asked, scandalized.

He didn't have to say anything, because she already knew his answer: yes.

CHAPTER SEVENTEEN

JOSH DIDN'T THINK Helena appreciated his valiant rescue.

When he saw the badger go after her, he'd reacted on instinct. His attempt to grab the animal by the scruff had backfired. Instead of thanking him for trying, she'd scolded him and treated him like he was stupid.

He *was* stupid. But that was beside the point.

Blood trickled down his left arm and dripped from his fingertips as he and Helena exited the ruins of the shop. He wiped his hand against his thigh in annoyance. The bites hurt—that little fucker had sharp teeth—and Helena's indifference added insult to injury.

"I'll drive," she said.

He fished the keys out of his pocket with a wince. The honey badger weighed about twenty pounds, tops. He felt as if he'd gone a few rounds with a grizzly. His arms were scratched raw and chewed to shreds. Now that the adrenaline had started to wear off, he was woozy. His knees wobbled as he opened the passenger door and eased into the seat. That was all he needed, to faint after being attacked by a glorified rodent.

Then he'd look weak *and* stupid.

Helena drove the short distance to the animal hospital. "I'll grab some bandages."

"Why bother? They'll just get wet when I wash up."

She ignored him and hopped out, returning a minute later with a box of first-aid supplies. He really needed a shower now. The mixture of blood, dirt and rabid-badger dander made his skin itch. But he didn't argue as she wrapped his arms in gauze. He endured the contact, hoping she wouldn't notice how shaken up he was. When she cut the strip of gauze and tied it to his wrist, he saw that her hands weren't steady, either.

Maybe not so indifferent, after all.

"I'll put on a permanent bandage later," she said.

He shrugged, as if it didn't matter. Tough guys shrugged off flesh wounds. They spat out loose teeth and dragged broken legs behind them. Hoo-yah.

Taking a deep breath, he channeled his navy training. SWCC didn't show fear or weakness. They had nerves of steel and muscles to match. Just as he was regaining his composure, an angry roar echoed through the park. The sound sent a fresh chill down his spine. No rest for the wicked.

"That's Tau," Helena said, listening.

"He sounds mad."

"It could be the cage he's upset about, but he usually doesn't roar like that unless he's protecting food."

"Do you think Zuma took the bait?"

"Maybe."

"We should check it out while there's still enough light."

She glanced at his mummy arms. "Are you sure you're up to it?"

"Of course I'm up to it," he said, feigning surprise. "What more do I have to do to prove to you that I'm a badass? I've taken nonstop abuse from wild females over the past few days. I'm still standing."

"You're sitting."

"Yeah, but I do my best work lying down."

Her lips twitched with reluctant humor. He was growing on her. He'd like to grow on her some more. "I guess we could ride the Skylift."

"*You* want to ride the Skylift?"

"It's quicker and safer, especially at dusk."

He couldn't argue that.

She drove to the loading dock, checking for Bambang before they exited the vehicle. They brought the guns, just in case. He felt bruised and bitten, but no longer in danger of keeling over. He should probably eat a snack, however. There were two broken vending machines by the entrance to the Skylift.

"You want something?" he asked her.

"Whatever you're having."

He grabbed two Snickers bars and soda. That should tide them over until dinner. Shoving the snacks in his shirt pocket, he hit the go button and helped her climb into one of the tram cars. Then he joined her, and they were off.

The aerial tram was relaxing for him. It was slow. It didn't climb to dizzying heights or sail through the air at top speeds. He popped open the soda and settled into his seat, watching Helena for signs of anxiety. Her mouth looked tense. Her dirty hands gripped the safety railing too tight. He couldn't blame her for being scared, after this morning.

He passed the soda to her. "Here. It can help with nausea."

"Caffeine?"

"Sodium bicarbonate."

She accepted the offering and took a sip. "Thanks, Dr. Josh."

Several inappropriate ideas about playing doctor sprang to mind, so he considered himself fully recovered. He unwrapped one of the candy bars and bit into it with relish. She watched him, moistening her lips.

"I brought you one," he said.

"I'll eat it after the ride."

He offered her his chocolate bar. She surprised him by leaning forward to take a bite. Of course, it looked sexual. But he also enjoyed the sharing aspect, and the fact that she felt comfortable enough to let him feed her. They finished the candy bar and the soda before they arrived at Heart of Africa.

She had a better view of the ground from her side. He didn't want to scare her by tipping the tram car, so he stayed still while she examined the area.

"The meat's gone," she said, excited. "She took it!"

He was able to get a glimpse of the area as they passed by. There was a drag mark near Tau's cage, and the bait itself was gone. Instead of celebrating, he kept his eyes peeled for Zuma. Unfortunately, he didn't catch sight of the lioness, and it was getting dark. "Will the drugs wear off by morning?"

"No. They're the long-acting kind. She'll be drowsy, if not completely out, for at least twenty-four hours."

He held up his palm, impressed by her foresight. She slapped him a high-five. This was damned good news. Tau was caged. Zuma was drugged, presumably. They'd fixed the fence and freed a badger. Wild hyenas might be terrorizing the city streets, but that was beyond their scope. For now, the zoo seemed calm.

It was the best they could hope for.

Josh was looking forward to rinsing off the blood and sweat. He could let Helena nurse his wounds. Then he'd cook her dinner. Maybe if he played his cards right, she'd reconsider hooking up with him. He'd promised not to touch her—unless she wanted him to. So the option was still on the table, as far as he was concerned.

He studied her as they rode back to the dock, contemplating what she'd said about men trying to make her feel small. He couldn't blame her for suspecting him of doing that. He'd ignored her discomfort and continued ribbing her over the years. Now that he knew about her father's death, and the kids who'd teased her for being somber, and the asshole who'd tried to put his hands on her, he regretted his actions.

The story about the old creeper at the stables infuriated him. Josh was aware that women were the victim of harassment and attacks too often. But Helena was so tough that he couldn't imagine anyone messing with her. She looked like she chewed nails for breakfast. It had never occurred to him that her size and strength might make her a *more* likely target. There were men who couldn't stand being on a level playing field with women.

Weak men, in his opinion.

Josh hadn't meant to belittle Helena with his jokes. He wasn't trying to take her down a peg. He wanted her underneath him, yeah, but not in a passive-aggressive, grudge-fuck way. His caveman instincts weren't about putting her in her place.

Were they?

He didn't think so. Some guys had pent-up anger or trust issues. Josh wasn't one of them. He loved his mother and sister. He hadn't been betrayed by any ex-girlfriends. He'd never slept around out of spite.

On the other hand, if sleeping around was so great, why had he stopped? He hadn't been waiting for Helena to drop her boyfriend. Even if his desire for her had been a factor, on a subconscious level, he had other reasons. He wasn't just bored; he'd changed. Chloe's situation with Lyle was part of it. Josh hated Lyle for hurting Chloe, and her experience had caused him to reevaluate his own actions toward women.

Josh had avoided commitment for a reason. He'd made the choice to have one-night stands and short flings; they hadn't just fallen into his lap. After fulfilling his navy service, he'd wanted to have fun and live it up. He'd relished the freedom of doing his own thing, surfing when the mood struck, chilling out when it didn't. Working hard but not breaking his back. Low stress and low stakes. No serious relationships, no dependents. No one expecting him to be a military hero.

He wasn't sure he liked what he saw when he looked at himself from this perspective. Maybe Helena was right, and he was just a goofball jackass who got lucky by making women laugh.

Well, fine. If that's what he was, he'd embrace it. He hadn't heard any complaints when she'd put her hand on his dick. Her sharp intake of breath was pure compliment. He'd enjoyed it. So why was he scowling?

As soon as they reached the loading dock, he jumped out and hit the switch. It was all clear, so they headed to the truck. She gave a concerned glance as she climbed behind the wheel. "I didn't think to bring any pain pills."

"I'm okay."

"It's no trouble to go back."

"You can dart me after the shower."

She smiled at this, no longer so guarded with her expressions. "I should give you an antibiotic injection, actually."

"Will I turn into a flying monkey?"

"Only if we do it after midnight."

He couldn't resist smiling back at her. Helena's dry, quirky sense of humor was like a cherry on top of her other good qualities. He enjoyed bantering with her almost as much as he enjoyed kissing her.

The greenhouse was on the other side of the loading dock, past the butterfly exhibit and garden trail, at the edge of the Lost Jungle. It was the area of the park where they did educational activities and hosted the bird show. There were a number of displays about recycling and alternative energy sources. The state-of-the-art greenhouse wasn't open to the public, and it wasn't just a showcase. A lot of the zoo's produce was grown right here. As an environmental science major, Josh was proud of that.

It was dark, so he brought a flashlight from the truck, along with the rifle. There was a rain cache system and a storage tank outside the greenhouse. Inside, there were drip lines hanging from the ceiling and an industrial-sized sink in the corner.

He did a quick inspection of the interior. The roof and side panels were made of polycarbonate, not glass. Although the building had sustained damage, it didn't appear unsafe. There were no doped-up wildcats or feral honey badgers lurking in the shadows.

"Okay," he said, waving her in.

Helena came inside and glanced around. She was carrying the extra clothes in a tote bag with a gorilla decal. She went to the sink and turned on the water, testing its temperature.

"Warm?" he asked.

"Lukewarm."

He'd take it.

The sink wasn't large enough to bathe in, so she grabbed an empty plastic washbasin, placing it on the floor by the sink. Then she attached a garden hose to the faucet. "There," she said, seeming pleased with her invention. "It's like a standing bath, and we can just lean over the sink to wash our hair."

Those words triggered a very explicit fantasy of her, wet and naked, bent at the waist. Water streamed down her pale back, glistening over her sleek curves.

Great. Now he was rock-hard.

"You might need help," she said.

He needed help, all right. Her helping hand, soapy and slick.

"Do you want me to hold it for you?"

"Yes." God, yes.

She gave him an expectant look, and he realized she was waiting for him to strip down. She'd offered to hold the *hose* for him. She'd wash him like a car or...an elephant. He pictured Obi's gargantuan member, rearing up and spraying wild.

"No," he said, choking out a laugh. He could manage the hose on his own. "Sorry, I meant to say no."

"No?"

"You go ahead. I'll stand outside."

She frowned as he limped toward the exit. "Are you sure?"

"I'm sure."

He left the flashlight in a flat of geraniums by the door. Then he guarded the front of the greenhouse like a sentry.

If he wanted to look, he only had to glance over his shoulder. The transparent panels wouldn't hide her body from his view.

He clenched his teeth at the sound of running water, plagued by visions of her slippery skin and sudsy breasts.

Get a grip, Josh.

He'd love to get a grip. On her hips as she rode him.

Taking a deep breath, he tried to focus on something else. He thought of elephant cocks again, but that wasn't gross enough to turn him off. Then he imagined getting attacked by a honey badger while naked.

There. That did the trick.

He stretched his neck and scanned the area. It was dangerous, being out here after dark. Visibility was limited, and they weren't far from the ruins of the reptile house. He hoped Bambang wasn't prowling around. Komodo dragons were like Godzilla, scary as shit. The bandage tugged at Josh's wrist, reminding him of his nightmare. An uneasy feeling niggled at him. He hadn't checked every nook and cranny of the greenhouse.

What had Helena said about snakes? They were attracted to heat sources.

He was about to call out a warning when she screamed like a banshee. The sound sent chills down his spine.

Abandoning his post, he rushed inside the greenhouse to help her. She had shampoo dripping into her eyes, and there was something on her shoulders that resembled a black whip. She grabbed the offending creature and flung it, still shrieking.

Josh couldn't light up the thing with his rifle and risk a ricochet on the concrete floor. He was about to stomp it to bits when he recognized the material as hosing from the rainwater collection system. It must have fallen from the damaged roof.

She wiped her eyes, shivering. "What is that?"

"Soaker hose."

"What?"

"It's a type of hose with a porous surface. Feels kind of like snakeskin. I'd have freaked, too."

She edged away from him, one hand between her legs. The other covered her left breast, leaving the right bare. She only had two hands, and he seemed to have about a dozen eyes. They were all over her.

She had a beautiful body, smooth and pale and well-proportioned, like a goddess sculpted from marble. But he'd known she had gorgeous skin and luscious curves already. What really amazed him was her level of fitness. There were sleek muscles in her stomach and arms. Not deeply carved abs or bulging biceps, but clear definition. It was sexy as hell. This was a woman who could run a marathon. A woman who did hard physical labor, and could carry her own weight on her shoulders.

He was enamored with her softer parts, too. The plumpness of her breasts, her trembling mouth. Strands of wet hair clung to her face, dripping on her shoulders and chest. She looked like a hot girl from a horror movie, naked and terrified. And he was the horny audience member, getting off on it.

Fresh arousal thrummed in his veins, making it difficult to look away. He wanted her taut belly against his, her strong legs locked around his waist. Her tight body clenching around his as she cried out in pleasure.

She retreated a few steps, still trembling. There was no invitation in her expression, just wariness and residual fear. She was shaken up, speechless. That was the only reason she hadn't protested to his rude staring.

It took a Herculean effort to avert his gaze and move to the door. "I'll stand right here while you finish."

She must have nodded her acceptance. A moment later, she turned the faucet back on. He pictured her bent over and rinsing, water dripping from her breasts. He wondered how it would feel to have her. If she'd be slick and hot, gripping him like a vise. No amount of badger-imagining could ease his hard-on. It jutted at the front of his pants, stiff and persistent. Lukewarm water wasn't going to help, either. He needed ice-cold.

When she was done, she gathered her things and reappeared at his side. She was wearing basic gray pajama bottoms and a tank top that said Life's a Zoo! across the front. He could see her nipples through it.

"Your turn," she said, taking a seat on a wooden crate by the door.

He removed the gun strap and gave her the rifle, hoping his erection wasn't too obvious. Then he approached the sink, setting aside his belt, radio and cell phone. He took his time removing his boots and stripping down to his boxers.

"I forgot to empty the basin," she said, apologetic.

He hardly minded. He'd drink her bathwater. He'd lick her clean. Instead of emptying the basin, which wasn't full, he dropped his shorts and stepped into it. He was still half-hard. She didn't peek, but he wouldn't have objected if she had.

Turnabout was fair play.

Hanging his head over the sink, he turned on the water, soaking his hair and body. It felt cool against his overheated skin, and his badger bites stung like hell. Both sensations caused his erection to wilt a little more, which was a relief. He winced in discomfort as he scrubbed his arms. Then he lathered his torso, running an absent hand over his dick and balls. He caught a hint of movement from Helena's corner. He glanced her way and realized she'd been watching him, at least for a second.

Christ. That wasn't going to help him stay soft.

He washed his hair with the same soap he'd used on his body. Then he rinsed from head to toe and called it good. Toweling off, he found the extra set of clothes she'd brought. T-shirt, giraffe boxer shorts, plain gray pajama pants. He'd forgotten about socks.

Instead of putting the stinky ones back on, he stuck his bare feet into his boots, not bothering to lace them, and collected his belongings.

He kept an eye out for predators as they headed back to the truck. She got behind the wheel and turned on the engine. "There's some instant soup in the employee lounge. We can have that instead of steaks. Less work."

"Fine."

"I'll take care of those bite wounds first."

He grunted in response, like a caveman. The only thing he cared about right now was diving between her legs. He wanted to eat *her* for dinner. Feast for hours. Maybe he could carry on an intelligent conversation when his boner-stupor wore off.

"I guess I should've thanked you earlier."

"For what?"

"Trying to protect me from the honey badger."

He shrugged, feeling surly.

"You also rushed into the greenhouse when I screamed."

"What did you think I'd do, run the other way?"

"No. I knew you wouldn't."

For some reason, her sincere gratitude irked him. Now that he had it, he didn't want it. No, scratch that—he didn't *deserve* it. "The sight of your wet, naked body was well worth the trouble."

"That's not why you did it."

"So what? I still liked it. I'm hard again, just thinking about it."

That shut her up. He didn't know why he wanted to shut her up. Maybe because he couldn't kiss her or touch her, or do anything else to her. Maybe because he was beginning to realize how much she meant to him. He'd finally found a woman who made him want to be a better man. And he couldn't have her.

CHAPTER EIGHTEEN

THE TENSION BETWEEN them was palpable.

Helena parked outside the staff building and exited the vehicle, troubled by Josh's confrontational attitude. She'd never seen him so heated. As much as she'd like to give him space to cool down, she couldn't put off treatment of his wounds. Animal bites had to be flushed to reduce the chance of infection.

She understood what was bothering him, of course. She felt the same sexual frustration, the same need to be touched. Her pulse throbbed with desire. The act of stripping bare, getting wet and soaping her body in his close proximity had felt unbearably sensual. Although the false alarm with the hose had diminished her arousal, sneaking a peek at him had brought it raging back to the forefront.

Speaking of forefronts...guh. He was gorgeous underneath his clothes. All lean muscles, strength and sinew. The total package.

Face hot, she walked through the staff area and picked up the lantern before entering the animal hospital. He followed her in silence. His eyes weren't dancing with mischief. They had a predatory glint that made her stomach flutter with awareness. It was difficult to meet his gaze, after what he'd said.

I'm hard again, just thinking about it.

She believed him. She didn't need to look down to see the evidence—desire was coming off him in waves.

I'll make it good, Helena. I'll do you right.

"Where do you want me?" he asked.

A couple of thrilling possibilities sprang to mind. Against the wall, with her legs around his waist. Or on the edge of the exam table, with him pounding into her. Better yet, they could get down on all fours and go at it, animal style. That would probably suit his mood. It would definitely suit hers. She was slick with desire, primed for action. She wanted to be well-used. Some biting and hair-pulling wouldn't be amiss.

"There," she said, pointing to a wooden stool by the table. He didn't strike her as the rough type, but maybe he was. He seemed very capable of giving a woman whatever she needed in the bedroom.

He sat down on the stool and pulled his shirt over his head. In addition to the bite wounds on his arms, he had some nasty scratches on his side.

She turned to the cabinet to collect the first-aid supplies. Saline, a syringe, towels, antibiotic ointment, bandages. She also found some mild pain relievers. They wouldn't kick in for a while, but she gave him two, with a bottle of water.

"I have to flush the wounds," she said.

"Go ahead."

Clearing her throat, she filled a syringe with saline and twisted off the capped needle. Then she grabbed a towel to absorb the extra fluid. "This is going to hurt."

"Good."

She couldn't interpret the flip answer, but she assumed he was just being stoic. Holding the towel underneath a nasty bite on his left biceps, she placed the syringe tip at the puncture site and pressed the plunger, irrigating the wound with saline. His hissed intake of breath and bunched shoulder muscles didn't denote pleasure. Which was probably for the best. Maybe the discomfort would take his mind off sex.

He had four or five bites on this arm, and multiple punctures that needed to be flushed until the fluid ran clear. They'd be here a while.

"Tell me about your sister," she said, hitting the wound again.

His reaction was less pronounced this time. He'd steeled himself against the pain. "What about her?"

"Is she older or younger?"

"She's twenty-three."

Helena had to remind herself that he was twenty-nine. "When did she move in with you?"

"About a year ago."

"How did that come about?"

"She wanted a fresh start. She was getting over a bad relationship. Her boyfriend was—" he sucked in another breath as she continued the treatment "—an asshole. And a drug addict. He stole her money."

"Did she do drugs, too?"

"I don't know."

"Why not?"

"I never asked her."

"You weren't concerned?"

"I was more concerned about her mental health. She took a bunch of my mom's sleeping pills once, when Emma was a newborn."

Helena stopped flushing. "Did she have postpartum depression?"

"I guess so. She was on medication for a few months. Then she got better, and she asked if she could stay with me while she finished college. My mom was getting on her nerves, trying to do everything for her."

"Did she need help?"

"Only at first. Then she needed space, and a change of scenery."

"How's it working out?"

"Good. I mean, it was. Until now."

She switched to his other side, her chest tightening in sympathy. He was worried for his sister and niece, plagued by second thoughts. "You're protective of her."

"Someone has to be."

"I always wanted a sister," she said. "Or a brother. I didn't care which one."

He didn't say anything, but his eyes met hers in silent understanding. He seemed to see through her, into that empty place she kept guarded so well. She turned to refill the syringe and get a fresh towel. When she placed it under his forearm, she noticed his gaze shifting to her breasts. The thin tank top did little to cover her. Feeling exposed in more ways than one, she irrigated the last bite in a clumsy rush.

He winced in discomfort, his attention returning to her face.

"Sorry," she said, her lips twitching.

"You did that on purpose."

"Did what?"

"You're enjoying this."

"I am not," she said, setting the syringe aside. Maybe she'd been punishing him a little, but she wasn't a sadist.

He gave her perky nipples a pointed stare, as if they were proof of his claim. Although she couldn't deny her arousal, it had nothing to do with hurting him. She'd been turned on before they started. He was shirtless and sexy, which didn't help. His raw masculinity appealed to her. So did his beautiful torso, etched from hours of surfing and swimming, paddling through the waves. He had well-developed biceps, broad shoulders, a taut abdomen. He looked strong enough to haul her over his shoulder and carry her away.

She flashed back to the glimpse she'd gotten of his lower body. The side view had been excellent. His penis had been thick and not quite soft, full of possibility. She'd imagined taking him into her mouth like that.

Flustered, she tore open a Betadine packet and swiped the scratches on his side. His stomach muscles were clenched, his jaw tight. There was a dark strip of hair leading down into his waistband. The flannel pants he was wearing couldn't hide his swelling erection.

If anyone was getting off on this, it was him.

She moved around to examine his back, clearing her throat. He had a few more scratches there. She found herself lingering over them, wanting to press a kiss between his shoulder blades. Resisting the urge, she applied antibiotic ointment to his wounds and covered the worst of the bites with adhesive bandages.

When she was finished, she crossed her arms over her chest. Her nipples hadn't softened. Neither had his cock.

"Why don't you let me give you what you want?" he asked in a low voice.

She pulled her gaze away from his erection, resentful. He was so annoying, with his hard body and direct sexual offers.

"How long has it been, six months?"

"I have a vibrator," she said. "Bigger than you."

He arched a brow at this claim. "Does it hold you all night?"

"I don't like to be held."

A hint of emotion flitted across his features. When she recognized it as pity, she turned to the cabinet in dismay. Pressure built behind her eyes. She placed the first-aid supplies on the shelf with shaking hands.

"He's not coming back, is he?"

She took a deep breath, realizing what she had to do. Telling Josh about her relationship struggles with Mitch would be difficult, but she was desperate. Now that her guard was down, she needed a new barrier between them.

"I don't know why you're staying true to him," Josh said. "He left you."

"He didn't have a choice," she said, facing him.

"Why not?"

"He was unemployed for almost a year. After six months, his savings ran out, and I was paying most of the bills. I didn't mind, but he was miserable. He said he didn't feel like a man anymore. He became more and more withdrawn. I was tired of him shutting me out. If he hadn't taken the job, we wouldn't be together."

"You're not together," Josh said. "You just haven't accepted it yet."

"What if he was deployed?"

"He's not deployed, Helena. Don't ever make that comparison."

She threw her hands in the air. "I just meant that there was no easy solution! I couldn't go with him, and he couldn't stay."

Josh was quiet for a moment, mulling it over. "Are you hanging on because you love him, or because you can't let go?"

She couldn't answer that. She didn't know.

"Don't you want more out of life? Companionship, at the very least. Or a family?"

Damn him. She glanced away, hating him for hitting the nail on the head. This conversation wasn't going the way she'd expected, but she'd already committed. Giving up wasn't in her repertoire. She had to just dig in.

"You do," he said in awe. "You want a family."

"Is that so hard to believe?"

"No."

"Don't lie."

"I thought the elephants were your family."

She didn't correct him this time. Whether she treated the animals like family was beside the point. She'd been at the park since college graduation. She was dedicated to this herd, and she loved her work. Leaving after ten years would be incredibly difficult. The Denver Zoo didn't have a pachyderm program, so her expertise would be wasted there. Assuming they were willing to hire her, she'd have to start over in another department.

Two years ago, when their relationship had been solid, she might have considered it. Then everything fell apart.

"Before Mitch got laid off, I was working around the clock," she said, dragging a hand through her hair. "Shani was about to give birth, and it's a difficult process. Some nights, I slept on a cot in the elephant barn. Then Mbali was born, and I worried about her. Newborn calves are very susceptible to illness."

He waited, listening.

"I had a few dizzy spells and I was extremely tired. Mitch joked that I was pregnant."

"Were you?"

She shook her head. "I took one of those at-home pregnancy tests. When it came out negative, he was so relieved. That's when I realized...I wasn't."

"Did you tell him that?"

"No. It was clear that he wasn't going to change his mind about kids, even though I had. A few weeks later, he lost his job."

"This is all the more reason to end it, Helena."

She swallowed hard, uncertain. "I need to talk to him in person and see how I feel. After six years, I owe him that much."

Josh absorbed this information without reacting, but his body language suggested that he accepted her words. He seemed calmer now, less volatile. No longer ready to pounce on her. "When are you going to talk to him?"

The prospect made her nauseous. "Soon."

"And then you'll go out with me?"

"Let's not get ahead of ourselves."

"What would he say if you told him about us?"

"He'd want to kill you," she said bluntly.

He nodded and rose from the chair, putting his shirt back on. He was so confident that he assumed this would all work out in his favor. She'd break up with Mitch and fall at Josh's feet. They'd have lots of sweaty, enthusiastic sex.

Until he got bored and moved on.

She didn't press her luck by admitting that she'd never date him, even if Mitch wasn't in the picture. Josh was everything Mitch wasn't. Young, hungry, careless, fun. His touch felt like an antidote for the problems in her relationship.

But it came with a killer hangover, and she was already beginning to suffer from the effects.

She couldn't explain all of her issues with Mitch to Josh. Their sex life was none of his business, and it wasn't fair to throw Mitch under the bus. Mitch had been a caring, generous partner. They were a good match on a physical level. But they'd hit a snag after her pregnancy scare, and another after he lost his job. His libido had flagged, along with his confidence. He'd stopped initiating contact, and she hadn't wanted to take the lead every time. They'd gone weeks, then months, without intimacy.

The offer in Denver had revitalized him. He'd made love to her for hours before he left, as if he was afraid he'd never see her again. Although she'd appreciated his attempt to keep their romance alive, it had felt more like a goodbye than a fresh start.

And—this was the kicker—she'd been happier without him. She'd relished the freedom of their empty apartment. She'd spent the following weekend with her vibrator. It had been sadly neglected during Mitch's unemployment. He'd been home every day, and she hadn't wanted to pleasure herself while he was moping on the couch. As terrible as it sounded, she'd preferred the device to him.

She'd talked to Gwen about her troubles with Mitch, expressing doubts about their long-distance relationship.

"You need to be single for a while," Gwen had said. "Go out and have fun."

Although Gwen had meant well, Helena had disregarded this advice. Gwen was a social butterfly. Helena wasn't. She had no interest in playing the field or being single again. What she really longed for was comfort and stability.

After Mitch had been gone a few months, she'd started to miss him. Maybe not him, specifically, but someone. A man in her bed, sharing her space. Shaving in front of the mirror, sitting next to her in the evenings.

Josh had been right about her vibrator. It wasn't enough. She wanted more. A sex toy couldn't give her companionship, and Mitch wouldn't give her a family. If Josh thought he could fill in those gaps, he was kidding himself. Since when had he held a woman all night? Probably never. He wasn't the steady-guy type. He didn't have a serious bone in his body. It was sweet that he loved his sister and niece, but that didn't mean he was ready to settle down. Some men were too wild to tame. Her father, for example.

The thought trigged a stab of panic in the pit of her stomach. It felt like a plane buzzing through her chest, spiraling out of control.

"Are you hungry?" Josh asked, studying her face.

She let out a slow breath and nodded.

"Let's find that soup you were talking about. When this is over, I'll buy you the best steak in town."

That sounded great. Too bad she'd never take him up on the offer.

They went back to the staff area to heat up the soup in the microwave. She used the restroom and grabbed a sweatshirt from her locker.

Josh charged his phone and turned on the radio while they ate. There was some new information about freeway closures and evacuation routes. Basically, every major road in the downtown area was impassable to vehicles.

Her appetite was off for several reasons. She was overwhelmed and on edge. Her favorite stress reliever was out of the question. She hadn't slept well the night before, and she felt too jittery to rest tonight. A thousand concerns vied for her attention. They'd seen a few planes and helicopters today, but she had no idea if any of the pilots had noticed their SOS signal. The radios were silent and the cell phones showed no activity.

"Do you want the rest of your soup?" he asked.

"Go for it."

He picked up the cup and forked out noodles. She hoped they'd get some assistance tomorrow. The zoo animals had never gone without food or fresh water. Even though they were capable of surviving without both for extended periods, they weren't used to it. Many had been born in captivity. Their needs had always been catered to by humans.

The honey badger was a case in point. She'd gone searching for food. Other animals in damaged enclosures would do the same.

"Stop," Josh said, tossing the empty soup cups in the trash.

"Stop what?"

"Worrying so much. You don't have to carry the world on your shoulders."

"I'm responsible for the entire park right now."

"We are," he corrected. "You and me."

"You're not a wildlife expert," she said. "You can't fully appreciate the extent of the problems."

"It's not healthy to stress out over things you can't control."

"Oh, okay. I'll just rewire my brain then."

He smiled at her sarcasm. "You could try to focus on what we accomplished today. We got a lot done."

She sighed, raking a hand through her hair.

"You cured your fear of heights with that awesome stunt on the tram."

"I thought you cured me with your magic ear."

"I helped."

She wasn't cured, and he knew it. But she'd taken a step in that direction. Talking about her father hadn't killed her. Neither had riding on the tram. Both seemed like small potatoes compared to the other dangers she'd faced.

"I also tackled a wild badger for you and saved you from a dangling hose," he said, thumping a fist against his chest. *"Semper fortis."*

"What does that mean?"

"Always courageous."

She laughed, reassessing his performance today. All joking aside, he'd been indispensable. He'd darted Tau from the tram, and that wasn't an easy shot. He'd assisted her with moving the lion into a cage and dragging Greg's body to shelter. She couldn't have completed those tasks on her own, or even started the fence repair. Josh wasn't just a strong back, either. He had a strong mind.

"We make a great team," he said, reaching under the table for a whiskey bottle in a black-and-gold box. "Let's drink."

"Where did that come from?"

"The director's liquor cabinet," he said. "This is good shit."

"Is it?"

"It should be. He's filthy rich."

She rarely drank wine or beer, let alone hard alcohol. Never *pilfered* hard alcohol, straight from the bottle. But she was tempted. It had been a long day. She'd survived a number of horrors, including a Komodo dragon and a runaway tram. She'd dragged her boss's body into a shed. Helped Josh build a fence. Been attacked by a rubber hose. Treated Josh's wounds and smothered her desires.

She'd never needed a drink more.

He tilted the bottle invitingly. "Come on, Hellie. Take a walk on the wild side."

CHAPTER NINETEEN

CHLOE DUCKED INTO the bathroom with the oversized dress.

Mateo had put a candle on the sink to illuminate the space. She studied her bright eyes and flushed cheeks in the mirror.

What was she doing?

She was making herself available, that's what she was doing. She was painting a fuck-me sign on her forehead. He'd be a fool not to assume she'd welcome his advances. And she would, if her daughter wasn't in the room. Then again, Emma slept like a rock. She probably wouldn't wake up until morning. They had plenty of time.

Should she...? Would he expect her to...?

No, she decided. He didn't expect anything. He was just finding a way to have fun in a terrible situation. Trying on strangers' clothes was the same to him as doing a flip into the pool. It wasn't a date, or an invitation for sex.

It felt like a date, though. He'd brought wineglasses and candles.

She scolded herself for being ridiculous and hooked the dress on the back of the door. Removing her T-shirt and yoga pants, she put on the dress. It was gorgeously made, if voluminous, with a long skirt and delicate cap sleeves.

She wished she had the body to fill it out. The cups of the bodice sagged against her thin chest like two empty bags. She looked like a little girl who'd been playing in her mother's closet.

There was a makeup case on the counter. She found toothpaste, which she used, and a hint of lip gloss. Then she smudged on some charcoal eye shadow and surveyed the results, ruffling her short hair. Not bad.

Butterflies in her stomach, she went out to greet him. He was standing in front of the full-length mirror on the opposite wall, wearing a white button-down shirt and baggy pants that were several sizes too large. Without the belt, his pants would have fallen down. There was a black silk tie hanging around his neck.

He turned to check her out, his eyes appreciative. When he saw the ill-fitting bodice of her dress, he laughed.

She flushed, feeling self-conscious.

"Que bonita eres," he said, his gaze on her face. Clearing his throat, he donned the suit jacket and spread his arms. *"Y yo, cómo te paresco?"*

She guessed that he was asking her how he looked. The clothes fit him about as well as the dress fit her, but she couldn't fault his form. His dark coloring made a striking contrast to the snowy white shirt. She also liked the juxtaposition of his formal attire and Mohawk hairstyle. "Very handsome," she said.

After a moment of wrestling with the tie, he tossed it aside. Chloe picked it up, struck by inspiration. She secured it around her chest and formed a bow. Then she scooted the bow around to the back and adjusted the bodice, tucking in the extra material. The result left a lot of skin showing, including the lacy edge of her bra.

"Mejor," he said, nodding.

He needed help with his outfit, too. She divested him of his jacket. Then she rolled up the loose sleeves of his shirt, exposing his forearms. Much better.

They stood side by side in front of the mirror. Her hemline was too short and his pants were too long. But they were kind of cute together. She was pale champagne next to his stark black and white. Barefoot, he topped her by about two inches.

"Mira estos guapos," he said, putting his arm around her.

Although she had no idea what that meant, his pleasure was so infectious she laughed, sharing it with him. When she moved her gaze from their reflection to his face, he turned his head toward her. Their mouths were inches apart. Her heart pounded with anticipation. She could kiss him again. Slower this time, with more feeling.

She froze, struck by uncertainty. This morning, she'd acted on impulse to put him at ease. He'd had his hand in her bra and his erection against her bottom. He'd initiated contact, albeit unwittingly. They'd both been half-asleep.

Now they were wide awake, with a bed nearby. Kissing him might send the wrong message.

Emma made a babbling sound in her sleep, shattering the spell. Mateo dropped his hand from her lower back. Chloe crossed the room to check on Emma. She was fine, if a bit warm. The curls at her hairline were damp. After touching Emma's forehead, which was cool, Chloe removed the thicker blanket and tucked the sheet around her.

Mateo watched from a distance, his hands in his pockets. She went back to the table and sat down, resting her foot on the nightstand. It felt good to elevate her injured leg. "Sit down," she murmured, gesturing to the chair opposite her.

He sat, sipping lukewarm Perrier. They listened to more music. Tragic, romantic songs of star-crossed lovers.

"Tell me about your brother," she said. "If you don't mind."

He shrugged.

"When did he die?"

There was a notepad and a pen on the nightstand. He wrote *18* on it.

"He was eighteen?"

"Yes."

"What happened to him?"

His pen hovered above the paper. The question was too complicated.

"Car accident? Illness?"

Instead of answering, he set down the pen and reached for her hand. Grasping her wrist, he turned it over and pointed at her faint scars. She pulled her hand back, feeling the blood drain from her face.

"Suicide?" she whispered.

"Sí."

She didn't know what to say. He must hate her. His own brother—his *twin* brother—had committed suicide. She'd sort of attempted the same, and lived. She was sitting here instead of his twin. What strange twist of fate had swept Mateo toward her, of all people? She was ashamed and humbled in his presence.

"Why?" she asked. "Why did he do it?"

He brought his fingertips to the center of his chest and then spread them out, like an explosion.

"Broken heart?"

After a short pause, he touched his temple, as well.

Broken head. Mental illness.

Her eyes filled with tears. "I'm so sorry."

"Ay, mamita," he said, pressing his fingertips to his eyelids. *"No me hagas llorar."*

"You must think I'm terrible."

He frowned and lowered his hand. "No. *Nunca.*"

She tried not to cry, but it was too much. He'd done everything in his power to help her and Emma. Chloe owed him their lives. Tears spilled down her cheeks and splashed on the surface of the table. He handed her a tissue.

"Thank you."

He didn't give his usual response. His gaze moved to the dark cityscape, which glowed orange in several places, like hot embers. Chloe looked with him, her chest aching. It was as if they were watching the world die.

A song came on the radio that he seemed to recognize. Another ballad, beautifully sad. He glanced at the face of the alarm clock, which blinked 12:00. They hadn't set the time, having only a vague idea of what it was. After a moment of contemplation, he rose to his feet and held out his hand to her, palm up. *"Bailamos?"*

She inferred by his body language that he was asking her to dance. He said something else, gesturing to her injured leg. It was a great excuse for her to decline, but she didn't want to. She hadn't slow-danced with a man...ever. Pulse racing, she eased her foot off the chair, grasped his strong hand and stood.

It was awkward, at first. He held her waist with a light touch, keeping distance between them like a boy in junior high school. She stiffly rested her hands on his shoulders. They shuffled back and forth on the carpet without rhythm. When she stepped on his foot, it was warm and alive, jarring her senses. He smiled at her blunder, which broke the tension. She settled into the music and the sway of his body.

The song changed but they stayed together. Twining her arms around his neck eased some of the pressure on her sore leg. At least, that was her initial justification. Then it just felt too good to stop.

She was aware of the low neckline of her dress, and how her raised arms lifted her breasts higher. The slippery satin draped over the legs of his suit pants. Her belly rubbed against his in a delicious slide. His hands felt hot at her waist, searing through the fabric.

She lost track of how many songs they danced to. They melded together, clinging to each other for comfort and support. Everything else drifted away. The devastation outside. Her sleeping child on the bed. The barriers between them.

Dancing so close had a predictable physical effect: they both got aroused. Her breasts plumped against the constrictive tie, her nipples tingling. The flesh between her legs felt swollen and sensitive. His erection was unmistakable. He could pretend he didn't notice her reaction. She couldn't do the same.

He stopped dancing, his fingers flexing at her hips. He wanted to let his hands roam all over her body. She saw it in his eyes. But what he said was something polite and quiet, like "maybe we shouldn't...."

She placed her fingertips on his jaw, feeling the slight scrape of stubble there. Then she kissed his tense mouth in demurral. Yes, they should.

He didn't have to be talked in to it. Thank God. He kissed her back with only the slightest hesitation, as if he couldn't quite believe what was happening. She squirmed against him, lips parted in invitation. He slanted his mouth over hers and plunged his tongue inside. Stroking her, tasting her, filling her sweetly.

She curled her tongue around his, trembling with excitement. He smelled faintly of smoke and chlorine, which was a strange aphrodisiac. It drove her crazy, nevertheless. She moaned into his mouth, wanting to lick his hot skin.

His hands shifted to her bottom, cupping her through the silky fabric. He groaned, lifting her against his erection and letting her slide down. That was incredibly good. She gripped his neck and held on as he repeated the action. After three times, it was too much to bear. He turned her toward the bed, but he didn't push her down. He broke the kiss, panting.

Asking.

She felt the edge of the mattress at the backs of her knees. His heart pounded against her chest and his erection throbbed against her lower abdomen. She didn't want to let go of his neck, so she tugged him forward. He reclaimed her mouth as they fell across the bed together. The bounce reverberated through her injured thigh, but the discomfort was fleeting. He kissed it away, squeezing her satin-covered hip.

They kissed for as long as they danced, or longer. He didn't press for more. In fact, he stretched out on his back and brought her on top of him. This action took the weight off her leg and let her set the pace. Her dress inched up her thighs. His hands followed, exploring her bottom through the fabric of her panties. She was frustrated by the layers of clothing. She wanted nothing between them.

His fingertips slid under her panties. The feel of his hand on her bare skin was electric. Escalating. He paused, as if gauging her response. She made it easy for him to interpret. Kissing him harder, she fumbled to release the buttons on his shirt. Posh as he looked, she was ready to rip the garment off of him.

He chuckled at her eagerness. Removing his hand from her panties, he helped her with the buttons. When she pushed it off his arms and splayed her hands over his chest, he drew in a sharp breath. She grasped his shoulders and lay back against the pillows, urging him to get on top of her. He made a growling sound, deep in his throat, and covered her mouth with his. She parted her lips and spread her thighs for him.

This position was a game-changer. The time for languid kissing had passed. He buried his tongue in her mouth and thrust against her. His erection nudged her swollen sex, sending sparks of pleasure through her body. She moaned and wrapped her legs around his waist, gripping his shoulders, begging for more. His hand traveled up her thigh, perhaps to divulge her of her panties. Instead, he encountered her bandage. And hesitated.

He lifted his head to study her. His lips were wet from her mouth, his eyes black. She glanced at Emma, who was still sleeping. Then she returned her attention to Mateo. He was staring at the bodice of her dress, which had slipped down. She fumbled with the tie and tugged the dress over her head.

He groaned at the sight of her in nothing but a bra and panties. The lace cups of her bra didn't cover much, but she didn't have much to cover. Their mouths met again, hot and eager. He shifted to his side and put his hands all over her, palming her hip and her breast. His thumb brushed her nipple. She shuddered with arousal.

He kissed her neck, pushing the bra strap off her shoulder. When she didn't protest, he tugged the fabric down completely, baring her breasts. He didn't appear disappointed by her size. He moistened his lips in anticipation, as if her nipples were some rare exotic fruit. She tensed as he put his mouth on her, sucking gently.

It felt odd. Especially the suction. She worried that her milk might let down. Which was ridiculous, as she hadn't breast-fed for months.

"No," she said, uncomfortable. "Don't."

He stopped at once, stricken.

She didn't know how to explain. In her experience, men had fragile egos about sex. Constant erections and fragile egos. Maybe that combination balanced out with age. Lyle had gotten defensive over the gentlest of corrections. Once he'd told her to shut up until he was finished, as if she was interfering with the porno playing in his mind. She'd felt more like a masturbatory aid than a partner.

Mateo was clearly right here with her, not imagining someone else. But when he grabbed her discarded dress and gave it to her, she realized he'd misinterpreted her wishes. He thought she was calling a halt.

She tossed the dress aside, hoping she hadn't blown it. "I just meant…no mouth. Here." She touched her nipples. "It feels like…" She glanced at Emma.

Understanding dawned. "No mouth."

"Hands are okay." She lifted his to her breast. "See?"

"*Sí.*"

"Mouth here," he said, brushing his lips over hers.

She melted against him. "Yes."

Oh, yes.

They resumed kissing and touching, learning each other. She found that he had boundaries, too. He didn't let her hands slip below his waist, and he kept his pants on. He seemed to want to focus on her pleasure.

No one had ever done that for her.

They didn't have any condoms, so intercourse was out. She suspected that he was worried about her injured leg, because he was careful not to jostle her. His touch danced across her skin like magic. His mouth was bold and delicious. She clung to him, panting and aching and wanting more.

It had been almost three years since she'd had sex. She hadn't been comfortable with her body during the second half of her pregnancy, and neither had Lyle. Their encounters hadn't been very satisfying before, either. The only way she'd reached climax with him was by her own hand. Did that count?

Mateo murmured something to her and tugged at the waistband of her panties. She assisted him by taking them off. He slid one fingertip inside her, testing her heat. She gasped and spread her thighs wider.

Please.

He gave her what she wanted, at his own pace. His fingers caressed and penetrated, taking her to the brink. She trembled with anticipation as he circled her clitoris in slow motions. She gripped his wrist, almost there. As if sensing her capitulation, he covered her mouth with his. She came with a muffled cry, her eyes squeezed shut and her stomach quivering. Although she didn't see stars, it was a near thing.

Wow.

When she opened her eyes, Mateo was watching her with a satisfied smile.

"You enjoyed that, didn't you?" she said.

"Claro."

She had her legs akimbo and her bra tangled around her waist, like a shameless hussy. It felt pretty great.

"Otra vez?" he offered.

She giggled, knowing what that meant. After checking on Emma, she reached for his belt. "What about you?"

He didn't stop her, but he seemed conflicted.

"Just my hand," she whispered.

Easily convinced, he helped her with the fly of his pants. She decided that basic briefs were sexy. Especially when he was in them. He lowered the waistband for her.

She curled her fingers around his shaft, thrilled. It had been a long time since she'd fondled a penis. He was bigger than Lyle, and he felt different in her hand. His erection didn't slide through her closed fist the same way.

Mateo covered her hand with his, demonstrating what he liked. She made a firmer grip. He worked her fist up and down.

Oooh.

He was hard and smooth and hot. Stroking him was easier than stroking Lyle, for whatever reason. She pumped faster, enjoying it. His eyes moved from her hand to her breasts, which jiggled as she pleasured him. That was hot, too. She liked watching him watch her. He seemed captivated by what she was doing. Mesmerized. She had this strong man in the palm of her hand, literally. Sweat broke out on his forehead and a crease formed between his brows. His abdomen clenched.

He grabbed her discarded panties and spilled into them with a strangled groan. She kept her grip on his pulsing flesh. He didn't soften much.

When it was over, he tossed her panties aside and collapsed against the pillows, his fly still open. She snuggled up next to him. After a short rest, he went to the bathroom. Then he brought her the yoga pants and T-shirt, along with a bottle of water. He was very considerate, even after he came. She donned the clothes and sipped the water, smiling. He blew out the candles and joined her in bed, kissing her temple.

She drifted off in his arms a few moments later, warm and content.

CHAPTER TWENTY

HELENA WATCHED JOSH tear off the label and unscrew the cap.

He took a measured sip, grimacing as he swallowed. Although he didn't cough or sputter, his reaction wasn't that of an accomplished drinker. Maybe he wasn't used to straight alcohol without ice or soda.

"Too strong?" she asked.

"It'll put hair on your chest," he rasped, passing her the bottle.

"Just what I need." She studied the liquid inside the rim, wrinkling her nose when the fumes assailed her nostrils.

"What are you doing, smelling it?"

"Is that not recommended?"

He shrugged.

She tipped the bottle to her mouth, holding her elbow high and craning her neck forward. The whiskey tasted awful and burned her throat. She choked it down with a shudder and wiped her lips with the sleeve of her jacket.

He laughed, taking the bottle back. "You drink like a girl."

"I am a girl."

"I know," he said, smiling to himself.

She didn't think he meant to be flirtatious. It just came naturally to him. She wasn't offended by his enjoyment of her "girlish" inexperience, or by his veiled reference to seeing her naked. His attention warmed her as much as the shot of whiskey. She liked his cocky sense of humor, his charming smile, the uneven stubble on his jaw. His honey-brown eyes. She studied the bandages on his arms, hoping the pain relievers had kicked in.

"I forgot the antibiotic injection," she said, straightening.

He screwed the cap back on the bottle. "Fuck it."

"No, you'll get an infection."

"Where does it go?"

"Exactly where you think."

Swearing under his breath, he stood with her. She grabbed the lantern before they returned to the treatment area, aka "torture chamber," where she found a new syringe and a vial of amoxicillin. "How much do you weigh?"

"One-eighty."

More than she'd figured. After drawing up the proper amount, she turned to him. "Lower your pants a little."

He didn't protest or make any sexual innuendoes. Sighing, he tugged down the waistband of his pants and boxer shorts, revealing most of his right buttock. He had a tan line across his lower back. Below, he was pale and firm.

His muscle twitched as she stuck him, clenching the same way it would when he thrust inside a woman. The sight was enough to induce hot flashes. She removed the needle and pressed a cotton ball against the spot. "Hold this here for a minute."

His fingertips replaced hers. "Was it good for you?"

She put the needle in the sharps container. "It wasn't bad."

"I can't say I enjoyed it."

"You tensed up, so that didn't help."

"Rookie mistake."

She crossed her arms over her chest, smiling.

After he pulled his pants back up and tucked the cotton ball into his pocket, they returned to the staff lounge. She took a seat next to him, contemplating the whiskey bottle. Having another round wasn't a good idea. He was hard enough to resist while they were sober. She couldn't afford to get tipsy, and they had a lot to do tomorrow. On the other hand, if she drank to excess, her worries would fade and he'd leave her alone.

She shook her head in disgust at this train of thought. Was she really so afraid of losing control—and making the wrong choice— that she'd choose oblivion instead? What a stupid plan. She might miscalculate the number of drinks, change her mind and jump on him. She might do that anyway.

After months without sex, and a long stretch of feeling unwanted, she was vulnerable. Josh's desire for her was a powerful aphrodisiac.

He unscrewed the cap and helped himself, not conflicted in the least. When he offered her the bottle again, she declined. This didn't faze him, either. He set the whiskey aside, amiable. He wasn't trying to ply her with liquor. There was a clear difference between his knee-jerk flirting and his blatant sexual advances. She hadn't considered it before, but now that she'd seen him in action, she understood. He didn't mean anything by the former, and the latter was impossible to misinterpret.

In her experience, people got easier to read as she became more comfortable with them. Josh was no exception. She doubted he'd curb all of his suggestive comments, but she trusted him to keep his hands to himself. He'd accepted her reasons for saying no, if only because he thought he'd have her later.

She didn't tell him that they'd never be together. He wasn't appropriate for a one-night stand or a long-term relationship. It was better that they remain coworkers. She could even consider him a friend.

"Why elephants?" he asked.

"What do you mean?"

"Did you want to run away to the circus as a kid?"

"Oh. No, not at all. I did see my first elephant at a circus, and he was in musth. You know what that is?"

"In heat?"

"It's similar to estrus in females. A hormonal surge. Male elephants have glands near their eyes that weep during musth, so I thought he was crying. He looked sad, and the ringleader hit him with a bull-hook. I was horrified. My dad spent the rest of the evening trying to win me a stuffed animal."

"Did he?"

"I can't remember," she said. "I know he bought me a candy apple, and I refused to ride on the Ferris wheel."

"He sounds like a fun dad."

She glanced away, uncomfortable with the subject. "I didn't plan on working with elephants. I wanted to be an equine vet, but then I got interested in exotic animals. Zookeeping suited me better."

"Why?"

"Well, look at the staff. We're all a bunch of misfits."

He couldn't argue that. After a pause, he picked up his cell phone and scrolled through some photos. Helena leaned closer and looked with him. There was a recent picture of his niece at the zoo. She was wearing a polka-dot sun hat, pointing at a giraffe.

"I got mad at her the night before the earthquake," he said, staring at the photo. "She'd climbed on my desk while Chloe was busy and found one of my comics. There were torn pages scattered all over the floor. I yelled at Emma, and she started crying. Chloe called me an asshole, and I slammed the door."

Her heart ached for him. "You're not an asshole."

"I do a pretty good impression of one."

She wanted to put her arm around him and rest her head on his shoulder. They'd formed a bond over the past few days, which was unusual for her. The natural reserve that protected her from getting hurt by people also prevented her from connecting with them.

Instead of reaching out to him, she picked up the whiskey bottle and unscrewed the cap. To hell with it. She took a sip and passed it on, coughing. He accepted the liquid comfort and tossed back a swig. They shared another round, drowning their sorrows. It went down a lot smoother on the third try than the first two.

"I still don't think they're gone," he said, recapping the bottle. "I have a gut feeling. Maybe it's stupid to believe in that, but I do."

"It's not stupid," she said.

"When your dad died, did you feel something?"

As she considered that question, she was struck by an epiphany: her father's death had left the empty place inside her. Mitch's abandonment had made the hole bigger. She couldn't believe she'd never thought of it that way before. But then, it was hard to examine the root of an unacknowledged problem.

"I didn't have a premonition or anything," she said, replaying that awful morning in her mind. "Two men came to the door to break the news to my mom. Her face went white, and she sat down. When she told me what happened, I didn't cry at first. But I felt the pain in my chest and I knew it was true."

Her story seemed to resonate with him. He hadn't wavered in his belief that his sister and niece were alive. Although Helena didn't trust her own gut feelings, she admired his faith in his. It wasn't healthy to worry about things you couldn't control, like he'd said earlier, and anticipating the worst was a miserable exercise.

He put down his cell phone and they sat side by side, listening to the radio. Although they'd had a hard day, she wasn't ready to end it. Sitting with him made her feel better. She was grateful for his company.

"What kinds of comics do you read?" she asked.

His brows rose at the question. "The superhero kind."

"Superman?"

"Wonder Woman is my favorite."

"Really?"

"Sure."

"Why do you like her?"

"She's hot, and kicks ass."

She smiled at his description. "I didn't know jocks read comic books."

"I'm secretly a geek."

"Since when?"

"High school."

"You weren't the star quarterback, dating the top cheerleader?"

"I went on a lot of fantasy dates with Wonder Woman. That's about it."

"No real girls?"

"Not until the end of my senior year."

"That's why you're funny," she said. If he'd been popular and dreamy as a teenager, he might not have developed the same personality.

He shrugged.

"What happened on these fantasy dates?"

"You don't want to know."

"Is it dirty?" she asked, intrigued.

His gaze dropped to her mouth and lingered there. "I'll tell you, but you have to share one of your fantasies."

She must have been tipsy, because she said, "Okay."

"Your sexual fantasies," he insisted.

"I get it."

He cleared his throat, hesitating a little. "Remember that these are from a fourteen-year-old's brain."

She smothered a giggle, intrigued.

"Wonder Woman appears in my room," he said. "She can astrally project and arrive in spirit form, but usually she just flies in the window."

"How convenient."

He inclined his head. "Sometimes she needs help saving the world and I have the key or the secret code or whatever. Then she embraces me in gratitude and one thing leads to another. Other times she's under a spell and the only way to break it is by having sex with me. Then there's the basic horny-for-no-reason scenario."

"What does she do to you?"

"Everything."

She laughed at his vague answer. "You don't turn into a superhero?"

"No."

"Why not?"

"I don't know. The part I like is that she's this extraordinary being with special powers, and she wants me."

"That is incredibly geeky," she said.

"I told you."

Suddenly it was her turn, but she didn't want to play anymore. His fantasy was cute. What if he thought hers was weird or gross?

"Go on," he said. "I won't judge."

"Of course you will."

"You could tell me you wanted to fuck an elephant, and I'd think it was hot."

She moistened her lips, nervous.

"Is that it? You want to fuck an elephant?"

"No!"

"I'm teasing you. Spill it."

"I have one about being abducted by aliens."

"Female aliens?"

She laughed, shaking her head. "They're sort of unrecognizable monsters."

"Where do they take you?"

"Into a lab where they do experiments."

"Sexual experiments?"

"Yes."

"Do you resist?"

"I can't, really. I'm restrained."

He didn't appear disgusted by her strange fantasy. If anything, he seemed to be filing the information away for future reference.

Good thing she was never going to sleep with him. She didn't have to worry about him trying to do some wicked experiments on her, or tying her to an exam table, naked.

Whew. Was it hot in here? She took off her jacket, forgetting that she was wearing only a thin tank top underneath. He must not have looked his fill earlier, because he perused her body again with interest.

"You're a lightweight," he said.

"I weigh quite a bit, actually."

"How drunk are you?"

She held her forefinger and thumb about an inch apart. He used his fingers to widen that distance, making her laugh again. She couldn't stop staring at him. He had a great smile, full of light and mischief. It made a pleasant contrast with his tanned complexion and the dark shadow of stubble on his jaw.

"What happened to your mustache?" she asked.

He stroked his upper lip. "Why, did you like it?"

At the time, she'd found it silly and annoying, drawing too much attention to his mouth. But when she pictured it now, she felt a flutter of feminine curiosity. How would it feel against her throat, her breasts, her inner thighs?

She tore her gaze away from him and examined the surface of the table, her cheeks hot. Someone had placed a sticker on the edge that advertised a local sports bar. It was popular with zoo employees, Josh included. They called quitting time "beer-thirty."

She couldn't tell him that there was no future for them. If she wanted a casual affair, she wouldn't have it with a coworker. He wasn't boyfriend material, either. His favorite saying was *hakuna matata*: no worries. No responsibilities.

"I can grow it back for you," he offered. "I'd do it in a heartbeat. I'd do just about anything you asked me to."

She believed him—and she had to get out of here before she took him up on that offer. "I'm going to bed."

"Don't trust yourself around me?"

Instead of bantering with him, she pushed away from the table. She didn't sway on her feet as she stood. Squaring her shoulders haughtily, she strode toward the ladies room. Five steps later, she realized it was too dark to see in there.

So much for her grand exit.

"Forget something?" he asked.

"I need a flashlight."

"Take the lantern."

She picked it up and went down the hall. Inside the bathroom, she placed the lantern on the sink and studied her reflection in the broken shards of mirror. Her eyes were wide and her heart pounded with trepidation. She wasn't standing tough; she was running scared.

Josh appeared in the doorway.

She whirled away from the sink. "What do you want?"

"The same thing you do, I imagine," he said, walking into an open stall.

"What's wrong with the men's room?"

"It's damaged."

He didn't bother to shut the door behind him. Gritting her teeth, she entered the last stall and locked it. His cheerful whistle and easy stream annoyed her. Even his pee sounded carefree. After she was finished, they returned to the staff room together. She grabbed a bottle of water and continued to the animal hospital. She couldn't stop him from following her. There was only one place to sleep.

Moving her cot would look cowardly, but she contemplated it anyway. She was too agitated to lie down.

"You're never going to go out with me, are you?" he asked.

She set the lantern on the floor, stalling. Once again, she'd misjudged his ability to read between the lines. He hadn't assumed everything would work out his way. He'd known she was putting him off to avoid confrontation.

"You won't take a chance on a real connection. After you break up with Mitch, you'll date another guy just like him. Another robot in a man's body."

"You don't even know him."

"He's a cold fish."

"He's *mature*."

"I've seen you together. He doesn't suit you."

"And you do?"

He nodded, confident as ever. "You're a cool customer. I like that about you, but you need someone hot-blooded to warm you up. That's why it didn't work out with Mitch. He's not the right man for you. I am."

She shook her head in disbelief. "Your ego is off the charts."

"There's something special between us."

"The only thing between us is physical attraction."

"Prove it."

"How?"

"Go out with me."

"It's not a good idea, Josh."

"Why?"

"We work together."

"I'll quit."

He was joking, as usual. There was no rule about fraternizing between employees. "You're too young for me."

"I'm twenty-nine, Helena."

"Going on twenty-one."

"Bullshit," he said, his eyes glinting with anger. "I was busting my ass in the navy when I was twenty-one. I spent my birthday working an eighteen-hour shift, so fuck you and your insulting misconceptions."

"You're reckless," she said, grasping at straws. "Life's a big joke to you. You'll probably hit your head surfing again and drown."

It was a terrible thing to say. She had no idea why she'd said it. She was a terrible person. A scared, small, terrible person.

"You think I'm like your father," he said softly.

Her throat tightened with panic. She felt the falling sensation again, as if the floor had dropped out from under her feet. Her father had been loud, charismatic, playful. Larger than life. Josh was the same type of man, big and bold in his affections. She could picture him throwing baseballs all night to win a teddy bear for a little girl. The thought of loving someone like that again, and giving her heart without reservation, terrified her.

"Has it ever occurred to you that *you're* like him?" Josh asked.

"Me?" she sputtered.

"Elephants kill more keepers than any other zoo animal. You said it yourself."

"That was ten years ago, in the days of free contact."

"Before you started?"

She didn't answer. The park had been transitioning from free to protected contact the year she got hired. She'd had some close calls. Working with elephants was always risky. They could be incredibly difficult to manage.

The difference between loving wild animals and loving wild people was simple. She took care of the animals from a safe distance, and never crossed the barrier between them. She also didn't expect them to return her affections or stay by her side. They had to be free of human entanglements.

Romantic relationships were more complicated.

God help a woman who fell for a handsome charmer like Josh. His love would be as all-consuming as his kiss. And he'd leave her with nothing but that cold, empty place inside her.

"You entered a deadly profession, and you love it," he said.

She crossed her arms over her chest. "So what?"

"I'm not reckless. I'm adventurous, and so are you. You're making excuses not to go out with me because you're afraid of the way I make you feel."

"I feel nothing!"

He closed the distance between them, bracing his hand on the cage wall behind her. "Liar," he said, directly to her face.

Helena saw red. He thought he could crowd her space and insult her? He was lucky they were in a cage, not muck-filled stables. The fact that he was telling the truth didn't matter. If she didn't win this battle, he'd take everything. "I won't go out with you," she said, grabbing the front of his shirt. "I'll never go out with you."

A muscle in his jaw flexed. He didn't try to escape from her grasp.

"But I will fuck you," she said, her lips inches from his. "Just this once."

He put his hand on her throat, brushing his thumb over the hollow. Her pulse throbbed against his fingertips. "I don't want to fuck you once. I want to fuck you over and over again, until the end of time."

"Too bad."

He was furious enough to say no. She could see it in his flared nostrils and tense mouth. "You're going to regret this."

"Why?"

"Because you won't be able to walk when I'm done with you."

An illicit thrill raced down her spine. "Maybe I'll chew you to pieces first."

"You can try."

She shut him up with a kiss, relishing the challenge.

His response wasn't gentle. Helena gasped as he shoved her back against the cage door, taking control. His tongue plunged inside her mouth, plundering her depths. He tasted like whiskey, hot and wild and desperate.

She threaded her fingers through his hair and kissed him back with matching force. She wanted to devour him. Their mouths crushed together, tongues tangling, bodies slamming against perforated metal.

It hurt. So good.

His hands dove under the waistband of her pants, groping her bottom. The novelty panties didn't cover much. He lifted her against his erection with a low groan. She sucked on his tongue and clutched at his hair, rubbing herself along his rigid length.

He didn't waste time warming her up. She was already on fire for him, her body screaming for relief. Breaking the kiss, he yanked off his shirt. She removed her tank top, baring her breasts. He cupped both in his big hands, rolling his thumbs over her taut nipples. Her eyes drifted shut and she shuddered, awash with sensation.

He surprised her by dropping to his knees. In one swift motion, he tugged her pants and panties down her thighs. Then he put his open mouth to her. He kissed her sex with the same hunger and urgency as her mouth. He didn't seem concerned about tenderness or technique. He just ate her avidly, for his own pleasure.

She'd never felt anything like it.

His tongue swept over her clit, warm and wet. She whimpered, widening her stance to encourage him. A little more. Right there. Please.

He could have brought her off with a couple of well-placed licks, but he didn't. In fact, he paused, placing a tender kiss on her throbbing clit. Then he slid two fingers inside her. In and out, watching her face.

Oh, God.

She braced her hands on the cage behind her, bracing herself. Trembling to come. Again, a flick of his tongue would send her over the edge. Paired with his thrusting fingers, she'd have a screaming orgasm. He didn't let her.

Removing his fingers, which were shiny with her moisture, he rubbed them over his lips. Then he rose and kissed her mouth again. His cock jutted at the front of his pants, creating an irresistible diversion. When she reached out and squeezed him through the soft fabric, he groaned. Two could play at teasing. Not content to be a passive partner, she sank to her knees and lowered his waistband.

He didn't protest as she wrapped her hand around the base of his shaft and swirled her tongue around him. She didn't linger over soft licks or nibbling. Angling the tip into her mouth, she relaxed her throat and took him as deep as she could.

"Fuck," he panted, fisting his hand in her hair.

She moaned and sucked harder, lost in the delicious act. She liked being on her knees, getting him off, reducing him to incoherency.

He didn't let her pleasure him for long. Withdrawing from her mouth, he gripped the base of his cock and brushed the slippery head over her parted lips. She flicked her tongue over him, welcoming his release. But he pulled away and brought her to her feet. Framing her face with his hand, he swept his thumb across her wet mouth.

"You could have finished," she said.

"We just started."

She felt a flutter of trepidation. Maybe he was serious about using her hard. She couldn't wait.

He lifted her off her feet and carried her to the exam table, depositing her on the cool surface. Then he stripped her naked and proceeded to explore every inch of her body. She sat with her legs spread and her hands gripping the edge of the table, watching him. He penetrated her with his tongue and fingers, driving her crazy.

She made desperate sounds of pleasure as he pinched her nipples and suckled her clit.

He finally brought her to orgasm with a rough hand. Burying two fingers in her slippery sheathe, he alternated between thrusting deep and strumming her clit. She came in a hot rush, her hips bucking, a raw cry wrenching from her lips. He moved his slick fingers from her body to his, coating his penis with her moisture. She couldn't believe how wet she was. He stroked fast, bracing his free hand on the surface of the table. With a strangled groan, he bent forward, spurting all over her splayed thighs and swollen sex.

Whoa.

He'd just given her the most intense orgasm of her life. She was still humming with sensation when he brought her a clean washcloth. Dampening the towel with bottled water, he wiped himself first. Then he took care of her.

It was risky of him to come on her that way. Not as risky as coming inside her, but not exactly safe. She wasn't complaining, though—she'd loved it. She was thrilled by his lack of inhibitions, titillated by his touch. He poured a bit of water directly from the bottle, splashing her tingling flesh. She shuddered at the cool trickle of liquid. She felt like a lush tropical flower.

He took a drink from the bottle, contemplating her wet folds. "I'm not done with you."

She glanced down at the front of his pants. His penis looked heavy and full. She'd like to have it inside her.

"I don't have any condoms," he said. "Do you?"

"No."

"I guess we'll have to be creative."

She drank a sip of water, rehydrating. "I'm ready."

CHAPTER TWENTY-ONE

JOSH WOKE TO the sound of Helena sneaking away.

He lifted his head and squinted at her retreating form in the early morning light. She had a wool blanket wrapped around her nude body, exposing her pale shoulders. Tiptoeing across the floor, she gathered her belongings with one hand. The blanket fell down to her hips as she bent to pick up her zebra-striped panties. Then she slipped through the door, silent.

Josh knew a walk of shame when he saw one. His stomach clenched with regret. Not because she had a boyfriend, though he wasn't proud of that fact. His misgivings were more about her mental and emotional state. She'd been a little drunk last night. He'd challenged her to talk about her feelings when she was vulnerable. Instead of agreeing to a date, she'd offered sex. And he'd taken it, thinking with his dick instead of his brain.

Fuck.

She'd shared her body without reservations, letting him do anything he wanted. And he'd wanted quite a lot. He'd brought her off with his mouth and hands more than once. She'd returned the favor, sucking him dry. They'd both been voracious. She was the most responsive partner he'd ever had. But she'd also kept her heart guarded.

He might not get another opportunity to win her over. He'd squandered his time screwing her senseless instead of appealing to her emotions. And in doing so, he'd proved that some of her criticisms were true.

He had a weakness for beautiful women. His scruples about poaching were a joke. Basically, he was a horny bastard. That didn't mean his feelings for her weren't genuine. He just had to try harder to convince her that he was more than a good lay. He was a good man, and she could count on him.

He tossed aside the blanket and stood up, stretching his arms over his head. Between the fence repair, the honey-badger attack and their late-night activities, he was sore. He swept his shirt off the floor and put on his boots, not bothering to lace them. Then he went in search of food, coffee and Helena.

He found her in the ladies room. She was standing at the sink, splashing her face with bottled water.

"Morning," he said, walking into a stall.

She didn't respond.

He used the facilities quickly and came out, trying to gauge her mood. Her nose was red, as if she'd been crying. He didn't know what to say. He was sorry, but not *that* sorry. "How do you feel?"

"Like shit," she said.

"Headache?"

"My whole body aches."

So did his. He hoped he hadn't been too rough with her. Judging by her responses, she'd wanted it that way, but he might have overindulged her. "Did I hurt you?"

"No."

He used her soap and water to wash up. He probably had her scent all over him. She watched him with cool, bloodshot eyes. She looked beautiful and deadly, as if she wanted to murder his face.

God. She was hot.

He took a sip of water, studying her. "Do you want to talk about it?"

"About what?"

"The sex, Helena. The sex we had last night. For hours."

She grabbed the bottle away from him and strode out of the bathroom, rolling her eyes. "There's nothing to talk about. It was a mistake."

He had a rule against getting angry in the morning. It was inspired by years of surfing. Most things weren't worth losing his temper about, especially not before work. He didn't rise at dawn to thump his chest like an ape or fight with some jerk-off who dropped in on him. No bad vibes to start the day. *Hakuna matata.*

His no-worries rule flew out the window at her casual dismissal. He followed her to the staff room, watching as she poured water into a cup.

"So that's it?" he asked, incredulous.

"What do you want, a performance evaluation? You were okay."

"I was *okay?*"

She nodded, putting the cup in the microwave. "I've had better."

Maybe she had, but he didn't think so. Not because he was God's gift to women. He was just a regular guy, though he loved sex and the female body in an almost obsessive way. What had made it special wasn't his technique, or her enthusiasm. It was more than great chemistry. They'd forged a powerful bond over the past few days.

She was in denial, which meant…she was afraid.

"I haven't had better," he said honestly. "You've ruined me for other women."

"Very funny."

"I'm dead serious."

"I was drunk."

He tamped down his temper, with some difficulty. "Were you drunk when you tried to take off my pants in the loading dock?"

Her cheeks stained pink. "I miss Mitch."

Oh, no, she didn't. Oh, *hell* no.

"I'm a sexual person, and it's been a long time."

"So you used me as a stand-in for your boyfriend," Josh said, wondering if his head would pop right off his neck. "That's your story?"

"Didn't you do the same thing?"

"Fuck no."

"You've never looked at me and thought of Wonder Woman?"

He had, plenty of times. But not last night. "I don't close my eyes and fantasize about one woman when I'm with another, Helena. What kind of asshole does that? If she's not worth my full attention, I don't bother."

She shrugged, as if she didn't care either way. When she reached for her cup in the microwave, he gripped her upper arm to stop her. Hot liquid wasn't a good idea right now. He was furious enough to knock the cup across the room.

"I don't believe you thought of Mitch once last night," he said. "I don't think he fucks you half as good as I did."

"You didn't—"

"I did," he said, interrupting her. "I fucked you hard. And when I put my cock in you, you won't even remember his name."

She drew in a sharp breath. "You have no right to act so possessive."

"You said you were going to break up with him!"

"I said I'd talk to him."

"And how's he going to respond to this new development?"

She tried to jerk her arm out of his grasp, but he held tight. She knew as well as he did that her relationship was over. This was all a defensive maneuver, designed to push him away before he got too close.

"You're using Mitch as a crutch because you're afraid of getting hurt."

"If you don't take your hand off my arm, *you're* going to get hurt."

He released her, swearing. "This has nothing to do with Mitch. It's about you and me. You think I'm not good enough for you."

She didn't deny it.

"I can make you happy, Helena. I can take care of you."

"I don't need to be taken care of," she said.

"Just like you don't want to be held?"

Her mouth thinned with displeasure.

"You won't let me get close," he said. "You won't challenge yourself to *feel*."

She removed her cup from the microwave and added instant coffee. "It's pretty ironic for you to accuse me of not challenging myself."

"Why is that?"

"You wanted to be a big-shot navy SEAL—"

"SWCC," he corrected.

"Whatever," she said, stirring her coffee. "You have a college degree and military experience. This job doesn't challenge a man with your skills. You gave up on your dream after one setback."

"I didn't give up," he said through clenched teeth.

"You failed."

"That's right. I failed. And you're so out of touch with human emotions that you fantasize about aliens fucking you."

She flinched at the insult.

Josh felt an ugly surge of satisfaction at the sight. Instead of quitting while he was ahead, he twisted the knife. "Good luck on your dream of having a family. Maybe you and Mitch can adopt a half-robot, half-alien baby."

Her eyes narrowed with anger. For a moment, he thought he was going to get a faceful of hot coffee, or a resounding slap. He deserved both, and he welcomed her ire. He wanted to duke it out with her and resolve their differences. If she was willing to take a risk on him, he'd do anything for her. They could challenge each other.

She didn't lash out at him, however. Keeping her cool, she lifted the coffee to her lips and blew on the surface.

His gut clenched at the sight. That was when he knew his feelings went beyond infatuation, beyond explosive sexual chemistry, beyond respect and admiration. He was in love with her. And she wouldn't even lower herself to argue with him.

Maybe they were doomed, and she was unreachable. She ran a tight ship, protecting her heart so diligently that even she couldn't access it anymore. Nothing could get in or out. No one could penetrate her fortresses.

Josh wasn't a quitter, despite her accusations, but his optimism only went so far. He couldn't appeal to her emotions if she refused to acknowledge them. Helena was a stubborn woman, prickly and aloof. He liked her that way. He always had. The contrast between her icy veneer and the heat beneath excited him. Although she was well worth the fight, he couldn't win by overpowering her. He had to find another way inside.

So he backed down and regrouped. He didn't want to lose her by pushing too hard, or scare her away by professing his love. He just hoped he'd have another chance to get through to her before they got rescued.

He warmed up water for his own cup of coffee, giving her space. They had a lackluster breakfast of granola bars and bananas, just like the day before. While he was considering his next step, his cell phone chimed with a notification.

He almost flipped his chair over in his haste to check his messages. There wasn't just one text, but three. The most recent communication was from the zoo director, under the heading "help is on the way."

Halle-fucking-lujah.

He clicked to read the full message, with Helena at his side. The director, Tom Spears, was flying in with three colleagues and two keepers. The National Guard had dispatched a helicopter to the naval hospital to rescue several groups of patients. Tom would hitch a ride with the Guard and arrive with his crew shortly after 10:00 a.m. He expressed his profuse thanks to Josh and Helena, and requested details about Greg Patel.

"They're coming to help us," he said to Helena. "It's over."

Tears filled her eyes and she hugged him, forgetting their argument.

He was overwhelmed with relief, but also sad that their adventure had come to a close. He didn't know how to reach her.

As soon as they left the zoo, they'd be separated. They might not see each other for days or weeks while the park closed for repairs.

After she relayed the pertinent information about Greg and the code ones, she returned the phone to Josh. He checked the other two messages. The first was a short, happy note in all caps from Helena's mother. Josh grinned at this, sharing her excitement. The next message was from his parents:

Flying home now. No word from Chloe. Please respond when you can. We love you so much, mom and dad.

The smile fell off his face. His parents hadn't heard from his sister. After two full days, that wasn't good. It didn't necessarily mean that something terrible had happened to her, but it didn't bode well.

"She could be stuck in the city, like we are," Helena said. "There must be thousands of people in the same situation, cut off from communication."

He collapsed in his chair, stunned by the news. What if Chloe and Emma had been dead this whole time, while he'd been messing around with Helena, getting stupid on whiskey and thinking with his dick?

Helena sat down next to him. He couldn't bring himself to look at her. The whiskey bottle beckoned, but he couldn't go there, either. He had to be a responsible adult. It was time to grow up and face facts.

He *was* a failure.

Although he didn't appreciate having it pointed out to him, the truth was undeniable. He'd failed his scuba and water-rescue courses. He'd failed to advance in SWCC. He'd failed to achieve his lifelong goal.

That was okay with him, actually. He couldn't have tried harder. His inability to function in deep water wasn't a sign of weakness. It was just something in his body chemistry. A natural predisposition, like asthma. Even if he found a way to manage the condition, he was a poor candidate for the SWCC.

So he'd accepted the disappointment and moved on. His priorities had changed over the past ten years. When he was twenty, special-ops warfare had sounded awesome. He'd grown out of his skinny geek faze and overdosed on testosterone for a while. Like many young men, he'd reveled in his strength and physicality.

He'd mellowed since then. He still enjoyed being active, but he didn't want to shoot people for a living. Zoo security suited him just fine.

Maybe he'd been coasting for a few years, finding his way. Some of his friends had traveled around the world after college. Others hadn't even gone on to college. Starting a career wasn't easy these days, and there was nothing wrong with chilling out for a while. It was better than working himself into an early grave. He couldn't say he'd reached his full potential, however. As much as he hated to admit it, Helena was right.

He hadn't been "all he could be."

"If I'd stayed on reserves or transferred to the Coast Guard, I might have been part of the rescue efforts," he said, glancing at her. "I could've searched for them."

She looked stricken. "You don't know that."

"I don't know anything."

"They could be fine."

"They could be dead, too."

"You said you had a feeling they weren't."

"Yeah, well. I also had a feeling that you belonged with me, so maybe my gut feelings are bullshit."

She fell silent, her expression troubled.

Agonizing over a situation beyond his control wasn't going to help, and he didn't want to sit here anymore, waiting for his chest to explode. "Let's go check on Tau."

She nodded her agreement. They had several hours to kill before help arrived, and plenty of loose ends to take care of. While he tidied up the staff room, she sanitized the animal hospital, spraying disinfectant on things and folding the blankets. He didn't know what to do with the whiskey bottle, so he put it back in the box. After the director and his crew assessed the damages, they'd probably need a drink.

Helena flinched at the sight of the black-and-gold box. She couldn't get rid of this evidence as easily as the lingering scent of sex on the blankets. For some reason, that made him feel better. If she never went out with him, she'd probably regret it. She'd think about their night together every time she looked at his face. Every time he spoke, she'd remember how his mouth had felt on her.

They brought the rifle and tranquilizer gun with them outside to the truck. He climbed into the driver's seat while she took the passenger's. "Should we ride the tram again?"

"Whatever."

He wasn't keen on watching her eyes dart around and her cheeks pale with nausea. She was already hung over. The motion of the tram might make her throw up. "I'll just cruise around for a few minutes."

"Fine."

He'd gone only a few hundred feet when they came to an obstacle in the road: Bambang. Josh put on the brakes, wondering why the lizard wasn't moving.

"Pull up on my side," Helena said.

He skirted around Bambang and parked. "Is he dead?"

She rolled down the window to get a better look. "I think he's unconscious."

"From what?"

"I don't know. Give me something to poke him with."

He handed her his tactical baton. She leaned out to jab the prostrate lizard.

"He's not moving," she said. "Let's go get a cage to put him in."

Josh drove back to the storage yard and they loaded up another crate.

Helena put a leash around the lizard's body, under his arms. She used that to pull his front half while Josh took the tail end. They transferred him to the cage, huffing and puffing. Bam was a heavy bastard, unwieldy as hell, jaws dripping venomous saliva. When they locked him inside the crate, Josh breathed a sigh of relief.

"Do you think he tangled with King?" he asked.

"It's possible. Komodo dragons will attack and eat cobras."

Josh hadn't seen any wounds. Maybe Bambang had gotten into something toxic. Eucalyptus leaves had a slight narcotic effect. It was a running joke among the staff that the koalas were members of the Rastafari.

Helena's startled gaze met his. "The drugged meat," she said. "He must have eaten it. That's why Tau roared so loud."

Josh's heart sank at this news. If Bambang had taken the bait, Zuma was still fully alert and on the loose.

CHAPTER TWENTY-TWO

CHLOE WOKE IN A fog of pain and confusion.

She was alone in a hotel room, her head pounding and her throat dry. She felt awful, as if she'd been drugged. She hadn't been this jacked up since she'd spent a three-day weekend at the Coachella Festival.

There was a bottle of water on the nightstand. She fumbled for it and sat upright. When the room stopped spinning, she took a sip. Then she gulped down half the bottle, struck by a tremendous thirst.

Where was Emma? Where was *Mateo?*

Had last night really happened? It seemed like a dream. A sweet, hot dream, too good to be true. She rose to her feet and hobbled toward the balcony. The sliding glass door was open, diaphanous curtains fluttering in the breeze.

"Emma," Chloe croaked, starting to panic. "Emma!"

Mateo was standing by the pool with Emma in his arms. They both looked up at her. Mateo smiled and waved.

"Mama," Emma said.

It hadn't been a dream, Chloe realized. His smile was sort of self-satisfied, but not in an obnoxious way. He just seemed pleased, as if he considered himself lucky. She wondered what he expected from her.

Were they dating?

She hoped they were dating. He was hot and nice and fun to be with. Although the language barrier was a problem, it didn't have to be a deal breaker. They'd communicated well enough so far. He'd understood her just fine in bed.

He was also an extraordinary person. He'd saved her and Emma. Chloe was the lucky one to have crossed paths with this brave man at the exact moment she'd needed him. It was almost as if he'd been sent by God to rescue her.

The thought made her dizzy.

She grasped the back of a patio chair to steady herself and took a few deep breaths. She felt feverish and strange. Her cheeks were hot, but she was cold. She wanted to go back to bed and climb under the covers.

Mateo asked her a question, his brow furrowed with concern. She was concerned, too. She forced a smile and went back inside, stumbling toward the bathroom. Her panties were hanging on the towel rack. He must have washed them for her. She tugged down her yoga pants and sat on the commode, studying her injured thigh. Around the bandage, her skin was splotchy, throbbing with heat.

No wonder she felt like crap. Her wound was infected.

Now what?

She wasn't sure she'd make it the final blocks to the hospital. She didn't want to stay here with Emma while Mateo went for help.

They weren't as safe without him.

If Chloe's fever got worse, she'd be unable to take care of Emma. Letting him take Emma wasn't a good option, either. Chloe would go out of her mind with worry. He was obviously not her father, and he didn't speak English well enough to explain.

Chloe just had to do what she always did. Keep moving forward, one step at a time.

After using the bathroom, she put on her damp underwear. There was no way she'd go to the hospital without panties. Maybe she'd feel better after breakfast. A pain reliever would reduce her fever and discomfort for a few hours.

Everything would be okay.

When she came out of the bathroom, Mateo was there with Emma. Chloe sat down in the chair by the table and held out her arms to her baby. He delivered Emma to her lap. Chloe hugged her tight, trying not to worry.

"Sorry for…" He gestured to the balcony. He was apologizing for taking Emma away. He'd probably wanted to let Chloe sleep in, which was nice.

"Did you see the pool?" she asked Emma.

"Swim!"

"You went swimming?"

"No," Mateo said. "No swim. Just look."

There was a basket of treats at the center of the table. Crackers, fruit, blueberry muffins, diet soda. He must have brought it up with him. Chloe sat Emma in the other chair and offered her a muffin, unpeeling the paper cup for her.

"How are you?" he asked carefully.

She opened a package of crackers and a diet soda, murmuring a vague answer. She didn't know what to say about her worsening condition, but she had no regrets about their tryst. She'd never regret it, no matter what.

He watched her with cautious eyes, as if he feared she would denounce him.

"Thanks for washing my panties," she said.

It took him a moment to process her words. When he did, relief relaxed his features. "My pleasure," he said, his lips curving.

"I'm sure it was."

He laughed at her joke, rubbing a hand over his jaw. His gaze moved from her to the bed and back again. She hoped he didn't expect her to act like a blushing virgin. She had a child, after all. It was silly to pretend she hadn't enjoyed his touch. He was no virgin, either. He'd known exactly what he was doing.

Emma made a mess of her muffin, getting more on the floor than in her mouth. When she was finished, Mateo gave her the animal book from the thrift store. She pressed the buttons, making the tiger roar.

Chloe nibbled on crackers and sipped soda, anxious.

"Your leg...*te duele*?"

"I need medicine."

"A ver," he said, asking to see her wound.

She rose with reluctance and tugged down the waistband of her pants.

He sucked in a breath through his teeth. *"Híjole."* Reaching out, he tried to remove the bandage for a better look.

She didn't want him to see how bad it was, so she shied away from his hands and readjusted her clothes. He stood and paced the room, raking his fingers through his hair. His rapid-fire string of Spanish blistered her ears. He seemed angry, perhaps with himself, but the infection was hardly his fault.

"Maybe we can find a pharmacy," she said. "Medicine."

He paused, as if remembering something. Then he left the room and rushed downstairs. He returned with some trial-size packs of pain reliever/fever reducer tablets. Chloe accepted them with gratitude.

Mateo helped Emma get ready to leave. He must have tidied the room while Chloe was asleep, because the clothes they'd borrowed for last night's fashion show were hanging in the closet again. He'd also brought their belongings back from the pool. She put on her socks and boots, wincing at the pull in her leg.

Before they set off, she asked to look at the map again. She'd seen a pedestrian bridge that passed over the freeway on the east side of the park. It led to a short nature trail that appeared to be a quicker, safer route. They'd travel through a wooded area near the zoo and continue to the naval hospital.

"Here," she said, pointing to the dotted green line on the map. "A shortcut."

He nodded his agreement and put the map away. She needed his help to descend the stairs, so he took Emma down first and came back for Chloe. Even with the cane, she couldn't manage on her own.

Traveling across flat ground wasn't so bad. The first two blocks were bearable. She leaned heavily on her cane, feeling like a decrepit old lady. Emma was in a good mood, chirping to Mateo as she walked. Her words were unintelligible baby-talk to anyone but Chloe. He listened with one ear, his attention divided between Emma and their surroundings.

It wasn't as quiet in the sky today. There was a mix of clouds and smoke and aircraft overhead. Military planes and helicopters buzzed around, scoping the scene. Forty-eight hours since the original quake, order hadn't been restored, not by a long shot. But at least there was some activity. An indication that rescue workers were mobilizing forces.

When they reached the footbridge, Emma tried to wriggle her hand from Mateo's grasp and run ahead. This was a typical Emma move. In her quest for independence, she often attempted to bolt across parking lots and race around at busy stores. The potential for a breakaway was always high.

Mateo didn't know how to deal with an unruly child in a high-stakes situation. The bridge looked solid, but he couldn't let her go across by herself.

"Give her to me," Chloe said, resting her cane on the railing.

He carried Emma to her gladly.

"I go bridge!" Emma said.

"We'll go together," Chloe said. "I'll give you a licorice if you're good."

Emma wasn't used to getting treats so often. She watched while Mateo tested the bridge. Deeming it safe, he came back for Chloe and Emma. They went across together and entered the nature path on the other side. It was nice in the trees, quiet and peaceful. For the first time since the earthquake, they weren't surrounded by wreckage.

"Zoo," Emma said, as if she recognized the area. "Unco Josh!"

Mateo glanced at Chloe in question.

"My brother works at the zoo," she explained. "He's a security officer."

The wildlife park was full of meandering passages through lush gardens and cactus groves. Those trails were perfectly maintained, with more exotic plants than this path, but Emma probably associated nature walks with the zoo. Mateo carried her for a few minutes. When they came to a clearing, Emma wanted to get down and run again.

"Zoo," Emma repeated. "Horse."

Chloe followed her pointed finger across the clearing. "Oh, my God," she said, clapping a hand over her mouth.

There wasn't a horse in the distance. That would have been unusual and startling enough. This was an okapi. Chloe had seen the animals at the zoo many times. They were about the size of a horse, with odd coloring. Their hindquarters were striped and their backs were brown. They looked like a cross between a donkey and a zebra.

"Que es esto?" Mateo said, agog.

"It's an okapi."

"'Kapi," Emma said, delighted.

While they watched, the okapi lowered its head to nibble on the grass.

"It must have escaped from the zoo," Chloe said to Mateo, uneasy.

His brows rose with understanding. He glanced around, as if expecting to see more wild animals in the area.

Chloe's heart started pounding in her chest. She swayed on her feet, fighting another wave of nausea. She'd been cold this morning, but now she was hot. Her fever felt worse instead of better. Mateo said a bunch of words and gestured back the way they came. She wanted to keep moving forward. She also needed to rest. It was hard to decide. Insects buzzed around her ears, making her dizzy.

His voice sounded far away now, drifting across the meadow. Her vision blurred and she stumbled into darkness.

*

HELENA BOARDED THE Skylift again, her stomach roiling with nausea.

This was what hell must be like. Heights, motion, guilt and a hangover. With Josh staring at her on a never-ending loop of doom.

She couldn't believe what they'd done last night.

She'd woken up buck-naked in a cage with a coworker. What if a zoo official or a member of the National Guard had walked in on them this morning? Or in flagrante delicto? She'd never been more ashamed in her entire life.

She couldn't blame the alcohol, because she hadn't been that drunk. She couldn't blame him, either. He hadn't taken advantage of her. She'd made a conscious choice to sleep with him. The only person to blame was herself.

What was she going to say to Mitch?

This wasn't an accidental kiss after a near-fatal accident. They'd screwed each other silly. She'd had multiple orgasms. He'd done dirty things to her and promised to do more. It was the wildest, most passionate night of her life. They might not have had intercourse, but she'd cheated. She'd cheated hard.

Mitch would never forgive her. He wasn't the type of man to brush aside this kind of transgression, and they wouldn't part as friends. She had to accept that.

In her heart, she'd known it was over. They'd been on shaky ground for months. She'd fallen out of love with him. She wouldn't have gone to bed with Josh otherwise.

That didn't make it okay. There was no excuse for moving on from a committed relationship without informing the other person. She should have broken things off with Mitch before she'd ever considered having sex with Josh.

She felt awful.

Turning her gaze to the ground below, she looked for Zuma. There was no sign of the wily lioness as they drifted over Heart of Africa. Tau was sitting upright in his cage. It was a tight space, cramped and comfortable. They'd have to wait until the backup crew arrived to move him. While she surveyed the rest of the park, disturbed by the widespread damages and untidy enclosures, she replayed her argument with Josh.

He'd said some terrible things to her this morning. The part about the alien baby was a low blow. Mitch wasn't a robot. He was just reserved, like her. He didn't talk about his feelings much, and neither did she. They were mature adults, not angst-ridden teenagers. But maybe they'd needed more emotion to bind them. They'd *both* withdrawn. Instead of growing stronger through adversity, they'd grown apart.

Josh had been right about her relationship with Mitch. Josh had been right about everything. She hadn't thought of Mitch last night. She hadn't used Josh as a stand-in. She'd only said that to hurt him.

She *was* afraid he'd break her heart. He'd come dangerously close to doing it already. She was standing on a terrifying edge, ready to topple over. Another selfless gesture from him, a few more emotional exchanges, a simple kiss...and she'd be lost forever.

She glanced at Josh. He looked miserable. His sister and niece might be dead. She gripped the safety rail, contemplating a jump over the side of the tram. The heights didn't scare her as much as her feelings did.

"I'm sorry," she said, forcing herself to meet his eyes.

He cupped a hand over his ear, as if he hadn't heard her. "What was that?"

"I'm sorry," she repeated stiffly. "For calling you a failure."

"I am a failure," he said, shrugging. "Most of the trainees for SEALs and SWCC fail. What bothers me is your insinuation that I didn't work hard enough. My failure had nothing to do with lack of effort or personal weakness. You would have failed, too."

"They don't even let women try," she pointed out.

He ignored this fact. "You're strong enough to compete, but your fear of heights would have prevented you from advancing. Anyone who suffers from motion sickness or serious anxiety is a poor candidate for special ops."

She'd always wondered if motion sickness was part of her problem. Instead of getting a diagnosis, she'd avoided the whole issue.

"Maybe zoo security isn't the most challenging job I could get," he said. "That's what I like about it. If something goes wrong, I can dial 911. I don't have to carry a firearm or decide when to use deadly force."

She understood why that would appeal to him. "You're a natural at handling emergencies, though."

He accepted this compliment with a curt nod.

"I'm sure it's common for law officers to feel conflicted about using their weapons. Any conscientious person would shoot as a last resort."

"My hesitation cost a sailor his life."

"You could save another life in the future."

"Why do you care what I do for work?" he asked bluntly.

She started to say she didn't, but the denial died in her throat.

"If I left the zoo, you wouldn't have to see me every day and remember how many times I made you come. Is that it?"

"No," she said, flushing.

He held up his hand, indicating it was five. Five times.

"It was four, you jerk."

"Was it?" He rested his arm on the safety bar, smirking. "I lost track."

She knew damned well he hadn't lost track of the number. He was just trying to goad her into admitting that his performance last night had been a lot better than *okay*.

Annoyed with his smug attitude, she studied the park grounds again, scanning the area beyond the fence line for stray hyenas. She didn't want Josh to leave the zoo. The idea of him reenlisting or choosing a more dangerous profession gave her that buzzing-plane sensation in the pit of her stomach. If she never saw him again, she wouldn't be relieved.

She'd be devastated.

Oh, God. Her worst fear had materialized: She'd fallen for him.

Before she had a chance to digest this terrible news, she was confronted with something even worse. She caught a glimpse of stealthy motion in the woods near Birdie Trail. Zuma. While Helena watched in horror, the lioness crept across a short space between bushes. Then she crouched down again, waiting in the shadows.

"Zuma is outside the perimeter," she said, swallowing hard.

Josh looked over his shoulder. "You've got to be kidding me."

The tram car moved past a pole, blocking their view. Helena tried to get another look at the bushes at the edge of the nature trail, but it was no use. They began to descend toward the loading dock, dipping below the treetops.

"Are you sure you saw her?" Josh asked.

"I'm positive."

He raked a hand through his hair. "Fuck."

"We have to go after her."

"Can't we wait until the others get here?"

"No," she said, swallowing hard. This situation was far more pressing than the other code ten. They wouldn't have been able to track the hyena, even if they'd known which direction the animal had gone. Hyenas were also opportunistic scavengers who preferred easy meals and rarely killed humans. Lions, on the other hand, were responsible for hundreds of attacks every year. Zuma was an aggressive lioness with no fear of people. That made her extremely dangerous. "I think she's hunting."

"Hunting what?"

Helena could only guess. "Rabbits are everywhere this time of year. She could have a field day on rabbits."

"Maybe that will keep her busy."

"I wouldn't count on it. She might chase one away from the trail, or wander miles into the city. We can't wait and hope she stays close. Our best chance to catch her is to act now, before she gets away."

He swore under his breath, but he didn't protest. He knew she was right. As soon as they reached the dock, he jumped out and hit the button. She exited the tram car and followed him to the park's front entrance. While she unlocked the gate, he sent a quick text to the park's director about Zuma.

"I'm sorry, too," he said, putting his phone away.

"For what?"

"Getting defensive. Acting like an asshole. I hope you have a family and whatever else you want in life."

Her chest tightened with emotion. "I hope your sister and her little girl are okay."

"So do I," he said simply. "And no matter what happens between us, I'm glad we spent this time together. Not just because of last night. The earthquake and everything was fucked up, but I loved being stuck here with you."

"Likewise," she said, unable to lie. "You were a great partner."

"I think we deserve bonuses. Hazard pay."

"Definitely."

After she wiped the tears from her eyes, they headed toward Birdie Trail to complete their final mission.

CHAPTER TWENTY-THREE

JOSH CREPT FORWARD, rifle raised, his adrenaline pumping with every step.

Helena stayed on his six with the tranquilizer gun. He knew she wanted to use darts instead of bullets, but if something went wrong, he wouldn't hesitate to take the kill shot. There was no way he'd let the lioness charge at his woman.

He couldn't guess what their relationship would be like after this ordeal was over. Helena might retreat into her cool facade and never let him touch her again. She might move to Denver and play house with Mitch. If Josh's wildest dreams came true, she'd break down in tears, confess her passionate love for him and beg him to take her to bed.

It was a pretty awesome fantasy. His dates with Wonder Woman paled in comparison. The thought of spending the rest of his life with Helena appealed to him on every level. He'd been disinterested in casual sex for months. Giving up his bachelor status was no loss. He could go without flirting or ogling women in short shorts.

He couldn't go without Helena.

He'd do everything in his power to win her over, but he understood reality. Sometimes you didn't succeed no matter how hard you tried. It was a fact of life.

And for all his desperate, lovelorn wishes, he'd trade a future with Helena for the safety of his sister and niece in a heartbeat.

In a heartbeat.

They didn't encounter Zuma on the trail. Before they reached the area where Helena had seen the lioness, Josh spotted an unexpected inhabitant: an okapi. The donkey-like creature with zebra legs and hyena ears nibbled on grass in the middle of an open field.

Josh stopped short, making a halt signal behind his back. Helena followed his gaze to the okapi, her eyes widening. They hadn't even known an okapi had escaped an enclosure, let alone the zoo itself. After he searched their surroundings for signs of Zuma, Josh ducked behind a pair of nearby bushes with Helena. She pressed her fingertips to her lips. If the lioness was nearby, she'd hear them.

Josh had to assume that Zuma was hunting the okapi. Waiting to ambush the lioness was a better strategy than moving forward into unknown territory. Zuma had the edge on them in this setting. She was the superior tracker. She had acute senses and the ability to move in silence. If the lioness knew two humans were following her, she could evade them easily.

Helena tilted her head toward a nearby bush, indicating that she wanted to check it out. Then she lifted her palm, telling him to stay here.

He shook his head. Hell no.

She walked her fingertips across her palm and made a sweeping motion. Then she gestured to the okapi. Josh gathered that Helena thought she could flush Zuma out of the bushes and into the clearing. He didn't like that idea, either. He touched her tranquilizer gun and pointed at the okapi. If she darted the prey, the predator might come running.

Helena nixed this option. She raised two fingers, reminding him that she only had two tranquilizer darts.

Fuck.

While they debated with silent, frustrated gestures, the okapi spooked suddenly and bounded off, disappearing into a tree-lined canyon.

Josh and Helena froze.

A disturbance at the opposite edge of the clearing explained the okapi's swift departure. It wasn't Zuma. There was a dark-haired man in the distance, carrying a woman. She was either dead or unconscious, her arms slack. She had blonde hair, like Chloe, and a slender figure. The man was average-sized. He could barely handle her weight. A small, curly-haired toddler walked alongside them.

Oh, Jesus.

His stomach twisted as he realized…it *was* Chloe. It was Chloe and Emma.

The man carrying Chloe stepped into the clearing and strode forward, grimacing under the strain. Josh was about to stand up and shout a warning when Helena clutched his forearm. Her short fingernails dug into his skin.

He followed her horrified gaze to Zuma. The lioness had crept out of the bushes and entered the field.

Shit!

Josh scrambled to get into the ready position with his rifle. Helena did the same, aiming her tranquilizer gun. Zuma was less than fifty feet from them, staying low and heading the same direction as the okapi. Josh wasn't sure if the lioness had spotted any of the humans. Zuma seemed focused on her prey.

Now, he implored Helena silently. Shoot *now*.

Helena took the shot, and it was good. The dart sank into Zuma's hindquarters. The lioness startled, more sensitive to the sting than Tau had been. Josh's heart leapt into his throat. He curled his finger around the trigger, waiting for the animal to turn on them.

That didn't happen. Something worse did.

The man carrying Chloe had stopped in his tracks, alerted by the sound of the gunshot and the sight of a two-hundred-pound lioness. But Emma kept trucking, unaware of the danger. She wandered into Josh's crosshairs, directly behind the lioness.

He couldn't shoot.

Zuma didn't continue into the trees in search of the okapi. She didn't look toward the bushes where Josh and Helena were crouched. The lioness focused her attention on the opposite side of the clearing, drawn to Emma's movement.

No!

Josh was up and running before he'd even drawn the breath to shout.

The man holding Chloe dropped her unceremoniously on the grass and chased after Emma, sweeping the child off her feet in one smooth grab. Josh started yelling at the top of his lungs, waving the rifle over his head to get Zuma's attention. The lioness saw him coming and roared.

He still didn't have a good shot, and now he didn't have any cover. But he'd caught Zuma's eye, which was exactly what he wanted. He wanted her to attack him instead of Emma. And she did. She came at him so fast he didn't have a chance to blink. He tried to bring his rifle forward as the lioness charged.

Nope. Couldn't do it.

Time slipped into slow motion and he knew he was a goner. One second ticked by, maybe two, before she struck. He wasn't able to get his hands in the right position. The best he could manage was to hold the weapon horizontally in front of his body in a feeble attempt to protect his head and neck.

Zuma hit him like a freight train, knocking him flat on his back.

The breath rushed from his lungs and his elbows slammed against the ground. He almost lost his grip on the gun. He shook off the pain and held on. He held on tight, because the metal barrel was the only thing between him and certain death.

Saliva dripped onto his face and sharp teeth glanced off his knuckles as they thrashed around, rolling across the grass. It was surreal.

Zuma's growls sounded far away, like they were coming from somewhere else. People were screaming. Josh might have been one of them; his throat was raw with terror.

Helena appeared in his peripheral vision. Before he could tell her to get the fuck away, she pressed the barrel of the tranquilizer gun against Zuma's neck and pulled the trigger. The big cat let out a furious roar. She switched targets, leaping off him and batting at Helena with razor-sharp claws. Helena cried out and stumbled backward, falling down on the grass. She'd drawn the lioness's wrath, but she had no protection. The sleeve of her jacket was torn, revealing red gashes on her shoulder.

Zuma smelled blood and pounced. Helena screamed, lifting her arm to cover her face. They tumbled across the grass together, woman and cat.

"No," Josh yelled, sitting upright. He raised the rifle with shaking hands, but he couldn't shoot at the blur of motion.

Helena ended up underneath the lioness, on the ground. Josh scrambled to his feet and took aim, ready to deliver the kill shot. But then he noticed the lioness seemed sluggish. She wasn't tearing out Helena's throat. The direct injection of tranquilizers had already taken effect. The lioness weaved drunkenly, her head bobbing.

Seconds later, she slumped on top of Helena. Unconscious.

Josh set down his weapon and shoved the lioness aside. Zuma fell over in a slack heap, her tongue hanging out. Josh straddled Helena's waist and molded his hands around her face. She stared up at him, not speaking.

"Are you okay?" he asked.

"I think so."

He didn't see any wounds to her neck or her vital organs. Other than the bloody shoulder, she looked fine. Just shaken up.

They were both shaken up.

"I thought you were going to die," he said in a hoarse voice.

"I thought *you* were."

Pressure built behind his eyes as he pressed a kiss to her temple. Then he looked across the meadow. The man was still there, holding Emma. Chloe lay on the ground, motionless. "I have to check on my sister."

"That's your sister?"

He nodded, unable to believe it himself.

"I'll come with you."

Standing together, they headed toward Chloe. The wounds on Helena's upper arm and shoulder needed stitches, but she was going to be okay. As they walked across the clearing, Josh steeled himself for the possibility that his sister hadn't been so lucky. Then she moved, turning her head to watch his approach.

She was alive. His heart swelled with emotion.

"Unco Josh!" Emma said, pointing at him.

The man holding Emma let her down. She ran to Josh and he picked her up, hugging her to his chest. The tears he'd been fighting spilled over his cheeks. Chloe and Emma were alive. He'd known it all along.

"Kitty," she said.

He laughed at this understatement, his throat tight. "Big kitty." When he reached Chloe, he sank to his knees in the grass. Her cheeks were flushed and she appeared confused. He cupped his palm over her forehead. She was burning up.

"What happened?" she asked, moistening her lips.

He studied the stranger who'd been carrying Chloe. He was young and dark-skinned, with a strip of black hair on his mostly shaved head. He was examining the edges of the clearing as if he expected another lion to jump out.

"I think I fainted," Chloe said, closing her eyes.

"Mama ouchie," Emma said. "Mama sleep."

"More lions?" the stranger asked Helena.

"No more lions," she assured him.

"That's Mateo," Chloe said. "He saved us."

Josh rose to shake the stranger's hand. "I'm Josh. This is Helena."

Mateo nodded politely. *"Mucho gusto."*

Josh didn't understand how Chloe and Emma had ended up on this trail, or where they'd come from. "Why are you here?"

"Hospital," Mateo said, gesturing into the distance.

"You were going to the naval hospital?"

"*Sí.*"

Josh gathered that Mateo was from another country, maybe Mexico. It amazed him that a man who wasn't familiar with the area or the language would do so much to help his sister. Mateo would have had a very difficult time carrying Chloe all the way to the hospital. And yet, he'd seemed willing to try.

Josh contemplated picking her up to continue the journey. It wouldn't be easy, even if they shared the weight. He could get a stretcher or a wheelchair from the hospital and come back for her, but he didn't want to separate. While he considered their options, four National Guardsmen descended on the scene. They charged across the clearing, armed to the gills. Mateo stuck his arms up in surrender at the same time Josh waved in relief.

They were saved.

CHAPTER TWENTY-FOUR

HELENA SPENT THE rest of the morning at the naval hospital with Josh.

It was kind of a madhouse. Chloe had received IV fluids and antibiotics, but no treatment for her wounded leg. The same went for the deep scratches on Helena's upper arm and shoulder. Although one of the nurses had bandaged Helena's wounds, she'd have to wait for stitches. They were scheduled to be evacuated to another hospital soon. A helicopter would take them to Los Angeles or San Bernardino.

Chloe was going to be okay. Her fever was down and she hadn't lost consciousness again. Josh was helping take care of Emma. The little girl seemed happy and healthy.

Helena couldn't believe they were all safe. She'd almost had a heart attack when Josh raced across the meadow to attract Zuma's attention. Without making a conscious decision to, she'd leapt to her feet and followed him, breaking Greg's rule about entering a dangerous situation to help a coworker in trouble. Because he wasn't just a coworker to her. He was more, and he always would be.

She'd aimed the tranquilizer gun at Zuma's carotid artery, praying the needle would hit the mark and deliver the sedative directly into her bloodstream. While intramuscular injections took several minutes to work, the intravenous method was fast. But finding a vein under fur wasn't easy, under the best of circumstances.

Good thing she hadn't missed.

One of the National Guardsmen had been stationed in the field to watch over Zuma. Helena had met with the zoo director and spoken to a group of keepers about an hour ago. They planned to transfer the lioness into a cage, secure the park boundaries and round up the other code ones. They had their work cut out for them.

"Do you want me to stay?" Helena had asked the director.

"Absolutely not," he'd responded. "Get your wounds taken care of and rest for a few days."

She didn't argue, because she needed a break, but it was hard to give up the controls. She always visited the elephants, even when she took time off. Whenever she'd gone on vacation in the past, she'd stayed close to San Diego.

"They'll be fine," Josh said, interrupting her thoughts.

"Who?"

"Your herd. Mbali and the others."

They were waiting for the helicopter in the chaotic hospital lobby. Helena wasn't looking forward to the ride. She took a deep breath to calm her nerves. Emma was sitting in Josh's lap, reading a book about animal noises. She kept pressing the tiger button, listening to the growl over and over.

"She looks like you," Helena said, studying the little girl's sweet brown eyes. Mischief danced in them. "Your sister does, too."

"The Garrisons are handsome devils," he said.

That was true. Emma and Chloe were both adorable. Helena glanced across the room, where the young mother was napping in a rollaway hospital bed. Mateo hadn't left her side. "What do you think about Mateo?"

"I think he's a superhero."

She smiled at this high praise. "What do you think about him and your sister?"

"What do you mean?"

Helena was surprised he hadn't noticed. For the first time ever, she'd picked up on an emotional undercurrent that Josh wasn't aware of. "He didn't find her on the trail, you know. They've been traveling together for days."

Josh couldn't dispute this fact. Mateo had been carrying a backpack with diapers and toys for Emma. The book had been in it. "So?"

"He likes her," Helena said.

Josh studied the young man with suspicion. He was sitting in a chair by Chloe's bed, watching her sleep. "Hmm."

"You don't approve?"

"It's not that," he said, frowning. "I don't care who she dates. I just don't want her to get hurt again."

Helena's chest tightened at those words. If she hadn't already fallen for him, his love for his sister and niece would have tipped her over the edge.

The moment he'd run into the clearing, risking his life for them…done.

"You can't protect her from everything," Helena said.

"I can try."

"She's a grown woman."

He shook his head in disbelief. "She had braces and pigtails a few years ago."

"She had a baby of her own a few years ago."

"Mama," Emma said, pressing the tiger button.

Josh fell silent. He had some fresh scrapes on his elbows, his shirt was dirty, and his pajama pants were ripped at the knee. He was lucky he hadn't been mauled by Zuma. So was Helena. She was still wearing her zoo tank top and pajama bottoms, along with a jacket. One of her sleeves hung in bloody tatters, revealing her bandaged arm. They looked like a couple of escaped mental patients.

She smiled at the thought, moving her gaze from Josh's dirty clothes to his scruffy face. Despite his disheveled appearance, he was achingly handsome. He flipped the page for Emma and pressed a button to make a bird chirp. There was a tenderness in his expression that Helena found irresistible.

He glanced up from the book, noticing her perusal. "What?"

"Nothing."

"You seem upset."

"I've never been in a helicopter before," she said. "I'm terrified."

"Ask them to give you a valium."

"I don't want to go."

A crease formed between his brows. "I can't stay here with you. I have to help my sister and take care of Emma."

Maybe splitting up would be the best option. She needed time apart to gain some perspective, pull herself together. Mooning over him while he held a cute baby wasn't the cure for these runaway feelings.

"The entire hospital is evacuating, and you're injured," he said. "You'd rather walk to a rescue center alone and worry everyone?"

He was right. She hated it when he was right.

"Don't make me call your mother."

"You wouldn't."

"Try me." He issued this challenge with a smile, only half-serious. Teasing her was second nature to him. "It's a short trip to L.A.," he added. "You'll be fine. But if you want someone to relieve your tension, I'm available."

"You're holding a baby."

"I can multitask."

She laughed at his silly joke, raking a hand through her hair. Getting back to civilization meant a hot meal and a shower, cold drinks, a comfortable bed...and Mitch. When she imagined his reaction to her infidelity, she felt sick. He didn't like to lose. She hoped he wouldn't be too angry. Maybe he'd been waiting for an opportunity to break things off with her, and he'd be relieved by the news.

She didn't ask for a sedative, and she regretted this decision as soon as they boarded the helicopter. It was a large military craft with enough space for more than a dozen passengers. She sat down and put her headphones on, trying not to panic.

The L.A. hospitals were all full, so they headed to a facility in neighboring San Bernardino. Although the flight was short, as Josh promised, Helena suffered the duration with clenched fists and a tight stomach. Emma wasn't a fan, either. She cried the majority of the time. Josh and Mateo attempted to quiet her, to no avail. Chloe looked miserable. They were all glad to reach their destination.

The hospital was bursting at the seams with patients in greater need than Helena. Chloe went into surgery for her injured leg. The rest of them took turns playing with Emma in the waiting room. They all sent texts on Josh's cell phone.

Helena bit the bullet and messaged Mitch. She updated him on her condition and location, saying "we need to talk."

It was late afternoon when a nurse practitioner called Helena's name. Josh left Emma with Mateo and accompanied Helena to the cafeteria, which was being used as a treatment area. She had to remove her jacket and tank top. While she sat at a lunch table in her bra, clutching a surgical towel to her chest, the nurse cleaned her wounds and injected a numbing agent.

"I'll be back in a few minutes, after that takes effect," the nurse said.

"You don't have to stay," Helena said to Josh.

"I want to be here for you."

She adjusted the surgical towel over her breasts, uncomfortable. The hospital had run out of gowns, as well as beds. Although it was a little late for modesty, there was a big difference between whipping off her top during a whiskey-fueled sexual encounter and this. She felt emotionally naked, pinned by his gaze.

"You were great with the tranquilizer gun today," he said. "Quick thinking to pop Zuma in the neck."

"I had to do something."

"She would've killed me."

"Yes," Helena said, her throat closing up.

He took her by the hand and brought her knuckles to his lips. Tears filled her eyes at the romantic gesture. She was torn between pulling away from him and dragging him closer. The idea of letting her guard down completely and surrendering to these new feelings scared her. Before she could respond, a disgruntled voice interrupted them.

"What the fuck is this?"

Oh, God. It was Mitch.

He must have flown in from Denver after the earthquake. She didn't know how he'd found her in this madhouse of a hospital, but here he was. He looked back and forth between her and Josh, incredulous.

Josh didn't let go of her hand or move away from her. He shifted into a protective stance, giving a clear signal of possessiveness.

Mitch's eyes narrowed at the sight. He was an intimidating figure, broad-shouldered and square-jawed. His clothes were wrinkled and fatigue lines marred his forehead. He hadn't shaved in several days.

"Why don't you leave us alone to talk?" Helena murmured to Josh.

"Yeah," Mitch said, brimming with anger. "You should run while you can."

Josh didn't budge an inch. "I don't think so."

The nurse returned with the suture materials a second later. "Is there a problem?" she asked warily.

"We can take it outside," Josh said to Mitch.

Helena made a sound of protest, but Mitch loved that idea, and the nurse nodded her approval. Helena couldn't follow them and lose her chance to get treated. She could only watch, helpless, as they walked away, hyped up on testosterone.

The nurse placed a stainless steel tray on the table, offering Helena a tired smile. "Man trouble?"

Helena extended her numb arm, miserable. "I prefer animal trouble."

The woman laughed, snapping on a pair of gloves. "Looks like you've had more than your share of both. This is a lucky wound, though."

"It is?"

She wiped the area with disinfectant solution. "A few inches higher, and I'd be tagging your toe instead of stitching you up."

*

JOSH DIDN'T REMEMBER Mitch being so…big.

Or animated.

In his mind, Helena's boyfriend had been a cardboard cutout, a tall statue in the corner. Expressionless and bland. He rarely deigned to attend their work parties. When he did, he didn't interact with anyone, not even Helena. He was a nonentity.

Now that they were up close, Josh had to reevaluate his opinion. Mitch was a flesh-and-blood man, more than capable of showing anger. He was older than Josh by at least five years. He had severely short brown hair, thinning on top, and a nondescript style. He looked like he lifted weights.

Josh didn't lift weights. For all his military training, he wasn't a tough guy. He didn't want to fight Mitch.

And yet, here they were.

Josh had suggested going outside for a couple of reasons. If Mitch was planning to take a swing at him, he'd rather defend himself in an open space. Fighting inside a hospital was rude. They had personal issues to discuss that strangers didn't need to overhear.

Josh also had Helena's welfare to consider. She was injured and in distress. He couldn't stand the thought of Mitch yelling at her or calling her names. Josh was happy to step in and bear the brunt of Mitch's wrath.

He was also happy to be alive, to be honest. He was happy that Helena was alive, along with Chloe and Emma. This dispute with Mitch didn't matter much to him. If Helena decided to reconcile with her boyfriend, Josh would be heartbroken, but he'd have no regrets.

They passed Mateo and Emma in the hallway. Josh didn't pause to explain. He walked through the main doors and out to a courtyard, where a few dozen people were milling around. There was no private space to conduct their business, no secluded corner. When he reached a grassy area underneath a tree, he stopped and turned around. Mitch already had his hands clenched into fists.

"I just want to talk," Josh said, raising his palms.

"You think I came out here to talk?"

"Give me a chance to explain, and then you can take a free shot."

Mitch wasn't interested in this deal, judging by how fast his fist flew into Josh's face. Josh's head rocked back and pain exploded in his jaw. He stumbled backward, rattled. Mitch had a hell of a right cross.

Damn. Josh was already getting his ass kicked.

"Okay, that was your free shot," Josh said. "The next one won't be."

"Good."

"I didn't mean to take her away from you—"

Mitch punched him again. It wasn't a direct hit, because Josh got wise and sidestepped. He also lowered his shoulder and drove it into Mitch's stomach, taking the fight to the ground. Josh was lighter on his feet than Mitch, but Mitch was a better wrestler. They traded a few more blows, tumbling across the grass. After Josh's run-ins with various wild animals, Mitch's heavy fists felt like hammers on his skin.

Josh maneuvered Mitch into a choke hold, breathing hard. When Mitch finally broke free, they were both winded.

Mitch socked Josh once more in the gut, for good measure. But it didn't carry the same heat as his first strike. Josh moved out of range and sat upright, holding a hand to his aching stomach. Mitch didn't come after him again.

It was a draw.

"I remember you," Mitch panted. "I've shaken your hand, motherfucker."

Josh couldn't deny that they'd met before.

"You're that...*security guard.*"

Josh was a certified law enforcement officer, not a security guard. It rankled that so many people had contempt for his profession.

"You knew about me," Mitch said.

"I knew you left her."

Mitch's mouth twisted at this charge.

"I've always had a crush on her," Josh admitted. "I asked her out once and she said no. Did she tell you that?"

Mitch squinted into the distance, uncertain.

"It was a long time ago," Josh said. "The important part is that she wasn't interested because of you. But then you moved away, and the earthquake hit, and…things changed. We've been through a lot in the past few days."

Mitch closed the distance between them, grabbing Josh by the front of the shirt. "There's only one thing I need to know. Did you fuck her?"

Josh didn't want to lie. He *had* fucked her, whether he'd used his cock or not. Admitting it might be a game changer for Mitch. A lot of men wouldn't take back a woman who'd had sex with someone else. Even so, Josh was reluctant to share the intimate details. He couldn't betray Helena's confidence.

"I'll tell you this," Josh said. "I love her."

Mitch let go of Josh's shirt, appearing stunned. Mitch seemed to realize that this was the bigger issue. He might be able to forgive a sexual affair, but Helena's feelings for Josh were paramount. Would she continue to deny them?

"I haven't told her yet," Josh said. "If she picks you over me, I'll walk away. I won't interfere in your relationship."

"You won't interfere in our relationship, really? That's great, man. You're a real saint."

Josh revised his opinion of Helena's boyfriend again. He wasn't a robot. He was more of a sarcastic prick.

Mitch got up and dusted off. "If we weren't surrounded by injured, suffering people, I'd beat you to a pulp."

"Be my guest. Just don't lay a finger on Helena."

"Fuck you," Mitch said tiredly. "Fuck you for even saying that."

After Mitch left, Josh rose to his feet. They hadn't drawn a big crowd, but there were a number of curious onlookers. It was pretty embarrassing. Josh crossed the courtyard, his jaw aching. There was nothing more he could do to prove his love to Helena. Fighting with Mitch hadn't solved anything.

She had to make her own decision.

CHAPTER TWENTY-FIVE

HELENA GRITTED HER teeth as the nurse placed the final few sutures.

Although the local anesthetic had numbed the affected area, the lacerations on her shoulder went deep. She could feel the needle piercing her skin and the sutures pulling through her wounds. It was uncomfortable, to say the least.

Mitch returned to the cafeteria without Josh. He didn't look much worse for the wear. His clothes were dusty and he had a red mark on his left cheekbone. She was irritated with Josh for suggesting they go outside, and with Mitch for taking him up on the offer. It was pointless. She wasn't a prize to be bandied back and forth.

To his credit, Mitch's demeanor wasn't exactly victorious. If he'd won, he'd taken no pleasure in it. He was a competitive person, physical in many respects, but more of a thinker than a brawler. She couldn't have guessed how he'd react to her affair with Josh. Although his aggressive response didn't surprise her, a cold dismissal seemed more like him.

He didn't say anything, and the nurse continued working. When Helena winced in pain, he reached out to hold her hand. She accepted the gesture, swallowing hard.

After months apart, his hand felt like a foreign object. It was large and strong, pale from the cold Denver winter. His knuckles were scraped, like Josh's.

The nurse finished the sutures and placed a bandage over Helena's shoulder. Then she left them in the overflowing cafeteria, moving on to the next patient.

Helena let go of Mitch's hand and straightened her clothing. When she was decent, she met his gaze warily. "Did you fly in?"

"No, I drove straight through as soon as I heard."

She nodded, feeling miserable. "Long trip."

"Yeah."

"Have you slept?"

"I got a few hours last night. They wouldn't let civilians into the city, so I volunteered at one of the evacuation centers. Gwen was there. She left earlier today."

Helena was relieved to hear about her friend. "I'm glad she's okay."

He asked about her injury, and she gave him an abbreviated version of this morning's events. It was awkward to talk about Josh after Mitch had walked in on them together. "I don't know what to say."

"I think that's why we're in this position."

He was referring to their lack of communication. She couldn't argue. "I'm sorry."

"So am I."

She couldn't believe he'd driven all the way from Denver. Her betrayal must have felt like a slap in the face.

"I can't blame you for…whatever happened with that guy," Mitch said. "I don't like it, but I understand. I've been gone for months. Even before I left, we were struggling. I wasn't providing for you."

"I didn't care about that—"

"I wasn't satisfying you."

She fell silent, unable to disagree.

A muscle in his jaw flexed. "I knew you weren't happy, and I knew the long-distance thing wasn't working out, but I didn't expect this."

"Neither did I."

"I feel like a fool."

"No," she said, guilt-stricken. "You're not."

"I am. I left a beautiful woman alone and unfulfilled."

She shook her head in denial. He was killing her—and she deserved every word.

"I thought you'd miss me."

"I did."

"You have a funny way of showing it."

Her stomach clenched in regret. There was nothing she could say to make this better. No amount of apologizing would ease the hurt she'd caused.

"You didn't ask me to come back," he said.

"You didn't ask me to move to Denver, either."

"Would you have considered it?"

"No."

"You always loved your elephants more than me," he said with a wry smile.

"That's not true," she said, but it was a weak protest. When the going got tough between them, she'd retreated into work. Because, as dangerous as elephants could be, interacting with them felt safer. She could love them from afar. They didn't expect her to communicate or provide emotional support. They didn't count on her for anything but basic care.

He rubbed a hand over his mouth, pensive. "My boss has been looking into a new job site in Southern California. If everything works out, I might be able to transfer."

She stared at him in shock.

"I was hoping to surprise you with the news in person."

They'd scheduled a visit for early summer, because he hadn't been able to get away over the holidays. She'd been planning to talk with him then. If she'd known he was considering a return to the area, she might have felt better about their relationship. So much for her selfish wishes that Mitch would be relieved by the breakup.

"I can see that I shouldn't have waited," he said.

"Why did you?"

"I wasn't sure you wanted me back, to be honest. You've been distant. We haven't talked about staying together."

"We haven't talked much, period."

"I know," he said. "I take responsibility for that."

She didn't like the way he was maneuvering her into a passive role. She wasn't a dog who'd escaped and roamed the neighborhood because of a derelict owner. She was a woman who'd made a conscious choice to disregard their commitment. He had every right to be angry.

"This is my fault," he said.

"It's *not* your fault."

"I left you unattended."

"And I dug under the fence?"

His determined gaze met hers. "You made a mistake. I can overlook it."

She inhaled a sharp breath. "You can?"

"I still love you."

The words were like a dagger, straight through her heart. His forgiveness was so much harder to accept than his anger. She believed he meant what he said, but she also knew him. He was stubborn and competitive. He couldn't stand losing her to another man.

"Do you remember when I took that pregnancy test?" she asked.

"Of course."

"I was disappointed when it turned out negative."

He seemed baffled by this news. "Why?"

"I guess I changed my mind about having kids, after Mbali."

"You're kidding."

"No."

"I had no idea."

She hadn't told him for the same reason they hadn't talked about their other problems. Some differences were impossible to overcome. "I was going to say something about it, but then you lost your job, and we drifted apart. Instead of reaching out to you, I withdrew."

He didn't understand. He was the type of person who preferred to fix things on his own. Taking responsibility for her affair was his way of staying in control. "Why are you telling me this?"

She struggled with her answer. It didn't matter if Mitch came back to San Diego or reversed his stance about having a family. He was a good man, and she'd always care about him, but she didn't want to reunite with him. They couldn't salvage their relationship. "I should have been honest about my feelings back then. The only thing I can do is be honest now. I'm not in love with you anymore."

He flinched at those harsh words. "Maybe you never were."

She couldn't blame him for lashing out at her, but his lack of faith hurt. They hadn't been the most affectionate couple, but she'd loved him. She still loved him, in a way. It was like a fading pulse, almost indiscernible.

When she was with Josh, her heart galloped wildly.

Her feelings for Josh weren't going away anytime soon. She realized that now, and she was starting to adjust. The intensity of emotion scared her. It was the difference between riding the aerial tram and dangling from the side. That second experience had made the first seem tame.

She couldn't say she wasn't afraid of what the future might hold. Josh was more of a challenge than Mitch. He'd probably annoy her as often as he made her laugh. The highs would be higher and the lows would be lower. But he'd be a true partner, sharing his soul with her, working alongside her without taking over.

There were no guarantees, of course. They might burn out as fast as they'd flared up. Even if they did, she wouldn't regret her decision to end her relationship with Mitch. She wasn't right for him; they were too similar. He'd be an excellent match for someone else. When he found a woman who suited him, he'd recognize that.

For now, he was just pissed off. He walked away from Helena and strode through the cafeteria with his hands clenched into fists. Josh was waiting by the door. As Mitch passed by, he shoved Josh into the hallway, sending him sprawling.

Then he kept going and didn't look back.

*

JOSH COULDN'T BELIEVE IT.

She'd picked *him* over Mitch.

He'd watched their entire conversation from a distance, and he could read body language. Mitch was no dummy. He wanted to keep Helena for himself. Who wouldn't? She was a fine-ass woman, strong and smart and sexy. She managed elephants and wrestled lions. She was basically a dream come true, better than any comic-book fantasy.

And she wanted him, Josh Garrison.

Hoo-yah.

He didn't even care about Mitch's late hit. Josh scrambled to his feet, his blood pumping. Nothing could knock him down right now; he was high on emotion. He straightened the chair he'd tipped over in a clumsy rush.

Helena approached him with a smile. She was holding her jacket under one arm. Her left shoulder was bandaged, her tank top bloody and frayed.

He was suddenly unsure of himself. She might have told Mitch to take a hike, but that didn't mean she was ready for a replacement boyfriend. Mitch hadn't signed over her ownership papers in the process of trading punches.

"You need some ice," she said, touching the side of his face.

"You should see the other guy."

"I did."

"How'd he look?"

"Like the winner."

"I went easy on him."

She rolled her eyes at this lie.

"He wasn't the winner," Josh pointed out. "I'm the one here with you."

"Maybe that was his choice."

"No."

She glanced away, shrugging. She looked a little sad. Her conversation with Mitch couldn't have been pleasant.

"Is there anything I need to know?" he asked.

"Like what?"

"I won't stand for him calling you names."

"He didn't."

Josh was glad to hear it. "How's your shoulder?"

"Fine. I'll get the stitches out next week."

"You're lucky that swipe didn't hit you in the neck."

"That's what the nurse said."

He rubbed his sore jaw, contemplative. "Let's go find some ice."

They spent the next hour with Emma and Mateo while Chloe recovered from surgery. Volunteers passed out drinks and snacks in the waiting area, which was nice. The woman sitting next to Mateo chatted with him in Spanish. She had four children with her of various ages, and they all spoke English.

"Can you translate for me?" Josh asked the oldest boy. He had a lip ring and long bangs that he kept flipping to the side.

"Sure," he said, shrugging.

"I'm Josh."

"Daniel."

"Good to meet you, Daniel. I just want to know what happened to my sister."

Mateo told Daniel that he'd been on a bus with his soccer team, crossing over the Coronado Bridge. The earthquake struck, and some of the vehicles plummeted into the bay. One of them was a red car. His sister's. Mateo said he knew she had a chance to survive the fall because the bridge was only half-collapsed at this point. They were about fifty feet above the surface. He made a wave motion with his hand, indicating that the water below was choppy. He watched her car sink.

"My God," Helena murmured, leaning in to listen.

Mateo went on to say that he swam after Chloe, but he couldn't find her.

Josh interrupted him. "Wait. How did you get in the water?"

"I jump," Mateo said.

"No."

"Yes," he said, nodding. Mateo said that his teammates had discouraged him from climbing out of the bus. But he did it anyway, and he jumped off the side of the bridge. Seconds later, that section of the bridge fell into the bay, taking the bus with it. As far as he knew, none of the men on board had survived.

"Wow," Josh said.

Mateo fell silent for a moment, saddened by this loss. The woman next to him made a sign of the cross. Then he continued the story. By some miracle, the current swept him toward Chloe and Emma. When he saw that she had a child, he took Emma and swam to shore. Then he came back for Chloe.

And that was just the beginning of their adventures.

Mateo talked about hiding from the fires the first day, and traveling most of the next. This morning, Chloe had been feverish when she woke up. She shouldn't have been walking, he said. They were on Birdie Trail when she fainted.

"I don't know how to thank you," Josh said.

"No thanks necessary," Daniel answered, translating.

Josh shook Mateo's hand, and Daniel's hand. The story blew him away. Josh didn't think he'd have had the balls to jump off a bridge to save his own sister, let alone a complete stranger. He knew he couldn't rescue anyone from a sinking vehicle. What Mateo had done for Chloe and Emma was nothing short of amazing.

As evening fell on the third day after the earthquake, Emma drifted off in Josh's arms. Chloe was safe in the recovery room. Helena laced her fingers through his and rested her head on his shoulder, sharing the peaceful moment with him.

They were alive, and they were together, and that was more than enough.

CHAPTER TWENTY-SIX

CHLOE DOZED OFF and on, dreaming about wild animals.

In one, a crouching cat leapt from the bushes and onto the okapi's back, digging its powerful claws into zebra-striped hindquarters. In another, Emma pressed a button on her book to send the events into motion. When she made the tiger growl, the animal appeared before her, conjured from the page.

Chloe was told that her surgery had been a success. She got transferred to a smaller room. There were at least two other patients behind curtained partitions. A nurse helped her use the restroom and removed her IV. Chloe fell asleep again, waking at sunset.

Josh was there.

Tears flooded her eyes at the sight of him. She thought he'd been with her this morning by the nature trail, and later at the naval hospital. But dreams and reality had blurred together, leaving her confused about which was which. "Where's Emma?"

"In the waiting room, asleep."

"With Mateo?"

"Yes."

Josh offered her a sip of water from a straw and adjusted her bed so she could sit up. Then he took a seat by the windowsill. His clothes were dirty and torn. He had unruly stubble, scrapes on his face and bandages on his arms.

"You look terrible."

"I've had a rough day."

"What happened?"

"You don't remember?"

When she shook her head, he told her the story. Her stomach tightened as she imagined how close to death he'd come. How close Emma had come.

He cleared his throat, looking out the window. It was getting dark. There were other people in the room, talking to other patients. She couldn't see them, but she could hear their voices beyond the curtains. "Mom and Dad are on their way. They couldn't get a flight to L.A., so they're driving in."

Chloe pulled back the blanket to study her wound. It was puckered and L-shaped, with ugly black sutures. She'd have a scar there, much more pronounced than the ones on her arm. That was okay. This scar would be a source of pride, rather than shame. It would be a symbol of her will to live, a sign of strength.

"I'm sorry for yelling at you and Emma the other night," he said.

She had to stretch her mind to remember the minor incident. It seemed like months ago. "You're apologizing for that? What about the time you locked me in a closet so you could smoke pot with your friends in the backyard?"

"I'm serious."

"So am I. That was traumatic."

"I love you, Chloe."

She was touched by his sentimental declaration. He'd always been affectionate, but he didn't say those words often. He must have been really worried about them. "I love you, too," she said, blinking away tears.

"I can't thank Mateo enough for saving you guys."

She wondered what Mateo's plans were now that they were safe. He might go back to Panama and never return.

"We spoke through a translator earlier. He told me he jumped off the bridge for you."

"He jumped?"

"You didn't know?"

She shook her head in awe. The impact with the water could have killed him. He'd risked his life to rescue her.

"Would you have survived otherwise?"

"I doubt it. I was tangled in my cardigan, already weak from cold. I could barely hang on to Emma."

Josh nodded grimly.

"He practically carried us across the city."

"That's what I gathered. He seems pretty attached to you and Emma."

She wasn't sure how to respond. The feeling was mutual.

"Is he your new boyfriend?"

"Did he tell you that?" she asked, startled.

"No."

When Josh arched a brow, she realized he'd been teasing. Embarrassed, she adjusted the blanket over her lap.

"Something going on between you two?" he asked.

"Nothing you need to know about."

"Maybe I should go ask him what his intentions are."

"Stop."

He smiled, leaning back in his chair.

"I like him," she admitted. "I don't care what language he speaks. Do you think that's weird?"

"It's a little unorthodox."

"Mom wouldn't approve."

"She doesn't have to, does she?"

He was a good brother. She remembered seeing him with a woman earlier. "Is your coworker still here?"

"Yes. Her name is Helena."

"Something going on between you two?"

"I hope so." He glanced toward the doorway, as if eager to get back to her.

"You don't have to stay with me."

"I'll send in Romeo."

"Mateo," she corrected, her lips twitching. Then she touched her disheveled hair, trying to smooth the tangles. Mateo had already seen her wet, bedraggled, sick and unconscious, so maybe it didn't matter how she looked.

He arrived a few minutes later with a teenage boy.

"I'm Daniel," the boy said.

Chloe shook his hand. "Pleased to meet you."

"Mateo wanted me to translate."

"Oh." She didn't know if communicating this way would be more awkward, or less. "Okay."

There was only one chair, so Mateo offered it to Daniel. The boy sat down, arranging his bangs over his forehead. He was wearing a black T-shirt, shorts and black tennis shoes.

Mateo stood next to him. His white soccer jersey had some red licorice smudges on the sleeve. Like Josh, he looked a little rough around the edges. His eyes were dark with concern, his jaw shadowed with grains of stubble.

Still hot.

He was so handsome and appealing that she almost didn't want to ruin it by talking. Too much reality might break the magic spell.

There were questions she was afraid to ask. If he was going back to Panama. If he had a girlfriend.

"How are you?" he asked in English.

"Better."

"Good."

After a short pause, he spoke to Daniel in rapid-fire Spanish.

Daniel listened carefully and turned to Chloe. "He said he hopes he didn't make your leg worse with too much activity."

She blushed, unsure if he meant last night's activities or the walk this morning. "I'm fine. It was my choice to…be active."

Daniel translated for Mateo again. "He should have let you rest."

"I didn't want to rest," she said. "I enjoyed not resting."

Mateo smiled, needing no translation for this exchange. Chloe suspected that Daniel knew exactly what they were talking about. He was at least fourteen, and old enough to pick up on the subtext.

"Can you ask him where he's staying, and what his plans are?" she asked.

This question required a detailed response. Mateo said that he was in San Diego for an international soccer tournament. His team had spent the week at the local youth hostel. A scout had noticed him during one of the games and offered him a spot on an L.A. college team, along with a two-year scholarship. He'd accepted. Assuming the deal went through, he wasn't going home anytime soon.

Chloe was thrilled for him. "What about after that?"

Daniel listened to Mateo's answer. "He wants to play soccer. He doesn't care where."

Fair enough. "Will he miss Panama?"

"He will, but there are better opportunities for him in the U.S."

There was one more thing she had to know before this went any further. "Does he have a girlfriend back home?"

Mateo said something to Daniel and gestured toward the door.

"He says he can take it from here," Daniel said.

Chloe felt a twinge of anxiety. Before the boy walked away, she said, "Wait. Can you tell me what *mamita* means?"

Daniel smirked at the question. "Depends on who you're talking to. It can mean little girl, mother, or sexy lady."

"Thank you," Chloe said to Daniel. He was cute.

After Daniel left, Mateo brought the chair closer to her bedside and sat down. She reached out to hold his hand. "No girlfriend?"

"Solo tú."

"Only me?"

He nodded. *"Si quieres."*

If she wanted to be.

She didn't even have to think about it. Communication between them was bound to improve in the months to come. He'd only been here a few weeks and he already understood quite a bit of English. They'd make it work.

Maybe they were an unusual couple, but she was an unusual girl. She couldn't worry about strangers looking down on them, or even her mother. They had a special connection. They were both survivors. She liked his dark good looks and the sound of his voice, but his words and actions meant a lot more to her. He was brave, and strong, and kind. If people said they had nothing in common, they were wrong.

"Okay," she said, agreeing. "I will."

He grinned, squeezing her hand. Then he gestured to her leg. *"A ver?"*

When she showed him the jagged row of black stitches on her upper thigh, he swore under his breath.

"It looks worse than it feels," she said.

He braced a hand on her knee and kissed the soft skin above the sutures. She shooed him away and covered the exposed area with her hospital gown, flushing. If he kept that up, she was going to get feverish again.

"Mouth here?" he asked, lifting his lips to hers.

She twined her arms around his neck with a happy sigh. "Mouth here."

CHAPTER TWENTY-SEVEN

HELENA STAYED AT the hospital with Josh for several more hours.

She met his parents in the waiting area. They were an attractive couple, concerned for Chloe and frazzled from the long trip. Josh introduced Helena as his girlfriend, earning a dirty look from her. But he also introduced Mateo as Chloe's boyfriend, and they didn't seem to take that news seriously.

Josh told his parents he and Helena had to leave because she was injured and needed rest. Although she could use the sleep, she suspected that his motives for whisking her away weren't completely altruistic. He winked at her as they said goodbye, as if his plans for the night involved something other than relaxing.

The problem with sneaking off to be alone together was that they didn't have anywhere to go, other than a crowded evacuation center. Finding a hotel near the hospital was impossible. There wasn't a vacancy in all of Southern California, and transportation options were limited. Flights had been canceled and rental cars were booked. They ended up taking a tour bus to his hometown of San Luis Obispo.

Josh looked on the bright side. "At least my parents won't be there."

It was a long ride, more than four hours, but they made good use of the time. She curled up next to him and fell asleep. He drifted off, too. Before she knew it, they'd arrived at the bus station. From there, they took a cab to his house.

The Garrisons were comfortable, rather than rich. They had a modest home in a nice neighborhood. The front yard was perfectly manicured and the interior was spotless. There were pictures of Emma all over the walls. Josh went straight to the kitchen and drank juice out of the container like a rebellious teenager.

"No dog?" she asked, glancing around.

"My mom doesn't like dogs. Or cats."

"She seems a little high-strung."

He nodded in agreement. "My dad is pretty mellow, so they balance each other out. Are you hungry?"

"Starving."

His parents had been on vacation, so there wasn't much to choose from. He made scrambled eggs with cheese and olives. It was her first hot meal since the earthquake, and deliciously simple. After they both ate their fill, he took her on a tour. His dad had a study downstairs, and there was a wine cellar for his mom.

The bedrooms were upstairs. Chloe's room had an edgy, eclectic style, with lots of black and dark purple accents. There were stuffed animals on the bed and a crib in the corner. It was a mix of teen angst, young mother and Goth girl. Josh didn't linger here.

His room must have been redecorated in the past ten years. There were no rock 'n' roll posters on the walls or baseball trophies on the shelf. It was a basic guest space with a four-poster bed and a vaguely nautical theme.

"Where's Wonder Woman?" she asked.

He went to the desk and opened a drawer, rifling through the contents. When he found a frayed comic, he tossed it to her.

She flopped on the bed and flipped through the pages, giggling in delight. "Is this from your secret stash?"

"Not really a secret. They aren't porn."

The images weren't explicit, but they were plenty sexy. Scantily clad women brandished weapons and did high kicks. They were muscular and voluptuous, striking exaggerated poses. "You never read these one-handed?"

He laughed, shaking his head. "If I could have taken them into the shower, they might have had a little more stroke mileage."

"Who fights in a vinyl bikini?"

"Chain-mail bikinis are better," he agreed. "See-through."

Helena found a page with a catlike vixen on all fours. She left the book open on the bed and tried to mimic the posture. It was impossible to contort her body into the right shape. Josh laughed at her attempt, clearly enjoying the view.

"I can't get my tits to bounce up and my ass to pop out at the same time," she said, twisting her midsection.

"Arch your back more."

She looked over her shoulder at him. "Like this?"

"You're making me horny."

"Are there any pictures of Wonder Woman tied up?"

He joined her on the bed, gripping her hips tight and pressing himself against her upright bottom. "Let's take a shower, and we can recreate any scenario you like," he said, his hands roving over her breasts.

They stayed on the bed for a few minutes, kissing and touching. Then they moved into the bathroom, still entwined. He didn't want her stitches to get wet, so he filled the tub. They brushed their teeth while they waited, sharing the sink. When the tub was ready, he helped her climb inside. She groaned as the luxurious heat enveloped her. He settled in behind her, causing water to slosh over the rim.

"Uh-oh," he said. "I'm going to get grounded for that."

She laughed, resting her head on his shoulder. He soaped her breasts and toyed with her nipples, his erection nudging her buttocks. She thought he might let his fingertips wander south, but he didn't. He washed her hair carefully, pouring water from an empty vase. Although he was still hard, he didn't rush.

When he was finished, he pressed a tender kiss to her nape. "Scoot forward."

She did, giving him space to wash his own hair. He dumped water over his head and shampooed quickly, not bothering with conditioner.

She released the plug after he rinsed, letting the water drain. His cock bobbed above the surface. She wanted to turn around and plaster her wet, naked body against his. Instead he grabbed her hips and pulled her bottom into his lap. "Let's fuck like elephants," he said in her ear.

"Your dirty talk is terrible."

"Pretend I'm too big to fit inside you."

He was half-silly, half-serious. Her breath quickened as he cupped her breasts. "Elephants can't do it in a bathtub."

"What about a bed?"

She didn't say no, so he helped her out of the tub and dried her off with a towel. They returned to the bedroom. His erection was pretty impressive. Not elephant-sized, or too large for her to handle. Just right.

She crawled across the bed on all fours, torn between embarrassment and arousal. "If you were really an elephant, you'd have to test me first."

"How?"

"With your trunk."

He sank to his knees on the floor, running his hands along the backs of her thighs. She quivered with excitement as he nuzzled her sex from behind. He used his tongue to taste her, dipping inside. He went way beyond a sample, but she didn't complain. She rested her elbows on the bed and tilted her hips, spreading her legs wider. He indulged her unspoken request, kissing and nibbling her until she felt like screaming.

"I think you're ready," he said, rising to his feet.

She'd been ready before he started.

He gripped the base of his cock and rubbed the tip against her opening. His penis slid over her clitoris, back and forth through her slippery folds. It was maddening. She wanted him inside her, and he was everywhere else.

"Please," she whimpered.

"Please what? Spray you with my hose?"

She groaned and collapsed on her stomach. Her shoulder hurt, so she rolled over and parted her thighs. "Fuck me."

He studied her brazen display with lust-dark eyes, his cock shiny and straining. Then he found a condom in the same drawer as the comic book. After glancing at the date, he tore the package open and rolled it over his length.

"Hurry," she said, moistening her lips.

"I should have tied you up. You have no patience." He positioned himself over her, lifted her leg onto his shoulder and thrust into her.

"Oh, God."

"It's Josh."

"Unhh," she said, beyond words.

He withdrew and slid home, over and over again, filling her with glorious precision. It felt so good she couldn't do anything but make incoherent noises of encouragement, gritting her teeth in ecstasy.

Yes. More. Oh.

Instead of building to a powerful crescendo, he slowed down. He switched positions, fitting her legs around his waist and bracing his arms near her head. Her breasts bounced against his chest as he drove into her, hard and deep. Buried to the hilt, he touched his lips to her neck. "Can you get off like this, with just my cock in you?"

"No."

"Good," he said, panting.

"Why is that good?"

"I don't want you to come too fast."

She gasped, digging her nails into his skin. He continued to move in and out, thrusting his hands into her hair and his tongue into her mouth.

It didn't last forever, despite his best efforts. He went still above her, his shoulders quaking from the power of his release. After a long, sweaty moment of crushing her beneath his weight, he rolled away and disposed of the condom. Then he joined her in bed again.

"How was it?"

She studied his smirk with suspicion. "You forgot something."

"What's that?"

"I'm going to punch you."

He laughed, sliding his hand between her legs. "Is this it?"

She was swollen and sensitive, trembling with need. He dipped inside, getting his fingers slick with her arousal. Then he stroked her clitoris in rhythmic circles. She bit down on her lower lip to hold back a whimper.

"I like to watch your face when you come," he said, kissing her flushed cheek. "Your body is…fucking hot, but I love your mouth and the sexy little sounds you make. Your eyelashes flutter and you…"

She exploded under the sensual onslaught, gripping his wrist and crying out his name. The orgasm undulated through her, bright and bursting. It seemed to go on forever. His touch gentled but didn't waver, wrenching more pleasure from her shuddering flesh.

God.

She was a ball of wax with a heartbeat. Eyes closed, she lay there like a limp rag, rapturously spent.

"I love you," he said.

The words floated over her, feather-light. She felt a buzzing-plane sensation, but it was just her blood pounding with post-orgasmic bliss. Nothing could rattle her right now. "You can't spring that on me while I'm in a sex coma."

"I put you in the coma, so I think I can."

"It's cheating."

"Cheating would be saying it before I let you come."

That would *definitely* be playing dirty.

"I won't cheat, though," he said. "I don't need to cheat. I'll be the best time you ever had, not just the best fuck."

She opened her eyes to study him. He'd already been both, and he probably knew it. But she wasn't as free and easy with her feelings as he was. She wasn't going to say she loved him until she was ready. "You're overconfident, aren't you?"

"I'm just the right amount of confident."

"You said I wouldn't be able to walk when we were done."

"Can you walk?"

She laughed, too languid to move.

"I rest my case."

CHAPTER TWENTY-EIGHT

One month later

HELENA STOOD ON the stage next to Josh, touched by the thunderous applause of the crowd.

They'd both received public service awards in a large ceremony at Grape Day Park. There were much more deserving recipients among them. Firefighters and police officers and EMTs. As a zookeeper, Helena felt out of place. They were the real heroes, but she couldn't insult the mayor by refusing to participate.

It was a beautiful day, balmy and mild. Everyone on the stage had a unique story of bravery and often heartache. The dead were honored, as well as the living. Greg Patel was mentioned as having given his life in an attempt to protect others. Tears burned in Helena's eyes as his picture lingered on a screen above the stage. His family wasn't in attendance. She'd visited Greg's wife and daughters a few weeks ago to pay her respects. They were in mourning, and not going out in public.

Among the survivors was an EMT who'd been trapped in her ambulance when the freeway collapsed. Helena noticed how pretty the woman was when they were introduced.

There was another young lady in the audience who'd given birth in the rubble after the collapse. She was dark-haired and gorgeous, holding a healthy newborn baby.

After the ceremony, Helena and Josh parted ways to mingle with the crowd. Josh shook hands with the attractive women, but he didn't linger or flirt with them. Helena chatted with the zoo's director for a few minutes, and accepted a hug from Kim, her coworker. Every time she looked for Josh, he was watching her. It was a little disconcerting.

Gwen was here. She'd come to offer moral support, and because she liked social events. Helena had endured many parties simply by standing next to Gwen, who was friendly and vibrant enough for both of them. That was one of the reasons they got along so well. Gwen was also a bit of a misfit, like Helena. Today she was wearing a sleeveless print dress with a stretchy black belt. A koi fish tattoo glittered on her upper arm.

Gwen had encouraged Helena to spruce up her boring keeper uniform for the occasion. She'd paired her khaki blouse with a fitted skirt and high heels. She almost topped Josh with the extra boost in height. But he'd whistled with approval when he saw her, so she'd stood up straight and tall beside him.

"Your new boyfriend is hot," Gwen said, taking a sip of champagne.

Helena murmured an agreement.

Josh wore his security officer uniform with pride. His shirt was ironed and starched, his shoes polished. He'd gotten a haircut the other day. He'd always been handsome, but right now he was dazzling.

"How's it going between you two?"

"Good," Helena said, smiling to herself. She'd never been better.

They'd spent a few days at his parents' house, recuperating with Chloe. Helena's mother had wanted to visit, but Helena advised her to wait. Thousands of people had died in the earthquake and the city was in shambles. She hadn't been able to return to her apartment to assess the damages for more than a week.

The zoo was still closed for repairs. Freeways had been rerouted and construction was heavily underway throughout the downtown area. Helena had gone back to work. The elephants needed to be cared for, whether the wildlife park was open for business or not. Most of her coworkers were fine. Josh's security partner was here today, along with his wife. Josh hugged Cordell and kissed Amelia on the cheek.

Trent wasn't in the crowd, and neither was Louis. Trent had reunited with Melody after the earthquake, but they'd broken up since. Helena hadn't heard the whole story. Sometimes tragedy brought people together; other times it tore them apart.

Josh wasn't needed at the zoo, so he'd volunteered with the Red Cross. He'd been helping with the rescue and recovery efforts all month. Outside of work, they'd spent every waking moment together. She'd slept at his place more nights than she'd been home. He couldn't seem to get enough of her. She hadn't grown tired of him, either.

She didn't think she would.

Chloe had healed from her injury and returned to San Diego with Emma. Mateo was staying in L.A. with his new team, but he'd visited a few times. Last week, Josh and Helena had watched Emma while the young couple went on a date. They were taking it slow, which earned Josh's seal of approval.

Gwen drained her champagne glass quickly. "I have to tell you something," she said in a nervous rush.

"What?"

"You know I saw Mitch at the evacuation center."

Helena nodded. Gwen had mentioned it in passing. So had Mitch. He'd called Gwen after the earthquake to ask if she'd heard from Helena. They'd both volunteered at the same center while they were waiting for more news.

"We kind of…well, we were worried about you."

"I was fine."

"You were getting attacked by animals left and right."

That was an exaggeration. She'd also been drinking whiskey and having wild monkey sex with Josh.

"Mitch really pitched in to help," Gwen said. "We were working side by side for hours, and we talked a lot…."

"Mitch talked a lot?" Helena said. "My Mitch?"

"He's not your Mitch anymore."

"Oh," she said, taken aback. "Wow."

Gwen's pretty face contorted into a grimace. "I didn't mean it like that."

"Even if you did, I'm the last person to criticize."

"That's not true, Helena. I've been your best friend since sixth grade. I wouldn't make a move on your boyfriend."

Helena waited for her to continue, suspecting there was more to the story.

"The thing is…I knew it was over between you."

"Did you tell him that?"

"No," she said. "But I felt it, and I started looking at him in a new way. He was lifting heavy stuff, and getting sweaty, and…"

"You wanted him."

"Yes."

Helena didn't see the problem. Finding a man attractive wasn't a crime. "I'm not sure why you're telling me this if nothing happened."

"Something happened. After your breakup."

"I see," Helena said. Mitch had been angry. So angry he'd slept with her best friend.

"I feel awful," Gwen said.

"Because he used you?"

"No, I didn't mind that part. He was really sweet about it, actually."

"Sweet?"

"He's called me a few times. I'm thinking about going to visit him."

Helena raked a hand through her hair, unsure how to react. This was what Gwen had been getting at. If she'd had a one-night stand with Mitch, she could've kept it to herself. The real issue was that she wanted to *date* him.

"Are you mad?" Gwen asked.

Helena picked up a flute of champagne from a nearby tray. "No."

"I need another one of those."

Helena gave her a frosty glass. "I'm just…surprised. Is he planning to stay in Denver?"

"He doesn't know yet."

"And this thing between you two is serious."

"It might be."

Helena sipped her champagne, pondering this strange turn of events. "He'd better come back to San Diego," she said finally. "I don't want you to move away."

Gwen's dark eyes filled with tears. "You don't hate me?"

"No, Gwennie," Helena said, putting her arms around her friend. "I love you."

They broke apart, and Gwen found a napkin to dab her eyes. Josh excused himself from the crowd to join them.

"What's up?" he asked Helena.

"Gwen is dating Mitch."

"Your Mitch?"

"He's her Mitch now."

Josh arched a brow at Gwen. "Mitch has good taste."

Gwen laughed, wiping her eyes again.

"If he doesn't treat you right, let me know," Josh said. "I beat him up once and I'm not afraid to do it again."

"I'll keep that in mind," Gwen said, smiling.

Josh smiled back at her.

Gwen handed her empty glass to Helena. "I'm sorry," she said abruptly. "I need to go for a walk and clear my head."

"I'll come with you."

"No. Stay and enjoy yourself."

Although Helena protested, Gwen gave her a hug and left, clutching a red handbag under one arm. Her spike heels dug into the grass as she crossed the park. Then she strode down the sidewalk, hips swaying.

"Should I go after her?" Helena asked.

He shrugged. "She's a grown woman."

"I can see you noticed."

He moved his gaze from Gwen's curvy form to Helena's bemused face. He'd probably never stop admiring pretty ladies. "Have I told you how hot you look today?" he asked, sliding his arm around her waist.

"Nice save."

"When can we leave? I have something special planned."

Her stomach fluttered with anticipation. "You're ready to go?"

"Sure."

He took her out to dinner at a place called the Elephant Bar. It was a global fusion restaurant with a lot of elephant statues and tiki torches. They took their seats at a quiet table in the corner near a gold Buddha.

"I hope they don't serve elephant here," she said in a stage whisper.

"Maybe we can order King Cobra."

Almost all of the code ones had been recovered within days of the earthquake. Bambang, Zuma and Tau were safe and sound in their enclosures. The okapi, the cheetah and other escapees had been caught and returned. King was found in a drainage pipe near the flamingo pond. The only casualties were a pair of aggressive hyenas that had attacked injured humans in the downtown area. Both animals had been shot and killed.

Josh had taken her out for a steak dinner weeks ago, as promised. Tonight she ordered honey shrimp, while he tried the Mongolian beef. Her dish had a sweet, spicy sauce that was quite delicious. He watched her eat with pleasure, his eyes glittering.

"Do you want one?" she asked.

He leaned across the table to take a bite, licking the sauce from her fingers. When they were finished, he didn't seem in any hurry to leave. She got the impression that he wanted to talk to her about something important.

"I have an interview with the Coast Guard on Monday," he said. "They have openings in the San Diego division of maritime law enforcement."

She hadn't known he was considering a job change. "What about the zoo?"

"I'd have to resign."

"I thought you loved it there."

"I do," he said, meeting her gaze. "I like the combination of environmental science and public service. The Coast Guard can offer me that, too, but with more opportunities for advancement."

"And more opportunities to get shot at."

"There's a certain amount of danger involved," he admitted.

She studied the Buddha in the corner, annoyed with his happy face.

"You look upset."

"Should I be ecstatic?"

"You're the one who said I wasn't challenging myself."

"That was before I—" *Fell in love with you.*

"Before you what?"

They hadn't talked about love since the first night. He'd made good on his promise to keep her well-satisfied, in and out of the bedroom. She enjoyed his company. He didn't care about socializing with friends as much as she'd figured he would. They were both content to stay home and relax, or spend an afternoon at the beach.

He hadn't pressed her about the future, either. She'd been expecting him to. He seemed so crazy about her, so intent on winning her over. She wouldn't have been surprised if he'd brought her here to propose.

"Is this part of your campaign to convince me that we're meant to be together and you'll do anything for me?" she asked.

"I will do anything for you, but this is for me. It's what I want."

"Since when?"

"Since the whole city fell apart? I liked standing on that stage today, knowing I made a difference. I'm proud of what I've done so far, but I can do more. You were right about that. You were right about a lot of things."

She waited for him to continue, her pulse racing.

"My time in the navy was full of challenges and responsibilities. I was disappointed that I didn't make it through special-ops training. The death of my crewmate weighed heavily on me. Maybe I lost faith in myself. Since then I've avoided big commitments. I didn't want anyone depending on me, because I was afraid of letting them down."

Reaching across the table, she took his hand. "You didn't let me down. You didn't let your sister or Emma down."

"I'm glad," he said simply. "I don't know what I'd do without you."

She rubbed her thumb across his knuckles. He'd be a conscientious officer, not reckless or trigger-happy. He'd have to take some professional risks, but so did she. She couldn't let her fears hold him back. She couldn't let them hold *her* back, either.

They needed to have a serious conversation before they could take their relationship to the next level. She'd learned her lesson about failing to communicate with Mitch.

"Do you still have a gut feeling about me?" she asked, pulling her hand back. "That we belong together?"

"Of course I do. I love you, Helena. I'm not going to change my mind about that."

She inhaled a shaky breath. "I didn't believe in gut feelings after my father died. It was my way to protect myself from getting hurt. I was afraid to feel…too deeply. And then the earthquake hit, and you showed me what I was missing."

His eyes darkened with emotion.

"I'm still afraid, but it's not as bad as I thought it would be."

"It's not as bad as you thought it would be," he repeated, squinting into the distance. "That's quite a romantic declaration."

She surged ahead before she could bungle things further. "You were right about me, too. I was closed off and out of touch. It's not easy for me to share my feelings. But I'm trying, because I love you."

He straightened in his chair. "You what?"

"I love you," she said, swallowing hard.

"You love me."

"Yes."

He just stared at her in shock.

"Say something."

"I don't know what to say. I had all of these sneaky plans to win you over. I was going to invite you on a nice vacation and butter you up."

Tears of joy filled her eyes. This sharing-feelings thing was kind of liberating. She should do it more often. "We can go on a vacation."

His lips curved into a smile. "Yeah?"

"What else did you have planned?"

"Asking you to move in with me at the end of the summer."

They were already sleeping together every night. Shacking up with him wasn't that much of a stretch. "I'll think about it."

"Really?"

She nodded.

"Maybe I should just pop the question while you're in an agreeable mood."

Laughing, she glanced around the restaurant. It had romantic lighting. "I thought you might have brought me here to do that."

"You're kidding."

"No."

"You thought I'd propose in public, at a place like this?"

"You wouldn't?"

"Hell no. I'd take you somewhere classy, like Olive Garden."

She laughed again, shaking her head.

"Would you have said yes?"

"I don't know."

He scrubbed a hand down his face, stunned.

"What?"

"I can't believe this. You said you loved me, and you'll think about moving in with me, and you might even marry me someday. Am I dreaming?"

"You're not dreaming."

"Pinch me."

She got up from her chair and went to his side of the table. Sitting down on his lap, she twined her arms around his neck and brushed her lips over his. "How's that?"

"I didn't feel it."

She kissed him again, deeper this time.

"You're getting there," he murmured.

"I'm not going any further. Buddha is watching."

"Buddha doesn't mind."

"I do."

"I love you, Helena. I want to spend the rest of my life with you."

She wanted that, too. So she said yes, and he took her home, away from prying eyes to make her the happiest elephant keeper in San Diego.

* * * * *

Author's Note:

Thanks so much for reading *Wild*! This is my first self-published book. I hope you enjoyed it. If you have time, please consider writing an online review. Reviews help new readers find me.

You can read the Aftershock series from the beginning or in any order.

Aftershock (Aftershock #1)
Freefall (Aftershock #2)
Badlands (Aftershock #3)
Passion & Peril (novella)
Island Peril (novella) *ebook only
Backwoods (Aftershock #4)

Mitch and Gwen's story, "Wild for Him," will be available in ebook.

Like erotic romance? Check out *Riding Dirty*, the first in my new Dirty Eleven MC series. This book is available in digital with HQN.

I love hearing from readers. Feel free to visit me at my website, sign up for my newsletter or like me on Facebook.

http://www.jillsorenson.com
https://www.facebook.com/pages/Jill-Sorenson/

Made in the USA
Middletown, DE
08 January 2018